Dear Reader,

When I first wrote the CIRCLE K SISTERS, a three-book series was a big deal to me. I kind of stumbled across the Crawfords of Oklahoma when I was looking for a hero for the third book. A family with five boys and one girl fascinated me and, even after the original trilogy ended, I found myself going back to that family to write Lindsay's story as well as two more of the brothers' stories.

Then my editor offered me the opportunity to write a longer book, to explore the family in greater detail with this new release, *Hush*. Of course I jumped at the chance. Every family has good times. But they also have problems, and it's the way they deal with their problems that is the true test of a family. In *Hush*, the Crawfords face that test in a most unexpected way. I hope you will appreciate their struggle and enjoy the results.

There is an old saying, "That which doesn't kill us, makes us stronger." Here's to the Crawford family. May they always grow stronger. I hope the same is true for you and your family. Life doesn't go smoothly all of the time, but togetherness is the way to survive and grow stronger.

Best,

Judy Christenberry

JUDY
CHRISTENBERRY

hush

Published by Silhouette Books

America's Publisher of Contemporary Romance

SILHOUETTE BOOKS

HUSH

ISBN 0-373-21860-5

Copyright © 2003 by Judy Russell Christenberry

Visit Silhouette at www.eHarlequin.com

Printed in U.S.A.

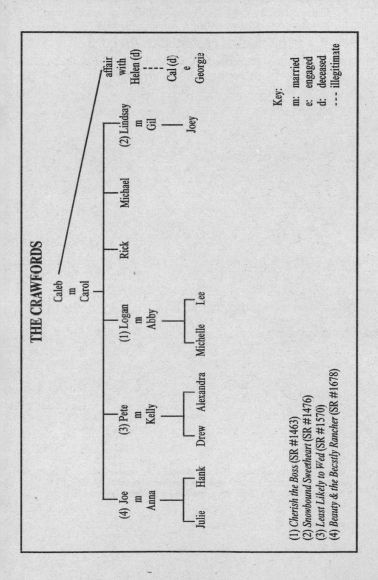

THE CRAWFORDS

Caleb
m
Carol — affair with Helen (d)

(4) Joe m Anna — (3) Pete m Kelly — (1) Logan m Abby — Rick — Michael — (2) Lindsay m Gil

Julie — Hank

Drew — Alexandra

Michelle — Lee

Joey

Cal (d) e Georgie

Key:
m: married
e: engaged
d: deceased
--- illegitimate

(1) *Cherish the Boss* (SR #1463)
(2) *Snowbound Sweetheart* (SR #1476)
(3) *Least Likely to Wed* (SR #1570)
(4) *Beauty & the Beastly Rancher* (SR #1678)

This book is dedicated to my editor,
Melissa Jeglinski, without whom it would
never have been written.

Chapter 1

Carol Crawford hummed along with the radio while she finished icing a chocolate cake, wanting it ready for when her husband and son came in to lunch. They were big, hardworking men. The extra calories associated with dessert weren't a problem, even for Caleb, her husband of thirty-eight years. He worked as hard on their ranch as he ever had.

A knock on the front door startled her. She wasn't expecting anyone, and certainly any members of her large family would have come in through the back, calling out as they entered. She swung open the door, her smile at the ready. Then she came to an abrupt halt.

"Hello, is this the Crawford home?" a young woman asked, almost in a whisper. She was leaning against the doorjamb, her advanced stage of pregnancy obvious to Carol. "I'm sorry. Could I come inside? I need to sit down."

Without hesitation, Carol helped her through the

door and down the hall to the kitchen, seating her at the table. Then she opened the refrigerator and poured a glass of cold milk. "Take a drink." Next she cut a piece of the just baked chocolate cake and placed it in front of her. "This will give you some needed energy."

The stranger did as Carol asked, taking several bites of the cake before she picked up the milk. As she ate, Carol studied her. The young woman was about six months pregnant, but other than her protruding stomach, she didn't have much meat on her bones. And she looked tired, as if she wasn't getting much sleep.

"Do you need to see a doctor?" Carol asked softly.

"No!" the girl exclaimed, her voice rising in alarm. "I'm fine. I just walked farther than I'd expected to. Someone told me your ranch was only a couple of miles out of town."

"Good heavens, you walked here from town? When did you start?"

The girl glanced at her cheap plastic watch. "About three hours ago."

"That's too much for you in your condition." Carol looked at the girl closely. "Excuse me, but do I know you?"

"No, ma'am. I don't even know the man I've come to see—Caleb Crawford. This is his place, isn't it?"

Carol stared at the girl, tension rising within her. "Yes, it is. What do you want with Caleb?"

"I'm sorry, but it's…it's private."

Carol thought of several things she wanted to say, number one being that she was Caleb's wife and he didn't keep anything from her. They'd made that decision a long time ago. Instead, she moved to the phone and dialed the number for the barn.

When Caleb answered, she asked him to come to

lunch early. "There's someone you need to talk to," she said. When he asked for more information, she hung up the phone.

Carol could only surmise that the young woman's business with Caleb had something to do with her baby. Carol wouldn't believe the father of this girl's child was Caleb. Though it might be one of their five boys. Three of them were happily married.

Dear God, she prayed, don't let it be one of them.

But one thing was clear, some kind of disaster was about to happen. She felt sure it didn't involve Caleb. Didn't she? They'd had a parting of the ways for a couple of months almost twenty-six years ago, and since then, she felt sure he'd been faithful to her.

"Caleb will be here in a few minutes," Carol told the girl. "Are you feeling better?"

"Yes, I am, thanks to your generosity. Mr. Crawford is lucky to have such a good housekeeper as you."

"I'm not his housekeeper. I'm his wife," Carol said firmly.

The young woman visibly swallowed. "Maybe I should, uh, call on Mr. Crawford some other time." She made an attempt to rise from the chair.

"I don't think so," Carol said, putting a hand on the girl's shoulder. "I think this needs to be cleared up now." She sat down beside the visitor.

Footsteps announced the arrival of Caleb and of Rick, their fourth son.

"What's going on, Carol? Why did you hang up on me?" Caleb asked, a note of complaint in his voice.

Carol gestured to the young woman. "You have a visitor."

Caleb drew a deep breath. "Okay. Hello, I'm Caleb Crawford. How can I help you?"

Before the young woman could speak, Carol said, "You don't recognize her?"

"No. I've never seen her before."

"How about you, Rick?" she asked.

"No, Mom."

"What's going on?" Caleb asked again.

The young woman stood up and both men stared at her protruding stomach.

"Mr. Crawford, perhaps if we spoke in private…" she suggested, looking longingly at the door.

"I don't think so. My husband and I don't have secrets," Carol said, her gaze fixed on her husband, not the girl.

Caleb spoke, but only to his son. "Rick, go wash up for lunch."

It was obvious Rick wanted to find out what was going on, but he knew when his father meant business. He left the room.

"What's your name, girl?" Caleb asked.

"Georgina—Georgie—Brown."

"Are you here about one of my sons?"

"Yes, I am."

"Which one?"

Carol held her breath.

"Cal."

It took a second for the name to register. Then Carol released her breath. "We don't have a son named Cal."

She looked at Caleb, expecting to see relief on his face. It was all a mistake. *This girl has no business with their family.*

But Caleb's face had gone pasty. "Caleb?" Carol asked.

"Come into the other room," he said to the young woman. "We'll talk privately."

"Caleb Crawford, have you forgotten? We don't keep secrets, remember?" Carol clenched her hands, trying to suppress the rising anger that threatened to break loose.

"I remember, Carol, and I'll tell you everything after I talk to her. But it will be easier to do it my way."

Her anger was boiling even more, but she said nothing else.

The young woman stood and shakily crossed to the door of the family room. Caleb followed her and closed the door behind them.

Georgie Brown felt sick to her stomach. Not for the first time, of course. The first three months of her pregnancy had been hellish. But lately she'd been okay. This morning she'd overdone it, walking so far on a warm day. And now she was causing problems for the nice woman who'd helped her recover. Georgie wished she'd never come to the Crawford ranch.

"So, my son Cal got you pregnant? Are you here because he abandoned you?" Mr. Crawford asked, his voice rough.

"Mr. Crawford, Cal didn't abandon me. He...he's dead. I'm sorry. I thought you would have heard by now." Obviously he hadn't known, since he turned even whiter than before.

After a minute, he asked, "When?"

"Three and a half months ago. He and Helen, his mother, were in Dallas when a drunk driver hit their car and killed both of them."

The man hung his head, his eyes closed. "So why are you here now?" he finally asked, his voice tight.

He wanted her gone, she knew, just like the woman in the kitchen. Georgie opened her purse, pulled out a folded piece of paper and handed it to him.

"What's this?" he asked. After reading it quickly, he looked at her. "Yes?"

"I—I lost my job, so I-have no insurance. My savings are almost gone, and I've got a minimum-wage job. I thought perhaps you could give me enough money from the trust fund to pay for the delivery of my baby."

"So you married Cal?"

"No. We were planning to marry, but he died before—"

"How do I know you're carrying his baby? You could be running a scam. Do you think I should believe you?"

His sudden anger frightened her. She got to her feet, none too steadily, and began walking toward the hallway that led to the front door.

"See my attorney if you want to collect on that money. But you won't get it without proof, young lady. I'm not going to be taken!"

She felt tears running down her face, so she kept her back to him. She'd been so hopeful! How silly of her. Now she'd have to work overtime. Or get a second job. Or just go into debt. She'd find some way to take care of her baby without having anything to do with Cal's father.

That was her last conscious thought as she fell to the floor of the wooden porch.

"Carol!" Caleb called, with a sense of urgency that brought his wife running.

He wasn't in the den, but standing on the front porch, staring down at Georgie's crumpled body.

"What happened?" Carol demanded, kneeling down to determine if the girl was still breathing. She stood and called her son. "Rick?"

When Rick appeared at the front door, she asked him to carry the young woman to the downstairs bedroom. Then she faced her husband. "What happened?"

"Damn it, woman, I don't know what happened. We—we argued. Then she stood up and walked out. I followed, and when I got to the door, she fell down. She's probably faking it for sympathy." He moved back as Rick carried the girl into the house.

"Put her in the bedroom behind the kitchen," Carol directed again.

"Why not just put her on the sofa? She'll come to in a minute and she can be on her way," Caleb suggested.

"Anxious to send her away, are you? Anxious to avoid the conversation we're going to have?"

"I'm anxious to be rid of a woman who's trying to scam me. I'm not a fool," Caleb assured her, his voice hard.

"I'm not certain of that," she said with a sniff, turning to follow Rick.

Caleb left the house, going back to the barn. He could do without Carol's taunts. He'd made a mistake once, but that had been long ago. He wasn't about to be chastised by his wife after being married to her all these years.

When Georgie came to, it was to find herself in an unfamiliar bed and to hear Mrs. Crawford talking on the bedside phone.

"Yes, I think she's just exhausted. But I wanted to check." Mrs. Crawford paused, then said, "Why, yes, she's awake. I'll ask her." Carol covered the phone with her hand and looked at Georgie. "It's the doctor. Have you felt your baby move yet?"

Georgie panicked. Could the fainting spell have hurt her baby? She clutched her stomach. Then she relaxed as she felt her child kick as hastily as ever. "Yes, yes, he's moving."

"The baby's moving, Doctor. Yes. Yes, we will." Mrs. Crawford hung up the phone and turned to Georgie. "The doctor thinks you're all right, though probably exhausted. He said to feed you well today and make sure you get a good night's sleep and then bring you in to see him tomorrow."

"No, I'm going home today. I don't have the time or money for this," Georgie told her.

"Nonsense. I'm Carol Crawford, Caleb's wife. And we're going to take care of you. Dear, can I ask. Who is Cal?"

After a moment, Georgie said, "He's the father of my baby. We were going to get married, but he died. A drunk driver killed him...and his mother."

"Was her name Helen?" Carol asked gently.

Georgie could tell that this might hurt Carol, but she nodded.

"So Cal was Caleb's son." Carol bowed her head for a moment before asking, "How did you know about Caleb? Why did you come to find him?"

"After Cal and Helen's deaths, I packed up the apartment we shared, and found papers about a trust fund among Cal's things. Seems your husband, Cal's father, had set aside some money for Cal when he reached twenty-five. But Cal died before he could collect and the money would then have gone to Cal's mother or Cal's child. I was surprised to find out about the trust, because Cal's stepfather had taken everything he thought might have any value, but obviously he missed this. He probably never knew the trust existed. I thought maybe Mr. Crawford would give me some money from the trust fund or loan it to me to help with the baby. I lost my insurance when I was laid off, and the only job I've been able to find is working at a fast-food restaurant. My savings are almost gone so… Obviously, I wasn't thinking clearly.''

"Don't you have any family?'' Carol asked.

"No. Cal and Helen were my only family.'' She tried to sit up, hoping to get out of there before she burst into tears. "Mrs. Crawford, I need to get back to Lawton right away. There's a bus that leaves at six-thirty.''

"Heading where?''

"To Dallas. I've always lived in Dallas.'' She tried to smile, but it wobbled a little.

"A city girl.''

"Yes.''

"Well, city girl, the doctor says you should stay in bed until morning. *If* you leave then, Rick will drive you into town.''

"But I don't want to cause you any problems. I mean any more problems. You've been so nice.''

"I'm going to bring you a tray for lunch. Then, after you've eaten, I'll tuck you in so you can sleep.''

"But I can't—''

"Hush, child. I don't think you have a choice.'' With those words, Carol left the room.

Georgie considered getting out of bed and slipping away, but she knew Carol wasn't going to let her go so easily. And maybe she should eat a good meal before she set out for Lawton. That way maybe she'd actually get there. She didn't think she could without a boost of energy.

Carol reappeared so swiftly, Georgie couldn't believe she'd managed to put together a meal. But the tray held a sandwich, a bowl of soup, a glass of milk and another piece of that delicious chocolate cake she'd tasted earlier.

"I can't eat all that, Mrs. Crawford, really."

"Call me Carol, dear. Eat as much as you want. But drink all the milk. I'll be back in a minute."

Georgie didn't know where Carol was going, but her stomach growled, telling her it wanted food. She picked up the sandwich and discovered it was roast beef. Before she knew it, she'd eaten the entire thing. She thought she ought to eat a few spoonfuls of the soup, not to be rude. Then she tasted the cake and discovered she couldn't resist it.

Carol came in as she was draining the glass of milk.

"Good girl. I hoped you'd eat." She removed the bed tray, setting it aside. "Rick is going to stay in the house while I run outside. If you need anything, you can call him. I'll be back shortly and we'll see how you're feeling."

"Carol, I can't thank you enough. You've been very kind. And I know my being here isn't easy for you."

"Don't worry about me. Just take care of your baby." Carol pulled the cover up around Georgie's shoulders. "Close your eyes and rest for a while."

Georgie did as Carol asked, planning to open her eyes once she left the room. But the woman didn't seem to be in a hurry. Georgie felt her body relaxing, but before she drifted off she heard Carol leave and say something to Rick in the kitchen.

"Rick, I'm going to the barn to talk to your father. Please wait here until I return, okay? I want someone around in case she awakens."

"But, Mom, I don't know anything about pregnant women!" Rick exclaimed, alarm in his voice.

"No, dear, but I'm reasonably sure you know how to call me in the barn."

Chapter 2

Caleb Crawford paced back and forth in the barn's center aisle, between the stalls where he kept the pregnant cows. How appropriate, he thought with disgust.

He knew Carol was going to cause a fuss about keeping Helen's pregnancy a secret. But he believed he'd done the right thing. He couldn't have let Helen go off, pregnant with his child, and not provide for them. And he wouldn't have dared to tell Carol that another woman was having his child—not when they had just reconciled.

The barn door creaked and Caleb stiffened as Carol entered, crossing the barn silently, her gaze fixed on him.

"Carol, whether you like it or not, I had to provide for the boy."

"I don't have any problem with the trust fund, Caleb. But it would have been nice to know you'd had a child in the first place. Now what about Cal's child?

Aren't you going to provide for it? Since he no longer can?''

"Of course I'll give the woman the trust fund money if the baby is Cal's. But there's no proof yet.''

"Didn't you hear her? She's been laid off. She has no insurance and she's on her feet working at a fast-food joint. That's not a job a pregnant woman should have. She has no family, either. Helen and Cal were her family and they're gone.''

"I know that's what she said, but I know Helen got married after our time together. Why isn't her husband considered part of this girl's family?''

Carol took another step closer. "I don't know. I don't want to talk about him. I want to talk about the lies you told me twenty-six years ago.''

Caleb's heart sank. He'd hoped to find a way out of facing up to this. It was a losing proposition. "Now, Carol, I've been faithful to you ever since that day I promised.''

"Have you?''

"Damn it! You know I have.''

"You gave me promises that you broke as soon as you made them. All these years, you've lived a lie. Did you think I would keep you from seeing your son? Did you think I would scorn the woman who'd trusted you, as I had, and denied her son a knowledge of acceptance from his family? Did you think I was that small?''

"No! I thought you'd refuse to have me back. It was you I wanted, not Helen. I'm ashamed to say I used her without thinking about her. I didn't want a life with Helen. I wanted a life with my children, our children, with you. I was afraid. So I'm sorry. But that's the last I'm going to say on the subject. I'll give this girl five hundred dollars and pay for her baby's delivery. Then, when the baby is born, if it's Cal's, she'll receive the trust fund. Now, not another word about it!'' He headed for the door of the barn.

"No." Carol's reply was soft but distinct.

"What?" he asked harshly.

"What that girl needs, more than anything, is family. I'm not sending her out into the world on her own."

"So you're willing to blacken my reputation throughout the entire neighborhood? Just so she'll have family?"

"What if this were Lindsay? Would you want someone to offer a few dollars and withhold what she needs most of all?"

"It wasn't just a few dollars. You tell me how much and I'll give it to her. But I'm going to protect my children. I'm not going to have our family gossiped about throughout the county."

"And Cal's baby, and its mother, are not your family?"

"Damn it! Carol, we'll find a home and put her in it. I don't want people to know."

"They won't know. We'll tell folks she's the widow of a distant cousin. She needed some help when he died. That will satisfy their curiosity."

"Okay, okay. And you and me? We're okay?"

"That's another matter. It will take me a little while to adjust. I thought you always told me the truth."

"You're being ridiculous."

"You consider it ridiculous to be upset about a secret you've kept for more than twenty-five years? You want to deny me time to adjust to what I now know?"

"You're my wife. It's your job to take care of me, not punish me like a child. So we'll go on as before, because you have no choice!" He knew at once he'd said the wrong thing and should apologize, but his pride was hurt. And he was scared. He couldn't admit that.

"I have no choice?" she asked, her voice soft, signifying she was at her most dangerous.

"Now, Carol, you know what I say is true. You can't—"

He stopped because she was no longer there to listen to him. She'd left the barn, without slamming any doors or crying any tears.

Carol was a strong woman. Together they'd built a strong family and a large fortune. More than that, he'd discovered happiness with her. And now he was on the brink of losing it.

What was he going to do?

When dinnertime rolled around, Carol set the table for herself, Rick and Caleb, figuring Georgie would sleep through it, since she hadn't awoken all afternoon. But Carol wasn't sure Caleb would come to the table. He was a stubborn man.

Well, she was tired of dwelling on his lies. They made her heart ache. She'd been honest with him when she'd said she needed time to think about what she had learned.

She went to the back porch and rang the dinner bell. She'd fixed a good hot meal for them. She had help for the cleaning and the laundry, but she preferred to do almost all the cooking herself.

The door opened and Rick came in, but Caleb was not with him. Carol's heart sank. "Where's your father?" she asked sharply.

"He's coming," Rick said nonchalantly. "Is the pregnant woman having dinner with us?"

"No, not tonight. She's still sleeping. And her name is Georgie."

"Won't all that resting make it hard for her to sleep tonight?"

"I think she'll sleep straight through till morning," Carol said, as she heard Caleb's footsteps in the kitchen. She turned to him, but Caleb didn't meet her gaze. He sat down in his usual chair, across from her place, and bowed his head to say the blessing. After a quick glance at each of them, Rick followed suit. So did Carol.

Dinner was a silent affair. Rick tried to start a conversation about the cutting horse he was training, but neither parent responded. He gave up and ate the rest of his meal in silence.

"Need me to baby-sit our guest this evening, Mom? If not, I think I'll go into Lawton. There's a good band I want to hear," he said as he wiped his hands with his napkin and put it on his empty plate.

"No, dear, but thanks for asking."

"Be careful," his father said.

"Sure, Dad." At twenty-eight, Rick tolerated his father's parental admonishments but didn't feel they were necessary.

Carol smiled at her son. Once Rick was gone, she began clearing the table.

"Carol, I'm not going to run away this time because we're fighting. This is my home. But I'm going to move into the guest bedroom down the hall. I don't want to force you to share the same air space."

His sarcasm hurt, but she only nodded. If he wanted to sleep by himself, she wasn't going to force him to remain close to her. At least she wouldn't wonder who he was with.

He left the room, and she continued doing the dishes automatically, while she thought about the events of the day. Maybe she should have let him get away with his lies, but she'd put such trust in his word, and all the time he'd been lying. That hurt.

No. She deserved some time to get past this. She gave a lot to her family, all she felt they needed. This time she was going to give to herself.

She finished the dishes and went to the family room, turning on the television. Then she reached behind the couch and got her knitting bag. She needed something to occupy her hands while she tried to figure out how to handle this situation.

Rick got in later than he'd intended. His father would let him hear about it in the morning. He smiled. That was one of the reasons he'd considered getting his own place, but he couldn't quite bring himself to leave. His parents enjoyed having him at the house, and it was convenient for him. So he'd let things go on as they had.

A sound interrupted his musings. He thought it had come from the bedroom behind the kitchen. Had his parents' houseguest woken up? He stepped to the closed door and knocked.

After what sounded like a gasp, there was complete silence.

"Lady? Georgie? Are you awake? Do you need something?"

Silence.

"I'm going to come in," Rick warned. He waited a few seconds and then opened the door, to find the woman out of bed and standing next to an open window in the dark. An open window? The temperature was in the forties. His mother wouldn't have opened the window. Why had this girl?

"I'm Rick, Carol and Caleb's son. We didn't get a chance to get acquainted before. How you feeling?" he asked softly.

"F-fine."

She did look better. In the light from the kitchen, he could tell her skin had more color and she didn't have such huge circles under her eyes. In fact, she looked much younger than she had.

"Are you hungry? Mom's cooking is almost as good in leftovers as it is at dinnertime."

"No...no, I'm full. I ate a lot of lunch."

"But that was over twelve hours ago."

"No, thank you," she said, her voice firmer this time.

"Your mother said you'd drive me to Lawton when...when I was ready."

Her cheeks flushed as she gazed at him with those huge blue eyes. Rick figured most any man would agree to whatever she asked, in spite of her pregnancy. "Sure, I'll be glad to help you out."

"Thank you," she said, with relief in her voice. "Okay, I'm ready."

Rick couldn't believe his ears. After blinking several times, he asked, "Now? You want to go now? It's two in the morning!"

"There's a bus at five-thirty. I can wait in the terminal."

"Well, I'll have to wake Mom and see if she approves of that plan. I suspect she'll think it's as bad as I do. I'm sure there's a bus a little later, so you can get up at a reasonable time and have breakfast. Then

I'll take you into town.'' He walked over to the window and closed it, locking it at the top.

"What are you doing?" she asked.

"I didn't want to forget to close the window. We're going to have a rainstorm in an hour or two. Those can be pretty heavy, get the room all wet. Mom would be upset."

Georgie's eyes widened and she looked outside nervously. "I don't see any clouds."

"You don't see any stars, either, do you? On a clear night, you can see a million stars out here, away from the city lights."

She leaned closer to the window to stare up at the sky before she turned, her eyes wide, to ask, "A million? Really?"

"Well," Rick said, a rueful grin on his face, "I've never actually counted them, but it seems like it."

"How wonderful that would be," she said with a sigh.

"You've always lived in the city?"

She nodded. "Yes. And I liked it, since there were usually lots of jobs available. But right now, with this economy, that's not the case anymore."

"So you don't have a job?"

"I do. But it doesn't pay much and I don't get insurance for the baby because I was already pregnant when I was hired."

"Tough situation. What are you going to do?"

Rick thought they were getting along well. But suddenly, everything changed. Her open expression disappeared, and she said firmly, "I'll manage."

"But—"

"Will you please take me to Lawton?"

"No, I won't. Not unless Mom says I should."

"And do you always do what your mother tells you?" Georgie asked in a sarcastic tone.

"She's a smart woman. I've learned the hard way about going against her."

"Fine."

Georgie stared at him awhile before saying, "Please leave."

"What are you going to do?"

When she didn't answer him, he said, "All right, I'll leave, but you'd better be here in the morning." He hoped his stern warning would keep her in place.

Rick headed up the stairs, but he didn't go to his bedroom. Instead, he went to his parents' and knocked softly on the door.

When his mother opened it, he said, "I hope I didn't wake Dad."

His mother gave him a strange look but calmly said, "No. He's still asleep. What's wrong?"

"Well, I got in kind of late and heard your guest up, so I went to check on her. She was fully dressed and had the bedroom window pushed up all the way, like she was about to leave through it. She asked me to take her to Lawton and I refused unless you okayed it. But she didn't want me to wake you."

"Good heavens, did she promise to stay through the night?"

"Well, no, but I closed and locked the window. I don't think she'll be able to get it open again."

Carol rolled her eyes. "I'd better go talk to her." She hurried past her son, heading for the stairs.

Rick was about to follow her, when he looked into the room to see if his dad was still asleep—and he realized his father wasn't in the bed. How strange. Rick had never known his parents to sleep apart, even when one of them was sick.

He left the bedroom and started back toward the stairs, but stopped when he heard slight snoring sounds coming from the guest bedroom. He opened the door and discovered his father asleep in the big bed. Quietly, Rick closed the door, worry in his heart. Something must be very wrong for his parents to be sleeping in separate rooms. And he had a distinct feeling it had something to do with the young woman in the down-stairs bedroom.

Georgie felt so much better after her long sleep and a sustaining meal. But it was time to leave the Crawford house, and since Rick already knew she was in-tending to go, she figured she might as well leave through the front door. She hurried outside, pulling on the sweater she'd removed yesterday in the late sum-mer heat.

A cold front was definitely moving through, for the temperature had dropped dramatically. She walked down the long driveway as quickly as she could in the dark, knowing she'd need to get out on the county road before she'd find a good place to hide.

She had just reached the end of the driveway when she heard a motor start up. Without hesitation, she hid behind some bushes that edged the road, staying low to the ground until the truck passed her by.

When she was certain the Crawfords' vehicle was well away, she struggled to her feet and moved back to the edge of the road, so she wouldn't trip on vege-tation in the darkness.

Ten minutes later, she saw the truck's headlights re-turning. Again she took cover and kept silent while the vehicle drove slowly down the road. When she saw it turn into their drive, Georgie stood and began walking once again.

Just then, large spatters of rain began to fall, accompanied by a strong wind. Hunching her shoulders, she pulled her sweater closer around her and continued to walk. She would just have to get wet. She wasn't going to stay where her baby's paternity was questioned and where her presence caused trouble for someone else. Carol was obviously a very kind and generous woman, and Georgie felt she deserved to be treated well in return.

Within a minute, Georgie was drenched, but she struggled on. It took so much concentrated effort just to stay upright and move forward that she didn't hear the truck behind her. When it pulled in front of her, she realized she hadn't seen it because the driver had turned off the lights.

Rick appeared beside her and scooped her into his arms without saying a word.

"Don't put me in the truck. I'm all wet!" she exclaimed.

He still said nothing, just swung her onto the seat, close to his mother.

"Don't worry about the truck," Carol said. "We've got to get you home and dried off so you don't catch pneumonia."

"Carol, I don't want to cause you any difficulty. Just drive me into town and I'll take the first bus home."

"But you don't have any family. You're staying with us. At least until the baby's born. I won't have it any other way."

Georgie shivered but said nothing more. Carol

wrapped an arm around her shoulder to help keep her warm.

When they got to the house, Carol sent Rick upstairs to get a nightgown out of her closet while she helped Georgie out of her wet clothes, then rubbed her down with a warm towel. He handed the nightgown in through the door and then went off, as instructed, to fix some warm milk for Georgie.

Carol came into the kitchen just as the milk was ready, and thanked her son for his help.

"How is she?" Rick asked.

"I hope all right. But she got completely chilled."

"Why is Georgie here? And why is Dad sleeping in the guest room?"

"Rick, there are some subjects that are better left alone. But if you must have answers, your father is the one to ask. He made some decisions that have resulted in problems." Without further explanation, she left Rick in the kitchen and took Georgie the warm milk. Then Carol headed up to her bedroom, where she slept alone for the first time in twenty-six years.

Chapter 3

Rick was the fourth of six siblings. When he had a problem, he frequently consulted one of his brothers. So the next morning, he headed to Pete's place, after he had called Joe and asked him to meet him there.

Pete was waiting in his kitchen when Rick and Joe arrived—coincidentally at the same time. "Come on in, guys. I've got the coffee on. What's up?" Pete asked.

Joe shrugged. "I don't know. It's Rick who arranged this meeting." He ambled forward to claim a cup of coffee.

Rick followed him, not looking either of his brothers in the eye. Now that it was time to reveal what had been going on at home, he wondered how to begin.

Kelly, Pete's wife, sailed into the kitchen, greeting her brothers-in-law as she did so. "I left out some coffee cake for you all. Sorry, but I've got to run. I'm taking Alexandra to work with me. I'll be back this afternoon after preschool gets out.'' She bent over and kissed Pete before leaving the house.

Rick looked enviously at his brother. "You're a lucky man, Pete.''

Joe, who was also happily married, nodded, adding, "Marriage is the best thing ever.''

"Yeah, I suppose. If you marry the right person. But it's hard to know who that is,'' Rick replied.

"Is that why we're here today? To discuss the merits of your latest woman? She's a looker, but she seems kind of full of herself,'' Joe said.

"No, that's not the reason,'' Rick replied. "It's Mom and Dad.''

Both his brothers sat straight and leaned toward him. "Well?'' Pete prompted.

"This pregnant woman came to the house yesterday to see Dad.''

"Are you saying Dad got a woman pregnant? I don't believe you,'' Pete exclaimed.

"No, he didn't recognize her. And before you ask, I didn't, either. And she wasn't claiming we did. She said the baby's father was someone named Cal.''

"Cal? Cal who?'' Joe asked.

"I don't know. But Dad did, and I think Mom did, too. They sent me away while Dad talked to the woman. Then apparently she fainted on the front porch. I carried her into the back bedroom and Mom fixed her a big meal. Then she slept for the whole evening.''

"So you want to know her identity?''

"Well, I know her name is Georgie. But what I really want to know is what she has to do with our folks. Because last night, I found out Dad slept in the guest room. I asked Mom what was going on and who Georgie was to them. She said I should ask Dad if I wanted answers to those questions." He sat back in his chair with a worried frown.

"So," Joe said, "did you ask him?"

"By myself? I don't think so. I thought you might like to hear the answers, too." He gazed at his older brothers hopefully.

Pete and Joe exchanged a glance. Then Joe asked, "How's Mom taking everything?"

"She seems upset."

"Does this Georgie person seem like she's out to hurt the folks." Pete asked.

"Hell, no! She's so young, so vulnerable. She kept saying she had to leave because she didn't want to hurt anyone, and how Mom had been so kind to her. She even tried running away last night, but we brought her back."

Joe hefted a big sigh. "Looks like we're going to have to go with Rick to talk to Dad."

"He won't like it," Pete warned.

"Like I don't know that," Joe said, sighing again. "Better get it over with." He stood and the other two followed him out of the kitchen.

The three men rode over to the ranch in Rick's truck. As they pulled up to their parents' house, a car came down the drive behind them.

"That looks like Mike's fancy car," Rick noted in surprise. Since their brother Michael lived in Oklahoma City, it was a surprise to see him during the week.

"I didn't know you'd called him," Pete said.

"I didn't." Rick responded.

The three brothers got out of the pickup and went to stand by Michael's car.

"Mike, what are you doing here?" Rick asked.

"I'm not real sure. Mom said Dad needed to talk to me, but she wouldn't tell me why."

"Was it about a pregnant woman?" Rick asked.

Michael raised his eyebrows. "No. Did one of you get a woman pregnant?"

"Well, I'm pretty sure I'm the one who got Anna pregnant," Joe said with a grin.

Michael laughed at him. "You're just bragging. You know what I mean."

"There's a pregnant woman staying at the house. Says her baby's daddy's name is Cal," Rick said, "but we don't know who Cal is."

Michael frowned. "Is Mom okay?"

Rick told him that their father had moved into the guest room.

"Why?" he asked, puzzlement in his voice.

"I asked Mom and she said to talk to Dad. I didn't want to do that by myself, so I enlisted Joe and Pete to back me up."

All four of them went into the house by the back door, calling out for their mother as they did so.

Carol shushed them as they entered the kitchen. "Georgie is still sleeping."

"Georgie?" Michael asked. "Is that the mystery girl you've got staying here?"

"She's...a family connection. She's skin and bones and six months pregnant."

"Where's Dad?" Joe asked.

"I believe he's stacking hay in the barn." Carol's voice was noticeably cooler.

"I guess we'll go talk to him, unless you want to answer some questions," Pete said, hoping his mother would do so. It was always easier to talk to her.

"No. They aren't my questions to answer."

"Okay. We'll see you later."

"Will you all stay for lunch?"

"Sure, Mom," Joe said, bending down to kiss her cheek.

When they were outside, Joe muttered, "She's upset about something."

"But she seemed okay," Michael said.

Joe gave him a look of pity at his naivete. Then he turned to Rick. "I'm glad you called us. Let's go find Dad."

They found their father in the barn and greeted him. Then Joe asked him to have a seat.

"I need to get this hay up out of the way," Caleb said in reply. "I'm bringing in a second crop soon."

Rick noticed their father didn't meet any of their gazes. "We'll help you, Dad, and have it done in no time," He said. "But we need to know what's going on."

Caleb stiffened. "If you're wondering about that pregnant woman, your mother is into her do-gooder thing, wanting to take care of her. I think she's gone overboard, offering to keep her here until she has the baby."

Carol did a lot of service work in the community. And sometimes their father protested about the people not deserving it. But he'd never before seemed so angry about her good-heartedness.

"Who is Cal?" Rick found himself asking.

His father glared at him. "None of your business."

"He's the father of Georgie's baby, but why does that affect us? Or is it Georgie who's connected to us? We want to know what's going on, and…and why you slept in the guest bedroom."

"That's something else that's none of your business," Caleb exclaimed, shortly.

It was Joe, the oldest Crawford sibling, who responded. "Dad, I think it affects us all. We'll be the objects of gossip we don't even understand. How can we protect our families if you don't answer these questions?"

"Damn it, Joe, just ignore the gossip," Caleb pleaded.

"Dad, Anna suffered from gossip with her first marriage. I'm not going to put her through that again, especially while she's carrying our baby. Who is this Cal?"

Caleb turned his back stubbornly, gazing out the barn door.

Pete cleared his throat. "Uh, Dad, we—"

"Fine! I'll answer your questions. Cal is my son!"

"You mean you were married before you met Mom?" Rick asked.

"No."

"You...got a girl pregnant in high school?" Pete asked, remembering how intent his father had been that his sons not get any women in trouble.

Caleb stopped the questions by raising his hand. "No. Do you remember, Joe, when you were about thirteen, I moved into town 'cause your mom and I had a big fight?"

"Yeah, I remember."

Caleb kept staring out the barn door. "I...I had an affair. When I realized what a mistake I was making, I told the woman I was going back to my wife, if she'd have me, and the woman told me she was pregnant."

No one moved. Rick thought the world of their dad.

He'd certainly been a good father. This revelation was such a shock.

Finally, Pete asked, "How could you, Dad? How could you do that to Mom?"

"I made a mistake, and I'm sorry. But that's all in the past—and better left there. I tried to get this Georgie to go away, but your mother wouldn't hear of it. She wants to ruin everything!"

Joe crossed his arms over his chest. "Dad, you know that's not true."

"Your mother is a stubborn woman."

"I won't argue with that," Joe agreed, "but she's worked hard for the two of you to succeed. I've patterned my marriage after yours, because I think two people who work as equal partners have the best chance of staying together."

"Look, this woman may be lying. She's probably a scam artist."

"Why did she come here? How did she know? Have you contacted this...Cal?"

"He's dead. She said Cal and his mom died in a car crash before she and Cal could marry."

"So she hoped you'd feel sorry for her?" Michael, a lawyer, asked, his gaze intent.

"No. I gave Helen a large sum of money and I established a trust fund for the baby. She never touched it. After their deaths, the young woman found the papers and hoped I'd give her some of the money for hospital expenses."

"Does she have proof that the baby is Cal's?" Michael asked.

"No."

"So what did you offer her?"

"I told her to speak to my lawyer, who set up the

trust. If she proved her baby was Cal's, then, yes, she could have the money."

"That's certainly fair," Michael agreed.

"But why is she here? Does she have a job?" Joe asked. "Or money for her medical needs? I think they wait until the baby is born for DNA testing, and she could be in real trouble if—"

"You sound like your mother!" Caleb exclaimed angrily.

Joe stared at him. "I'm not ashamed of that. Mom has a generous heart. Did she know about Cal?"

"No! I told her about Helen, but…"

"But you were afraid Mom wouldn't take you back if she knew you got another woman pregnant, right?" Rick stared at his father, looking for an answer.

"Yeah," Caleb finally said. "I messed up. But don't think I'm going to allow young pups like you to give me grief about something I can't change."

After several moments of silence, Michael said, "I'd better talk to Georgie. Dad, it might be wise to offer some kind of settlement."

"I offered—at least, I told your mother I would. But she insists on having the woman live with us, so she can embarrass me before all my neighbors. She's the one creating difficulties."

"We'll talk to her," Michael promised.

The brothers all trooped out of the barn.

"You going to tell Mom she can't take care of Georgie?" Rick asked his little brother.

"I'm going to talk to Mom and this woman and try to get the stories straight. It's not my place to tell Mom what she can and can't do," Michael said.

"Good," Rick said firmly.

"You think she's telling the truth?" Joe asked.

"Yeah," Rick replied. "She hadn't eaten much in a long time, I think, judging from the way she tucked into the meal Mom fixed her. And she'd walked all the way from Lawton. She had big shadows under her eyes and she seemed scared."

"Did she tell you anything about herself?"

"Mom told me she's working at some fast-food place 'cause she was laid off from her better paying job, and has no insurance and not much savings."

"That's tough," Pete said, and Rick knew he was thinking about his wife, Kelly. Her first husband had left her with a lot of debts and no insurance. If their sister, Lindsay, hadn't become partners with her to create their store, Oklahoma Chic, Kelly would've had a hard time making it. But at least Kelly had had help from her own mother.

"Has this girl got family?" Pete asked.

"Mom said no."

When they reached the house, they went into the kitchen and found Georgie sitting at the table eating some toast. She immediately looked alarmed and tried to rise, making her pregnancy obvious.

"Hi, Georgie, it's Rick. You remember me, don't you?" he asked.

"Yes, of course. Your mother went upstairs. I'll…I'll go in the bedroom."

"No, sit down and finish eating or we'll get in trouble with Mom," Rick said, smiling at her. "These are my brothers, Joe, Pete and Michael. I have to warn you—Michael is a lawyer."

The fright on Georgie's face took away all the humor Rick had intended. "Hey, I was just teasing," he hurriedly said.

"He's not a lawyer?" Georgie asked.

"Well, yeah, he is, but he's not going to do anything to you."

"Why does meeting a lawyer scare you?" Michael asked.

"Because you might say I'm trespassing. But I tried to leave. Rick and Carol brought me back." She sneezed.

Rick frowned. "Did you catch cold?"

"No, of course not," she said as she sneezed again.

"I heard that," Carol sang out as she came down the stairs, and Georgie looked guilty.

Carol entered the kitchen to find her sons all staring at her guest. "Goodness, I hope they introduced themselves, Georgie. I promise I tried to teach them manners."

"Mom, you know you did," Joe said with a grin.

Carol smiled back, her voice softening. "I know I did. I'm very fortunate with my children, Georgie. They are special."

Georgie smiled at her. "I'm not surprised, Carol."

"Mom, we want to ask Georgie a few questions. Is that all right?" Michael asked.

"That's up to her," Carol said, an edge of steel in her voice. "She's a guest in this house and only has to answer if she wants to." She looked at Georgie. "You hear me, child? If you don't want to answer, just say so."

Georgie nodded, a hint of fear in her eyes.

Rick sat down next to her. He patted her arm. "Everything will be fine."

She nodded again.

The other men sat down, too. Carol began pouring glasses of iced tea.

Michael cleared his throat. "I understand you claim Cal Crawford is the father of your baby."

"I know he is," she said quietly.

"You'll understand that we can't take your word for it, won't you?"

She nodded. "When I talked to the lawyer whose name is on Cal's trust fund papers, he said I would need DNA proof of my baby's paternity, but that the doctors advised waiting until after the baby was born."

"So you've already talked to a lawyer?"

"Just over the phone. Afterward, I came to talk to Mr. Crawford, thinking he might help me. I know I shouldn't have, that doing so was a mistake. Then Carol was worried about my health and wouldn't let me leave. But I'm doing better today, so I'll be able to catch the bus this afternoon."

"So you're willing to wait until the baby's birth and DNA testing before making a claim on the trust?"

"Yes."

"No!" Carol declared at the same time.

"Mom!" Michael protested.

Joe spoke up. "How are you going to pay for medical care?"

Georgie's cheeks turned bright red. "I'll manage."

"Yes, but how?" Joe persisted.

"I have a job," she said, raising her chin.

"What kind of job?" Pete asked.

"That's none of your business," she retorted, clenching her hands in her lap and staring at the table.

"We're not trying to be difficult," Joe said gently, "but your baby is our nephew. We want to be sure he is well cared for."

"Mr. Crawford, my child may be your nephew or niece, but he or she is *my* child. The only part of Cal that I will ever have. I'll do everything I can to make my child's life a happy one.''

"Have you seen a doctor?" Pete asked.

"Yes, I have."

Pete and Joe looked relieved, but Rick gazed at her intently. "When was the last time you saw this doctor?"

Georgie stared at him. Then she turned to Carol. "I need to get to Lawton to catch the bus, Carol. Would it be possible for you to drive me there? I'd appreciate it very much."

Chapter 4

Carol hurried to Georgie's side. "Honey, I don't want you to leave. We'll take care of you until the baby is born. We're going to be your family. It's the least we can do."

Georgie's warm smile lit up her face. "Carol, you are the sweetest woman in the world. But we both know your husband doesn't feel the same way. It would be poor repayment if I stayed and caused problems between you and Mr. Crawford. I promise I'll take care of my baby."

Before Carol could answer, Rick said, "Don't be ridiculous. You can barely take care of yourself."

All the warmth disappeared from Georgie's face. "I need to leave now. Thank you, Carol," she said as she stood. Then she went into the back bedroom, and came out with a shoulder bag and a sweater. She said nothing else as she went out the back door.

Rick leaped to his feet and hurried after her. "You can't leave!"

"Why not? Are you going to keep me here against my will?"

"Aw, come on, Georgie. You know we're only doing this for your own good."

"I am an adult, Rick Crawford. I get to decide how I live."

"Dad will give you some money if you'll wait a bit." Rick sounded as if he was offering the ultimate temptation.

She looked up at him, her chin firm. "I don't want your father's money."

"That's why you came here, isn't it?"

"I'd hoped he would want to help me. I thought... I guess I was looking for family for my baby. But your father has made it clear that he wants nothing to do with me or my child." Tears welled in her eyes, but she refused to let them fall. She turned and started walking again.

Rick hurried back into the house—to ask his mother what she wanted him to do, Georgie supposed. At last she was alone.

The day was a lot cooler than yesterday, so the walk should be a little easier. She was no worse off today than she had been then, in spite of her foolish hopes. She was alone, and that wasn't going to change. She would just need to work overtime as much as possible and find a cheap place to live, saving every penny she could. When the baby was born, she would do the paternity test and then contact the lawyer.

But she wouldn't come back to Oklahoma to visit the Crawfords. In spite of Carol's kindness, the rest of the family wanted nothing to do with her and her baby.

She heard a truck start up. Was Rick coming after her again? She wasn't going to get in the vehicle, even though she was already tired. She couldn't trust him.

"Georgie? Come on, I'll drive you to Lawton." Rick said as he pulled up beside her.

"No, thank you." She kept walking.

"Georgie, I don't think you're strong enough to make it all the way into town. Let me drive you."

"No, thank you. Now go away and leave me alone." She trudged on, finding it more and more difficult to put one foot in front of the other. But she'd make it. She had to.

Rick didn't speak to her again, but he continued to follow her, watching her every step. She could feel his gaze on her back. Getting away from these Crawfords was as difficult as getting flypaper off your shoe. Except for Caleb Crawford.

She stumbled over a tuft of grass and staggered. When she was steady again, she discovered Rick standing beside her.

"Are you all right?"

"Of course I am," she told him, her chin firmly in the air.

He laughed. "You remind me of my mother."

"Thank you. That's a lovely compliment."

"No, it's not. I was talking about her stubbornness."

"I still think it's a lovely compliment."

He shook his head. "I've got to get the truck."

"When you get it, head for home. Your following me is ridiculous." She hoped he'd believe her. It was becoming more and more difficult to resist accepting a ride to Lawton.

"Are you sure?" he asked, sounding anxious.

"I'm sure."

She kept walking, looking over her shoulder only once, when she heard the truck turn around. He was leaving. She was alone again.

Georgie sighed. Then her vision began wavering. She drew in a deep breath and let it out slowly. She was just tired. Everything would be all right. She stopped and waited a couple of minutes, then continued on.

Rick drove only a short distance down the road before turning around again. He was going to follow Georgie into town, but he'd keep a distance so she wouldn't notice him. He was worried because her face had seemed to be growing more pale by the minute.

He looked for her once he was turned around and was surprised when he couldn't find her. He sped up a little, amazed that she could walk so fast. Then his eye caught a movement at the side of the road and realized it was Georgie, lying on the grass. He slammed on his brakes and backed up beside her.

When he picked her up, he thought she'd wake up, but she didn't, and he wondered if she'd added a concussion to her list of problems. He pulled out his cellphone after he'd put her on the bench seat in his truck.

"Mom?" he asked as soon as she answered.

"Yes, Rick, did you get Georgie?"

"She must have passed out and fallen. She's not coming to. Shall I take her in to Patrick?" Patrick Wilson was their family physician.

"Oh my, yes. I'll call and let him know to meet you at the hospital."

Rick closed the passenger door. He got in on the driver's side, lifted Georgie's head and laid it on his thigh. Then he shifted into Drive and sped toward town.

He was surprised and pleased to find Patrick already waiting for him at the emergency entrance. The doctor and the nurse lifted Georgie from the truck and carefully placed her on a hospital gurney.

"She hasn't come to yet?"

"No. I'm afraid she may have a concussion, 'cause she fell on the pavement."

"What was she doing walking on the road?" Patrick asked as he bent to examine his patient.

"It's a long story."

"I'd like to hear it someday, but not now. I'll let you know what I discover," Patrick said as they entered the emergency room. He motioned to the empty chairs. "Wait out here."

"Can't I come with you?" Rick asked.

"Are you the father of the baby?"

"No!"

"Then wait out here."

Carol headed for the hospital as soon as she heard from Rick. Before she left, her other sons had told her that Caleb thought she wanted Georgie to stay on the ranch as a way of punishing him. So he would be embarrassed when anyone asked who Georgie was.

A ridiculous thought. Wasn't it? Carol had already figured out what to tell folks about Georgie, so they wouldn't understand her complex connection to Caleb. So of course she wasn't trying... Carol paused. Maybe she *was* trying to punish her husband. Without damaging his reputation. Because every time he saw Georgie, he'd be faced with a reminder of his infidelity.

She shook her head. The most important thing right

now was Georgie and the baby. The girl wasn't strong, and the last three months of her pregnancy would be the hardest. She needed help and she had no one but them to turn to.

Carol believed a strong family was the most important thing in the world. Whatever happened, members of her family pulled together. She couldn't imagine being all alone in the world and facing the birth of a baby.

When she got back home, she'd talk to Caleb. He had to understand how much Georgie needed them. He was not a mean man. He'd always been there for his six children. But he hadn't for his seventh. That was a discouraging thought.

When she reached the hospital, the receptionist gave her Georgie's room number, informing her that Dr. Wilson had admitted her. Carol didn't take that as a good sign.

Rick was sitting beside Georgie's bed when Carol entered the room.

"Dear, has she come to?" she asked him.

"No. Patrick said she has a mild concussion and is physically weak, which makes it harder for her to wake up. He says she needs a long rest and good food."

"I know. But we couldn't have kept her at the ranch against her will. And she is definitely stubborn."

"Takes one to know one," Rick said, grinning at his mother. Before she could respond to his teasing, the door opened and Patrick came in, followed by a nurse pushing a sonogram machine.

"Hello, Carol. If you two will step into the hallway, I'm going to make sure the baby is okay."

"I'll stay with her, Patrick. We're her family, after all," Carol said.

Patrick shrugged his shoulders. "Rick said the father is dead."

"Yes, he was a cousin of Caleb's."

"I see. Rick, go ahead and wait outside. But we're going to take a picture of the baby, one Georgie can show you herself later on." He nodded to the door.

Carol watched intently as the doctor and nurse set up the equipment. She knew Georgie would be devastated if anything was wrong with her baby.

"There he is," Patrick said, pointing to an image on the monitor.

"It's a boy?" Carol asked.

"Of course. If this baby is a Crawford, chances are slim it would be anything but. Remember, it took you six tries to get a girl."

"You're right. I hope the news pleases Georgie."

"Me, too. She doesn't seem to be having an easy time of it."

"No. She's been working too hard. She shouldn't be on her feet so much."

"She shouldn't be at all. I hope she's been eating right." After a minute, he said, "Any chance she can stay with you for a while? At least a month, but preferably until the baby is born?"

"I need to talk to you about that," Carol murmured. "I wanted her to stay, but she's very proud. I couldn't talk her into it. But she might stay on if she thinks leaving will endanger her baby. Could you convince her it would be better if she did?"

"Sure. And I won't be lying."

"Thank you, Patrick. I couldn't bear the thought of her going off on her own. She has no family but us."

Carol was satisfied that she'd found a way to convince Georgie to stay. But how would Caleb react? Not well. He talked about her own stubbornness, but Caleb Crawford could match her any day. Things around home were going to be difficult until he accepted Georgie's presence.

Georgie was thirsty. She struggled to come awake, but it seemed to be particularly difficult.

"Look. I think she's waking up. You'd better get Patrick," someone said.

"Thirsty," she managed to whisper, but she couldn't seem to open her eyes. It was too much effort.

"Georgie? Can you open your eyes?"

She knew that voice. Carol Crawford was here. For Carol, she'd make the effort. Struggling, Georgie finally opened her eyes a slit, just enough to know the light hurt. She managed to get those two words out and immediately the overhead light was turned off. She tried again and saw Carol's welcome face bending over her in the shadows.

"Hi, Carol," she whispered.

The door opened and another voice, one she didn't recognize, said, "The doctor's on his way."

"D-doctor?" She moved her hand to her stomach.

Carol seemed to understand her question. "The baby's okay, Georgie. The fall didn't hurt him."

Georgie relaxed a little, letting her eyes close once more. "Where am I?"

"In the hospital in Lawton. You passed out while walking back to town."

Her eyes widened as Georgie tried to sit up, but hands held her down in the bed. The overhead light, turned on again, made her flinch and narrow her gaze. "Let me go. I have to get out of the hospital. I can't pay—"

"It's all right, dear," Carol said. "It's all taken care of."

Georgie found Carol's face and stared at her desperately. "You don't understand. I can't pay—I have to save all my money for when the baby comes."

A male voice entered the discussion. "Your baby is going to come much too early if you don't obey my orders. I'm Dr. Wilson."

Georgie reached for her stomach again, comforted by the movement she felt there.

"Your baby is fine if we change a few things, like getting you more rest, a balanced diet and no stress. If you want your baby born healthy, you have to obey me. Carol has offered to have you stay with her until the infant comes."

"But I can't. Mr. Crawford—"

"Will welcome you when we explain everything," Carol said. "You mustn't let your pride get in the way of a safe delivery. The baby is the important thing now."

"But I'll promise to get more rest and eat a balanced diet at home. Then I won't be a problem for anyone." She looked eagerly at the doctor.

"I'm sorry, Georgie. But all evidence says that isn't going to happen. I know Carol will take good care of you. That will be best for your child. By the way, we took a sonogram earlier today. Would you like to see your baby?"

Distracted, she tried to sit up again, and the doctor moved to the side of the bed and pushed a button that raised the head. Then he grasped her wrist gently and took her pulse. "Look, don't talk."

He spread out the rolled up picture. Georgie gasped

as she saw her baby for the first time. "Can you tell if it's a boy or a girl?" she whispered.

"It's a boy. Makes sense, since your husband was a Crawford," the doctor said.

Georgie shifted her gaze from the paper to Carol. Who had told the doctor she was married? What was going on?

"He's right, you know," Carol said. "It wasn't until my sixth pregnancy that I had a girl. You haven't met her, but she's here with me. Lindsay, meet Georgie."

A pretty young woman greeted her with a warm smile much like her mother's. "I'm glad to meet you," Lindsay said.

Georgie started to tell Lindsay who she really was, but after a glance at Carol she simply said, "Thank you."

"We didn't know we had any cousins we hadn't already met. Where do you live?" the young woman asked.

"In Dallas. I guess my...husband is the city branch of the family." Obviously it was important to Carol that the identity of her baby's father be hushed up. And Georgie would never do anything to hurt Carol.

"Are there any more of you?" Lindsay asked.

"Crawfords? No. My husband's mother died with him in a car accident a few months ago."

"Oh, you poor dear. When is your baby due?"

The doctor stepped forward. "By my calculation, I'd guess between two and a half to three months. Right, Georgie?"

She nodded. "Can I leave now?"

"You've had enough excitement today. If you're very good, I'll let you go home tomorrow."

When Georgie's eyes lit up, Carol said, "He means

home to my house, Georgie. It's going to be your home for the next three months.''

Georgie closed her eyes. What could she say? It would seem unappreciative if she continued to protest. Yet to accept such an offer when she knew Mr. Crawford didn't want her there made her extremely uncomfortable. She opened her eyes. "I really appreciate your offer Carol, but your husband—''

"Owes you more than that.'' Carol's voice was firm, leaving no room for argument.

"Maybe if I stay a week, the doctor will decide I'm in good enough shape to return home.''

Carol smiled. "Maybe. We'll take it day by day.''

Chapter 5

The next day, Rick was working in the barn when he heard his mother call out for him. Since she didn't often enter the barn, he knew something had to be up. Sure enough, it had to do with Georgie.

Carol had just learned that Georgie was to be released from the hospital that afternoon. Apparently, all of the girl's belongings were still at the apartment she had shared with Cal and his mother. With the lease up in a few days, she had nowhere else to store them. Carol had volunteered Rick to drive into Dallas with Georgie to pick up her things and bring them back to the ranch tomorrow.

Rick didn't mind the drive to Dallas. Although he hadn't hit it off with Georgie, she was like a member of the family and she and her child needed protection. Heck, he might even enjoy getting to know her better during the drive.

Until his mother warned him she would try to lose him.

"What? What are you talking about, Mom? Why would she do that? Did she tell you she was planning to run again?"

"Of course not, dear. She has a lot of pride, and she thinks she can manage on her own. But Patrick said her baby is undersized because she's not getting enough to eat. So we mustn't let her stay there."

"So I'm going to be responsible for the health of the baby?" He was beginning to realize the day trip was not going to be a picnic.

"Yes," Carol said cheerfully, patting his arm. "I'm sure you'll do fine, Rick. You're a smart boy."

"Not too smart or I wouldn't have gotten caught in this mess."

"Quit grumbling," his mother ordered.

"What's he grumbling about?" Caleb asked, entering the barn in the midst of their conversation.

"It's nothing to concern yourself with," Carol assured him.

His father scowled. "I'll be the judge of that!" he snapped.

"No, you won't." She turned on her heel and marched out of the barn, leaving Rick to face his father.

"Uh, I need to get back to work," Rick muttered. Before he could take two steps, Caleb planted himself in front of him.

"What were you complaining about?"

Rick shrugged his shoulders and said, "Oh, just stuff Mom needs me to do. I wasn't really complaining." He gave his father a smile and tried to walk around him.

But Caleb wouldn't let him go. He grabbed Rick's arm to stop him from walking away.

"Dad, I'm taking tomorrow off to help out Mom, that's all."

"To do what?"

Rick hated the secretiveness going on between his parents. But he wasn't going to tell his father. "You need to ask Mom if you want to know." Then he pulled away and went back out to the corral.

Caleb could barely tolerate his son's response. But he didn't go after Rick. Forcing him to betray his mother's trust wouldn't be fair.

He headed for the house, his jaw squared. When he appeared in the kitchen, Carol didn't seem surprised.

"Hello, Caleb. Would you like a cup of coffee?"

He nodded and sat down. It almost felt like old times, coming in for a coffee break to talk over the morning's events.

Carol joined him at the table after she put a plate of cookies there, too. He automatically took one.

"It's not fair to put Rick between us," he growled.

"I'm glad you realize that," she said with a nod.

"So tell me what he's doing for you tomorrow."

"Why should I? According to you, secrets are okay."

"When did I ever—" He broke off and stared at her. "You're making a mountain out of a molehill!"

"No. I'm just keeping a secret. A small, inconsequential secret, unlike the knowledge of a child."

Caleb bent over, rubbing his forehead. "Carol, I was trying to protect you. It was better for you not to know. If you'd known, we wouldn't have had the past wonderful twenty-six years. We wouldn't have had Lindsay!"

"I am an adult, Caleb. Your lying to me makes all those years seem as if they were built on false promises. It would've been difficult to know the truth, yes, but I loved you. We could've had those years, and Lindsay, and you could've gotten to know your seventh child before he was killed in a car wreck."

"You say that now, but you wouldn't have forgiven me. I know that. It's easy to say you would have forgiven me now, when Helen's dead and we're both older. But not then."

She stared at him sadly. "I didn't realize how little you trusted me or my feelings for you. It's a wonder you came back at all."

"I couldn't leave!" he roared, frustrated. "We had five boys to raise!"

Tears escaped Carol's eyes and made their way down her face. She stood and turned her back to him, wiping them away with her apron. Then she slowly walked out of the kitchen and up the stairs, as if she'd aged fifty years.

When Rick came in for lunch, he knew at once something was wrong. Carol took pride in the meals she served her menfolk. Today she'd left him a note telling him to heat up the leftover lasagna or make himself a sandwich.

He put the lasagna in the microwave and then knocked on Georgie's door and opened it. "Have you had lunch?"

"Yes. Carol brought me a sandwich and a bowl of soup after we got home from the hospital."

"Did she seem all right?"

"No, she didn't. I asked her what was wrong and

she said something about chickens coming home to roost. I didn't know what she meant."

Rick didn't know, either. "Is there anything you need?"

"No, thank you."

He gave her a smile and closed her door.

He heard his father come in and wash his hands in the workroom. Rick returned to the kitchen and took the lasagna out of the microwave, dishing it onto two plates. His father came in as he was putting it on the table.

"Is that lunch?" Caleb asked.

"Yeah. What did you say to Mom?"

A guilty look on Caleb's face spoke louder than he did. "Nothing. I did nothing."

They both ate in silence. After lunch, Rick scrubbed their dishes and loaded them in the dishwasher. When the kitchen was as clean as he'd found it, he slowly climbed the stairs, then tapped on his mother's bedroom door. "Mom?"

"Yes?" she responded in a muffled voice.

"Are you sick?"

"No."

"May I come in?"

"No."

"Mom, I'm worried about you."

"I'm fine."

He knew she wasn't. He went downstairs again and headed for the phone. His little sister would be the best person to help in this situation. He dialed her store in Lawton.

Kelly, his sister-in-law, answered the phone. "Oklahoma Chic, this is Kelly. May I help you?"

"Yeah, I need to talk to Lindsay," he said gruffly.

"Rick? Is that you? Is something wrong?"

"Yeah. Mom's sick or something."

There was no response for several minutes until Lindsay picked up the phone. "Rick? What's wrong with Mom?"

"I don't know. She won't talk to me. It's connected to Georgie and that situation."

"Why would Georgie have anything to do with it? Dad doesn't mind an extra mouth to feed. If his cousin's widow needs help, he wouldn't turn her down."

"Damn, is that what Mom told you?"

"Yes," Lindsay said slowly. "Isn't that the truth?"

"No." He thought about telling her on the phone, but felt it would be better to give her the news in person. "Look, I'll come into town. Is there somewhere we can talk without being heard?"

"Yes, of course."

He hung up and hurried out the door.

Shoppers were slow that afternoon and Lindsay invited Kelly, their sister-in-law, to join them in the back room, while their manager watched the store. "I don't understand what's going on," Kelly said when Rick arrived, "but we don't keep secrets in our family. This is very strange."

Rick had no problem with Kelly joining them. After all, as he told the ladies, Pete knew most of what was going on.

Kelly stared at him. "Pete knows? But he didn't say anything to me about a problem."

Rick groaned. "Look, this isn't our secret. But Mom obviously needs some help, so I'm going to tell you."

When he finished his tale, both women stared at him, their mouths open.

Finally Lindsay said, "Dad had another son from an affair before I was born? And that son got Georgie pregnant, but died before they could marry? And Georgie is alone with no family and no money and Dad wanted to throw her out?"

"Basically."

Kelly shook her head. "Poor Carol. No wonder she doesn't feel up to par."

"No, you don't understand. She was fine until today. She's invited Georgie to stay at the ranch until the baby's born, which will be in about three months. But Dad said or did something this morning. See, Mom wants me to drive Georgie to Dallas to collect her belongings tomorrow. I was grumbling about it because Mom said Georgie would try to run away."

"Why?" Lindsay asked.

"Mom said she has too much pride. Anyway, Dad came in and wanted to know what I was doing for Mom. Mom told him it was a secret. She went to the house and he asked me. I told him to ask Mom."

"And?"

"I don't know what happened between them but Mom didn't fix lunch. She left a note to heat up the lasagna in the microwave. That was it. I went upstairs to check on her and she sounded terrible. But she wouldn't let me in, and said nothing was wrong."

"Oh, my," Lindsay said, well aware how unusual it was for their mother to behave like that.

"Did you ask Dad what happened?"

"Same answer—nothing. And he went back to the barn without checking on her."

"Can you manage without me, Kelly?" Lindsay asked.

"Of course. We'll be fine. Call me when you know what's wrong."

"Yes. Tell me, Rick, was Gil in on any of this?" Lindsay asked. Gil was her husband. He and Lindsay had a ranch near town.

"Nope. As far as I know, neither he nor Rafe have heard anything."

Kelly muttered, "Good." Rafe was Kelly's stepfather, who also happened to manage Gil's ranch.

"But Pete knew about it," Lindsay reminded Kelly.

"Yes," she acknowledged, anger in her voice, "and my loving husband said nothing about it to me."

"Mom?" Lindsay called as she slipped into her parents' bedroom. "Are you all right?"

"Yes, dear," said her mother who normally never took naps or even got in bed during the day. "What are you doing here?"

"Rick came to see me. He's worried about you."

"Nothing's wrong," Carol said, sitting up a bit.

"Mom, you don't take to your bed unless you're on your last legs. Do I need to call the doctor?" Lindsay could tell her mother had been crying, and that worried her a great deal.

"No. I don't think he can cure a broken heart."

"Mom, what are you talking about?"

"I've discovered that the past twenty-six years of my marriage have been a lie. Your father came back to me out of necessity because I had five children and Helen only had one. Simple mathematics."

"Oh, Mom! I'm sure Dad didn't mean—"

"I'm afraid he did. But don't worry. I'll recover...somehow."

Lindsay sat beside her mom and gave her a big hug. After a moment, she asked, "Are you going to divorce him?"

"I don't know."

Lindsay stayed with her mother for a while, until Carol insisted she was fine and that she needed to be alone. When Lindsay entered the kitchen, she found Rick and their father fixing themselves sandwiches for dinner.

Rick looked at her and then their dad, but he said nothing.

Caleb, however, spoke up. "How's your mother? Does she need a doctor?"

"No," Lindsay said slowly. She tried to hold back her anger, her pain, her mother's pain, but found she couldn't. "How could you, Dad?" The anguish in her voice would've upset him at any time, but now, with everything out of kilter, he looked stricken.

"It was twenty-six years ago, damn it! I made a mistake and I've said I'm sorry. What does she want me to do?"

Lindsay knew what her mother needed was reassurance and a big apology, but it wasn't up to her to tell her dad that. She shook her head and walked out but not before she heard her father say, "Damn females. They're impossible to understand."

Later that evening, Kelly waited until their children were in bed before she spoke to Pete about his parents. "Pete, do you remember me asking what Rick wanted when he came over yesterday?"

She'd gotten his attention. He regarded her cautiously, instead of the television he'd been watching. "Yeah."

"What did you tell me?"

"I said he had a problem with Dad he wanted some help with."

"Ah, I see. A family matter?"

"Well…yeah."

"How long do we have to be married before I'm part of the family?" she asked.

That question made him sit up in his chair. "Honey, you are family. My family."

"I am? And yet you didn't bother to tell me that you found out your father had an illegitimate son? That he betrayed your mother? That the young woman who turned up pregnant at your parents' house is carrying a Crawford baby?"

"I should've told you, but Dad…well, he was embarrassed and didn't want to tell us. So I figured we'd keep it between us guys and that would be better."

"Like he kept it from your mother?"

"He was afraid she wouldn't take him back."

"And how are things going now?"

"Fine."

"So why did Rick tell Lindsay your mother wouldn't come out of her bedroom and refused to let him in?"

"Is Mom sick? Did they call the doctor?"

"No, she refused. She said a doctor couldn't cure a broken heart."

"Kelly, what are you talking about? Mom wasn't that upset. She wants to keep Georgie at the ranch and take care of her. You know how Mom is."

"Lindsay asked Carol if she was going to divorce your father and she said she didn't know."

Pete looked stunned.

"Do you remember saying that you wanted our marriage to be as strong as your parents'?" Kelly asked her husband. "That we should always tell each other everything? No secrets?"

"Of course I do."

"But you didn't tell me what was going on."

"Honey, I didn't want you to be upset. I was trying to protect you."

"I want you to protect our children. I'd like you to respect *my* intellect. I would've felt sorry for your mother, but it wouldn't have affected our marriage, because you were keeping your word. I tell you everything, but if you're only going to tell me what you think I need to know, that changes things."

"Kelly, you're being silly."

"Like your mother was silly? Too silly to know the truth?"

Kelly watched her husband carefully. He opened his mouth to answer. Then he closed it again as if he had to think a bit before replying. "You're right. I promised the truth to you, and I want the truth in return. Dad was wrong to lie to Mom."

"Do you realize how hard it is to trust someone when they've lied to you? Think about your mother. She hasn't stopped loving your dad. But she can no longer trust him. And that's why her heart is broken."

"Damn. Does Dad understand that?"

"Of course not. I'll bet he hasn't apologized and asked her forgiveness, because he doesn't figure he did anything wrong. What do you think?"

"I know you're right."

Pete gathered Kelly into his arms, and she didn't

resist his tight embrace. "How did I get such a smart wife?" he asked, grinning.

"I'm smart because I suffered. But I don't want to suffer again. I want our marriage to last forever. But you have to respect me as I respect you. You see, I told you about your mom's response. If I had kept it a secret, you wouldn't have understood the situation. You couldn't help your father do and say the right things."

"Honey, don't expect miracles. Dad is stubborn."

"I know, because you are, too. But try."

"I will."

"It would be so sad if they divorced."

"Yeah," he agreed as he hugged her to him even more tightly.

Chapter 6

When Joe came in from the barn that evening, his wife was working at the sink, her back to him. Usually she met him at the door, but he figured she probably hadn't heard him enter. He sneaked up behind her and wrapped his hands around her big stomach. He loved feeling his baby kick against his hands. He was surprised when Anna didn't turn in his arms and give him a warm greeting.

Before he could ask her what was wrong, five-year-old Julie, followed by their toddler, Hank, came into the kitchen, hollering for him. Joe scooped Julie up and tossed her in the air while she squealed. Then it was Hank's turn. He screamed even louder.

And all the while, Joe noted, Anna still kept her back to him.

"Honey? What's wrong?" he asked.

She turned from the sink and carried the salad she'd

been making to the table. "Go wash up, Julie. Come here, Hank, and Mama will wash you."

"I'll do it. You don't need to be lifting Hank. He's a big boy," Joe said.

She stepped back and let him pick up her son. When he and Anna had married, Julie had just turned five and Hank was barely nine months old. Now they were having a third child. "Do you feel okay? You're not having any pains, are you?"

"No."

Joe knew something was wrong now. He put Hank in his high chair after he dried his face and hands. Then he began to help him eat his dinner, and encouraged Julie to eat hers. "If you kids do a good job on your food, I reckon you can have a bowl of ice cream while you watch television."

In fifteen minutes, Joe had the children in the den, watching television with their ice cream. When he came back to the kitchen, Anna had still not uttered a word. "Tell me what's wrong," he said.

"Like you told me what was wrong yesterday?" she asked coolly, meeting his eyes.

He shifted his gaze to the floor. "Who told you?" he asked gently.

"Lindsay. She wanted you to know that your mother might divorce your father."

"What? She must be kidding!"

"I wouldn't know, since I had no idea there was a problem."

The shock of the news from Lindsay was fading a little, and he caught the hint of danger lurking in Anna's words. "Honey, I didn't want to worry you. I figured Mom and Dad would figure things out. They get cross with each other occasionally, but they always work it out.''

"Did you think this was just something trivial I shouldn't know about? Your illegitimate brother and a woman pregnant with Caleb's grandchild?''

"No, of course not, but I didn't want you to worry. Our baby's due soon and I feared it might upset you.''

"Oh, it's upset me all right!'' Anna said.

"Mommy!'' Julie shrieked. "Hank spilled his ice cream!''

Anna bustled out of the kitchen with a towel in hand.

Joe gave up continuing their discussion until after both children had been tucked in bed.

As he was reading Julie a storybook, she asked, "Is Mommy okay?''

"I think I did something wrong. But don't worry. I'll tell her I'm sorry.''

"Good, 'cause Mommy always forgives me when I say that.''

"I know.'' Joe kissed her good-night. "That's because you are irresistible!''

"I know,'' Julie said with a grin.

"Watch it, young lady, or your mommy will be onto you.'' Not that he was worried. Julie was well behaved.

Anna was waiting for him in the den. He gave a sigh of relief at seeing her. "Okay, I know I've upset you. Is it because I didn't tell you about Mom and Dad's problems?''

"Yes,'' she said quietly.

He sat there debating what to say next when she spoke again. "If you didn't tell me because your father wanted it kept secret, that means you didn't trust *me* to keep the secret. Or you don't feel I'm actually part of the family.''

"All I can say for myself is that I didn't think," Joe admitted quietly. "It's a shameful thing that Dad did. I didn't want you to think any less of him or me."

She stared at him. Then, much to his relief, she fell into his arms. "That's the only excuse I'd accept, but don't let it happen again. You promised, after we messed up the first time, that we'd always be honest with each other."

He loved the feel of her against him. "Yeah, I did, 'cause I almost lost you just because I wasn't honest. I love you."

"I love you, too, no matter what your father did. Now, tell me all about it."

Later that night lying in bed, Joe figured that he'd place a call in the morning to his other brother, Logan. The third Crawford brother had married a lady rancher in Texas, near Wichita Falls. Their ranch was only a couple of hours away, and they saw Logan, Abby and their two children frequently. Joe thought Logan had the right to know what was going on.

Especially if their parents were headed for a divorce.

He couldn't believe his parents might separate. They had been so devoted to each other. At least he'd thought so. Yet his father had had a child by another woman. Joe didn't think his father had loved her, but he'd been careless.

Joe wondered if his brother's wife had reacted like Anna had. He smiled and pulled her a little closer to him as she slept.

He was a lucky man. And he wasn't likely to forget it.

Rick was glad he was in his truck, driving to Dallas with Georgie to pick up her things. At least he wasn't home being attacked on both sides, his father wanting to know what his wife was saying, and his mom trying to make sure Rick kept his mouth shut.

Besides, Georgie was fun company. They'd discussed the Cowboys, Dallas's pro football team, the Mavericks, pro basketball, and the Stars, pro hockey. Then he brought up the Rangers.

Georgie kept up the conversation. "I like baseball. It's fun to watch and it doesn't take all your attention. I usually do something else while the game is on."

"I didn't know there were girls who like to watch sports."

"I'm not an expert," she hurriedly assured him.

"Me, neither. Have you ever gone to see a game in person?" he asked.

"No. They're out of my budget."

"The prices are getting pretty high, but I'd like to go once or twice. Only I think I'd miss seeing instant replay."

Georgie laughed, which made her look much younger. Rick tried to think of other subjects that would bring that expression to her face. He brought up books, and she stared in surprise.

"I didn't think you would do much reading," she said, staring at him in amazement.

It was his turn to laugh. "That just shows that you don't know my mother very well. She insisted we read. And once we discovered pirate stories, my personal favorite, she couldn't buy me enough books."

"That's wonderful! Carol's a terrific mother."

"Yeah. How was your mother?"

The smile disappeared and Georgie turned away, staring out the window.

"Georgie?"

"Yes?"

"Aren't you going to tell me about your mother?"

"No. And I'm sorry, but I need to stop." She looked straight ahead.

"Don't apologize. Mom warned me. It's not a problem." He pulled off the four-lane highway into a gas station. He'd actually expected to stop more often. They were almost to the outskirts of Dallas. He'd asked her address earlier. She'd been reluctant to give it to him, which was strange, since he was taking her home.

She'd made no attempts to run away. Maybe his mother had been wrong. Even as he thought that, he realized Georgie had been gone about ten minutes. He walked over to the ladies' room and knocked on the door.

"Just a minute," someone hollered.

"Georgie? Is that you?"

The door opened and a middle-aged woman came out. "There's just me in there."

"Did a young blonde, about six months pregnant, come out when you went in?"

"Oh, you mean the one looking for a ride? There was a lady trucker in there and she agreed to take her."

"What? Do you know what her truck looked liked?"

"She said she was hauling pigs."

Rick scanned the area for any trucks carrying animals and saw one pulling out. He was pretty sure the driver was a woman, though he couldn't see Georgie inside the cab. He ran for his truck, irritated with the woman. What was wrong with her? Several times she'd expressed concern about causing trouble for Carol.

He drew up beside the truck, just close enough to

make certain Georgie was inside. Then he got behind the vehicle so she couldn't see him.

When they got to the spot on the freeway where he should have exited to go to her apartment, the truck pulled over, caution lights flashing. Rick slowed down and followed behind. When the truck started up again, leaving Georgie on the side of the road, waving good-bye, Rick pulled up beside her.

"You want a ride?" he asked.

Consternation marked her face. "How did you find me?"

"One of the ladies in the rest room told me. Come on, get in."

"Rick, you should've let me go. That way, your mother would think she'd done her best, but I wouldn't be a problem for her."

"Again, you don't know my mother. She'd have me down here searching every street in Dallas, looking for you. It will be easiest for me if you get in so we can get this done and go back home."

With a sigh, she pulled open the truck door. He extended a hand to help her crawl up on the high seat.

They drove without conversation, though she did give him directions to her apartment. Rick scanned the neighborhood with a critical eye as they pulled up. He wasn't impressed.

Once inside the building, she led him to apartment D and inserted the key. The door came open rather easily and Rick didn't think the lock looked very sturdy.

Georgie seemed eager to enter. He supposed this was home for her, no matter how run-down. Then she froze. "Someone's in there," she whispered.

Rick shoved her behind him and pushed the door

open. "Who's in here? Show yourself at once or I'll call the police!"

A disreputable looking man stepped out of the bedroom. "Who says so?"

"The owner. Or at least the lessee," Rick assured the man.

"If *she* told you that," the man said, pointing to Georgie, "she's lying. You check with the manager. Her name's not on the lease."

"Who are you?" Rick asked, noting Georgie's worried look.

"Name's Leon Dipp. I was Helen's husband. She leased this place for her son. And it's about time you showed up," he said to Georgie.

"What are you doing, going through my things?" Georgie asked angrily.

"I'm looking for what you must have already found. The paper about the trust fund. You know that belongs to me."

"How do you figure that?" Rick asked, studying the man.

"Who are you? This doesn't concern you, that's for sure. If she told you *she* had a trust fund, she's lying."

Leon walked closer and Georgie scuttled past him into the bedroom. The she screamed with rage. Rick raced in behind her, to find her standing in the middle of the room, holding a shirt that had been ripped in two. It looked like other items of clothing had been treated the same way.

"How dare you!" she cried as she raced to the door and glared at the man still standing there.

"I was looking for what belonged to me. Who knew where you'd hidden it?"

She started toward Leon, but Rick caught her arm.

"Go through your stuff, see if there's anything worth saving. I'll take care of him."

She gave him a look that said she didn't believe him, but she turned back to the mess on the floor. The man had done his best to destroy everything she owned, which, in Rick's eyes, was pitifully little.

"Look, my father set up the trust, and he's not going to release the money to you. It will only go to Georgie once she proves the baby is Cal's. You can forget getting any part of it."

The man stared at Rick and he stared back. When he saw a light come on in his eyes, Rick knew he'd thought of another angle. "Well, of course I intend to offer that poor child a home for her and her baby. I only made a mess in there because I was worried out of my mind about her."

"Right," Rick drawled, letting his disbelief show.

"It's true. I'll give you the address where he can send the money. I'll be taking good care of her and her baby." He wrote down his address on a piece of paper and handed it to Rick, who reluctantly took it.

"No need for you to stay and waste your time. I'll take care of the sweet thing. She'll be just fine. We'll send the proof after the baby is born."

Leon was so obvious, Rick couldn't believe the man thought he would believe him. He stuck his head in the small bedroom. "Georgie, this man says you're going to live with him."

Georgie let out a stream of profanity before she stopped herself and said clearly, "I wouldn't live anywhere near him, or trust him with anything so precious as my baby. He's horrible. He wants the money and nothing else. Don't believe a word he says."

As if Rick needed someone to tell him that. "Don't worry, honey, I won't."

He turned to Leon, whose eyes were filled with anger over Georgie's words. The man opened his mouth, to respond in kind, Rick was sure, but changed his mind as Rick glanced at him.

"The poor child didn't have a good upbringing," the man said. "Helen tried to help her because Cal was so in love with her, but she worried about her. I'll take care of her, I promise."

"I don't think she wants that kind of care. She's coming with me."

Rick stepped back into the bedroom and asked Georgie if she was ready.

"Yes. I have three boxes. Is that too much?"

He said no and reached for one. She did, too. He told her to leave them for him, but she insisted on carrying one, so he grabbed the third one as well and followed her out.

The man came after him. "She won't get the money. I'm hiring a lawyer. That money comes to me as Helen's surviving spouse. I know about these things. That money belongs to me and I'll get it in the end…one way or another."

Rick stopped suddenly and turned, and the man almost ran into him. "You'd better think about that, sir. I have four brothers as big as me, and a father who's still as strong as an ox. And one of my brothers is a lawyer. We're going to protect Georgie. After all, she's the mother of our nephew. If you come after her or the money, you'll have a fight on your hands. One you can't win."

Then he walked on to the truck. Georgie was watching him, a worried look on her face.

Quietly, he said, "Get in the truck and lock your door, honey. We're leaving this place." And he saw no reason to ever return. He arranged the boxes so nothing would blow out. Then he turned to look at Leon, who was glaring at him. "Are we clear on everything?"

"I'm not talking to you!"

"Suits me, but remember what I said."

He climbed into the truck and started the motor, pulling out quickly as the man shook his fist at them.

"Who was that man again?" Rick asked.

"Leon Dipp was married to Helen for the last ten years. I think he married her for the money she had invested. Toward the end of the marriage, when the money had run out, he treated her badly. When he heard about the trust fund, he tried to figure out how he could get his hands on it."

"How did he hear about it when you didn't?"

"Helen told him. But no one told me. After the accident, he was very nice to me. It was a relief when I figured out why."

"Strange how well it turned out for him, Helen and Cal both dying," Rick said slowly.

"You don't think…"

"I don't know, honey. I'm just guessing. But I'm glad I came down with you. I got the feeling he'd tie you up to get a chance at that money."

"You're probably right. I'm sorry I've been so much trouble. I didn't even think about him being there. And…and he ripped everything, even the baby clothes I'd sewn."

"You made baby clothes?"

"We didn't have a lot of money. It was cheaper that way."

He pulled over to the side of the freeway and took a piece of material she'd been holding. He held it up and saw a nightgown handsewn with neat stitches. "You didn't have a machine?"

"No, but I'm pretty fast," she assured him.

"You'll be even faster now. Mom has a new sewing machine. She'll let you use it. You may be able to repair some of the clothes. And Lindsay and Kelly may have some baby things they can loan you. Lindsay's baby boy is almost two, and Alexandra, Kelly and Pete's little girl, is almost a year old."

"That would be nice, but I couldn't take them because I'll be going back to Dallas after the baby is born."

"Why?"

"Because I don't have anyplace to live. I can't stay with your parents when your father doesn't want to ever see me again. Your mother is sweet to invite me, but I can only stay until I have the baby. And he may come early," she added, rubbing a palm over her stomach worriedly. "I hope not too early."

Rick caught her hand in his. "He'll be fine. Doc didn't see anything wrong, did he?"

"He said he was a little small."

"Was Cal a big man, like us?"

"Yes. He made me feel safe."

"Good for him. I'd say, in that neighborhood, you needed someone to make you feel safe."

"It's not that bad a neighborhood. I know a lot of people because I've been working about a month at the local fast-food restaurant. That's where everyone goes to eat around there."

"The food you'll get at home is a lot better for you. If you eat well in the next three months, I bet that little guy will grow like a weed. The only thing is, I think you're, too, uh, delicate to carry a big boy.''

''I'll manage, I promise. I promised myself that I'd do whatever it took to deliver my baby safely.''

''And that's why you need to stay with us until you do. We'll talk about what happens after that later.''

Georgie gave him a wary glance, but she said nothing else, leaning back in the corner and closing her eyes. As she nodded off, she dreamed about a magic carpet—or was it a truck?—delivering her back to a magical ranch, where a woman could raise a child to be healthy and strong.

Chapter 7

Georgie woke up to discover Rick's truck coming to a halt near Carol's front porch.

"Go on in," he said softly. "I'll bring your boxes."

"Oh, no. I'll help."

"Georgie, go on in." His voice was firm, and she nodded after a minute and entered the home through the back door. Carol was in the kitchen and greeted her warmly.

"Oh, Georgie, you made it back safe and sound."

"Yes, of course."

"Where's Rick?"

"He's bringing in what I had left," she said, fighting back tears again. He was bringing in scraps of material, the remains of her life. If, as Rick said, Carol would let her use her sewing machine, she could repair a few shirts and things.

"Rick...Rick said you have a sewing machine." She

watched Carol's face, trying to tell if the words bothered her.

"Yes, do you sew? I only use it to patch things, but you're welcome to it."

Georgie shook her head in amazement. "Carol, you are so generous. Aren't you afraid I'll break it?"

"Of course not. If you need help using it, I'll show you how. But even if something went wrong, Caleb can fix almost anything."

Georgie was about to respond when Rick and Caleb came in, carrying her boxes. Georgie scooted over to open the door to her room for them. Caleb set down his box and picked up one of the nightgowns she'd made—or at least half of it.

"Who did this?" he demanded. Carol, standing in the doorway, gasped when she saw the damage.

"Cal's stepfather," Georgie said.

"Why?" Carol asked, moving into the room. "Why would he do such a terrible thing?" She began looking at the pieces of material in the boxes. "Honey, all of these are ruined."

"No, not ruined. I can sew a lot of them back together. It will be all right."

"Answer Carol's question," Caleb ordered, staring at her.

Georgie gazed at him blankly, unable to remember what question he meant.

"Why would Cal's stepfather do such a thing?" he asked again.

She shrugged her shoulders. "Because he couldn't find the trust fund papers." She didn't add that he'd gone through her belongings the first time while she was at Helen and Cal's funerals, taking everything he could sell. He'd said she had nothing except what Cal had given her, so it all belonged to him.

"Why would he want the papers?" Caleb asked.

"He thinks he can get some money that way. I…I think he married Helen because she told him about the money she had. Helen had complained to us that most of her money was gone because he'd 'invested' it or spent it on himself. He drives a Porsche."

"Does he think I'm an idiot? That I'd okay giving the money to him?" Caleb asked.

She shrugged again.

Caleb turned to his wife. "Carol, take some money out of savings and get the girl some clothes, for her and the baby."

"No," Georgie said. "I'll repair the damage with Carol's sewing machine. I'll be fine, but thank you for your generosity. It's especially impressive when I know you don't want me here."

Caleb shot both his wife and Georgie dark looks and walked out of the bedroom and into the kitchen.

Rick followed his father and said, "That was nice of you, Dad."

"Yeah, sure. I'm protecting my reputation. If everyone believes she's a relative, I don't want them to think I let her run around in rags. I'll tell Carol—No, I won't. You'll tell your mother the reason. Okay?"

"Okay," Rick agreed. "But, Dad, there's something I need to discuss with you. Helen's death, hers and Cal's, sure was convenient for Helen's husband. She probably had insurance, but…I thought maybe we should call the police and discuss it with them."

"You think he had something to do with their deaths?"

"It's a possibility."

"He seems dangerous?"

"Oh, yeah. And he tried to get me to leave Georgie in his care. I bet she'd be dead the minute the trust fund was transferred."

"Can Georgie go back to Dallas without this man bothering her?"

"I don't know, Dad. She has no family or anyone to take care of her."

"Well, I don't want her here, but even I wouldn't send a pregnant woman off by herself to have a child, especially when he's my grandbaby. You did say it's a boy, didn't you?"

"Yeah, he's a healthy boy, though he's a little undersized, Patrick said."

"Hmm. You can't say Anna's baby is undersized, can you?" Caleb asked, smiling.

"No. But she's due real soon. Joe thinks it will be any minute," Rick said, remembering his brother's excitement.

"We seem to be a factory for turning out boys. You let me know if that little girl needs anything." Then he stomped out the door.

Rick grinned. He knew his father wouldn't be mean to Georgie once he understood her situation. She was hardly more than a child. She said she was twenty-one, which would make her seven years younger than himself. He'd keep an eye on her.

Carol left Georgie lying on her bed to rest. Then she called her daughter and daughters-in-law, asking each of them to go through their maternity wardrobe for things Georgie could borrow. Anna said if she'd wait a week or two, she could have her entire wardrobe, because Anna never wanted to see her maternity

clothes again. But she was laughing. At the end of a
pregnancy, most women had had enough of their limited wardrobe.

Then Carol made a quick trip into Lawton to buy
Georgie some undergarments, maternity jeans, a nice
pair of slacks and several maternity tops. She was back
home before Georgie woke up.

Rick and Caleb came in at their regular time for
dinner. She had the table set and a tasty meal for them,
as if everything was normal. But it wasn't.

There was no dinner conversation, for one thing.
Caleb never looked at her. She was wearing a new
dress, which he would usually notice. But not tonight.

"Did Rick tell you about Georgie's apartment and
that rotten man who was there tearing everything to
pieces?" she asked, staring at Caleb.

He looked at her, then returned his gaze to his plate.
"Yeah."

"Do you see now that we need to help her?"

"I could give her some money so she could take
care of herself," Caleb said sturdily, as if it would
solve all the problems.

Carol slapped her hand on the table. "Do you think
the almighty dollar is the answer to everything? Do you
really think money is the reason all our children are
respected in the community, that they grew up to be
good people? You're smarter than that, Caleb!"

"I'm glad to hear it," he replied, sarcasm in his
voice.

"Then why are you shoving her away?" Carol
asked.

"Because she reminds me of a mistake I made! And
I don't want to broadcast that mistake to our neighbors!
I didn't enjoy facing my sons. I don't see why I have

to be responsible for her mistakes, either!'' By the time he finished, his voice was almost a shout.

"Dad, shh," Rick warned.

"You shushing me, boy?" Caleb demanded, anger in his voice. "You and who else is gonna make me be quiet?"

Rick swallowed hard. "Dad, I've never known you to hurt someone on purpose. And I don't think Georgie made a mistake. She loved Cal and planned to marry him. It's not her fault he died, leaving her pregnant."

"Rick?" a soft voice called, and he spun around in his chair to discover Georgie standing in the doorway, her face pale.

Rick leaped to his feet and reached for her, afraid she'd pass out again. "Georgie, are you all right?"

"I'm fine. If Mr. Crawford will give me five hundred dollars, I'll disappear and never bother him again. That would be best for everyone."

Carol protested.

Rick said, "No, Georgie, that won't do. Five hundred wouldn't pay for even a month, much less the three you have ahead, and the delivery bills."

"I'll manage, Mr. Crawford, if that's what you want."

Caleb pulled out his checkbook and wrote her a check for one thousand dollars. "Don't go back to Cal's stepfather."

"No." She reached out and took the check. "I'll try to pay you back after…afterward."

Caleb waved his hand dismissively. "No need."

"Carol, I won't forget your kindness. And Rick, too." Then she turned and reentered her bedroom.

"Caleb, how could you!" Carol protested, an ache in her voice.

Rick, his eyes burning, glared at his father.

"You wanted me to help her, didn't you? Well, I did!"

"You didn't help her. You paid off your conscience!"

They all heard the back door close. Rick ran to the door and opened it. "Georgie! I'll drive you back to Dallas." Rick ran after her. The other two sat in silence.

Finally, Carol said, "You miserable, selfish man." She got up and went upstairs.

"I doubled the amount of the check!" he shouted after her, but that fact didn't seem to make any difference.

When Carol came down the stairs half an hour later, having heard Rick's truck in the driveway, she found the kitchen cleaned, obviously by Caleb. She supposed it was his attempt to placate her, but she began to think she'd never forgive him. When she thought of Georgie out on her own, with no family anywhere, she wanted to cry.

A half hour later, Rick entered the house and heard his mother call out to him. "Rick? Did she come back with you?"

"No, Mom," he said as he walked into the kitchen and gave Carol a hug. "I left her at the bus station. I talked my head off, but in the end, I couldn't convince her that Dad would ever change his mind. I didn't know what else to do."

"I know. We can't keep her prisoner. I just—just worry about her so."

"Yeah."

Carol gave her son another hug. "Thank you for trying."

"No problem, Mom," he said, his voice tight. They each went their separate way to their bedrooms.

Rick stood at the open door of his room. It had been his for as long as since he could remember. It had changed as his interests changed. He'd collected trains when he was a little boy. He still had a few.

When he'd discovered girls, he'd forgotten trains. There were several pictures of him with various girl-friends, taken by his mother. He'd been involved in football, playing wide receiver. There'd even been talk of a pro career, but he'd turned it down. A couple of footballs, each marked for a special event, were displayed around the room.

And throughout the years, he'd been crazy about horses. Pictures of his favorite horses were also on the walls.

As he stood there, he compared his room to that of Georgie in the apartment she had shared with Cal. It was an anonymous room, a place to stay. Not a place to grow and love and build a future. It seemed to emphasize more and more the life that his father had condemned Georgie to. As his mom had said, money wasn't what counted. Even if it did, it would take more than a thousand dollars to help Georgie get by.

Rick had had a hard time leaving her at the Lawton bus station, but she'd refused to let him wait with her until the next bus came through. She'd promised to be careful and had sent him away, her last words being another thank-you.

As if he'd done much to help. About all he'd done was give her a ride to Dallas in his truck. He recalled the few belongings she'd had and how they'd been ripped to rags. He remembered how she'd held two pieces of a baby blanket and told him she planned on sewing it back together. How brave she'd been.

He couldn't enter his safe, luxurious room, so he walked back down the stairs to the bedroom behind the kitchen. It seemed empty now. He went to the window, remembering how he'd told Georgie about the stars. Her eyes had widened and there'd been excitement in them. She'd looked so young, so innocent.

He whirled around and sat on the edge of the bed. When he stared down at the floor, he caught sight of something barely protruding from underneath the bed. He reached for it and found an old billfold. A man's billfold that had been used for so long the leather was shiny. Rick opened it and found money in it—a total of thirty-eight dollars and fifty-two cents.

He pictured her in the bus station, realizing she'd lost her billfold. Of course she had the check his father had—a check? No one would cash that check until morning.

Rick grabbed his keys and headed for his pickup, Georgie's billfold in his hand. She might insist on running away, but she could at least have her wallet with her. He'd make sure of that.

Georgie did a useless thing. She sat in a corner of the Lawton bus station and cried a few pitiful tears. She'd wanted to stay at the Crawford ranch for a while, at least. Rick and Carol were such warm, thoughtful people. She wanted that so much for her baby. So much that she'd lost sight of the truth—that wasn't a place for her and her baby. Caleb Crawford had made that obvious.

"Sorry, Cal," she said softly. "But I'll take good

care of him, I promise. Somehow.'' She rubbed her tummy. The baby had been restless tonight. After the drive to Dallas and back and all the disappointment and worry, she knew she needed to take it easy for the rest of the evening. When they announced the bus to Dallas, she remembered to go buy her ticket. She reached for her billfold but couldn't find it. Frantically she searched every inch of her purse. She found the check, but not her wallet.

She hurried up to the ticket window. ''Sir, I need a ticket for the Dallas bus, but I've lost my wallet. I have a check. If you could cash it, I can—''

''We don't cash strangers' checks.''

''It's a check from Caleb Crawford.''

The elderly man behind the window stared at her. ''Let me see it,'' he said. She willingly handed him the slip of paper. ''A thousand dollars? Did you steal this?''

''No! He gave it to me.''

''That's hard to believe. Why would he do that?''

She immediately used the story Carol had made up. ''I'm a distant relative of his. Well, my husband was. But he's dead. Mr. Crawford was just trying to help me out.''

''That's a good story, but I don't believe it.'' He reached for the phone. ''I'll have to call the police.''

''The police? No! Call Mr. Crawford. He'll tell you,'' she pleaded.

He ignored her. Georgie thought about running away, but without that check, she had nothing. She tried to control her panic. The police would contact Mr. Crawford, surely. If she could just be patient, she could take the next bus, in the morning. She tried to calm herself by taking deep breaths, but it didn't seem to be working.

The man warned her not to try to run. She told him she wouldn't, and stood to one side. She watched everyone board the bus and the coach pull away, wishing she was on it.

Two men in khaki uniforms came to the window. Georgie knew they were the law in Lawton, and she grew more and more nervous. When they began questioning her, she could hardly speak. To top it off, her stomach was beginning to hurt. She frowned. She'd never experienced such a pain.

The two law officers turned back to talk to the man, and she caught her breath. The pain went away, and she told herself she'd imagined it. Of course she had.

She stepped closer to the officers in an attempt to try again. "Sir, if you'll call Mr. Crawford, I'm sure he'll tell you he wrote the check."

One of the deputies took her arm. "Why don't we step inside the office and just give Mr. Crawford a call? If he corroborates your story, this gentleman will cash your check and you can be on your way," he said.

Before Georgie could move, another pain struck and she fell to her knees on the cold cement, shock and terror pumping through her.

"Lady, you okay?" the deputy asked.

Another pain, this one sharper, hit her. She felt as if she were being ripped apart. She screamed in surprise as much as in pain, and gave up the attempt to stand up. She lay down on her side, holding her stomach.

"Lady, is it time for your baby to arrive?" the other deputy asked, kneeling beside her.

"No! Too soon." She answered. "Please, get some help!"

The second deputy radioed for an ambulance.

Chapter 8

Carol Crawford had learned to deal with telephone calls in the middle of the night. With five boys, she'd had to. But she hadn't been prepared to get one tonight.

"Hello?" she said, her voice breathless as she answered.

"Mrs. Crawford, this is Lawton General Hospital. Dr. Wilson asked me to call you. A Miss Georgie Brown has been admitted for premature labor."

Carol felt as if she'd been punched in the stomach. "Oh! Oh, I'll be right there!" She hung up the phone and began grabbing clothes. It was only a little after eleven. Sometimes she stayed up that late, but being shaken out of sleep seemed to rob her of energy.

She was lacing up her tennis shoes, having found a sweatsuit to slip on, when the bedroom door opened.

"Who was it?" Caleb asked.

"Nothing. Go back to bed."

"Damn it, Carol! I'm not going to ignore one of my children being hurt."

She stared at him, then she said, "It's Georgie. She may be in labor."

He stood frozen. Then he began, "Maybe it would be—"

"Caleb, if you dare say it would be better for that baby to die, then don't plan on coming back to this house."

It was evident she meant every word she said, and Caleb couldn't blame her. He'd been thinking over his actions and even he realized how selfish he'd been.

"Come on. I'll drive you."

"No, thank you. I'll ask Rick to drive me."

"Rick went out a few minutes ago and hasn't come back."

Carol glared at him and said nothing.

Caleb went downstairs and got his keys and billfold. When she came down, he took her arm and led her to his pickup.

"I can drive my car."

"I'll drive." He opened the door and motioned her inside.

She acquiesced, knowing she was too upset to drive safely.

When they got to the hospital emergency room, they came to an abrupt halt when they saw Rick speaking with two police officers. Their son looked very upset.

"Rick!" Carol called him.

"Mom!" He hurried over and acknowledged his father, too.

Caleb stepped forward. "What's going on?"

"We were on the scene when Ms. Brown went into

labor," one of the officers said, as he walked over to stand next to Rick.

"On the scene of what?" Caleb asked. "Was Georgie in some kind of trouble?"

"She had a thousand dollar check from you, Mr. Crawford. The gentleman at the ticket booth didn't think it was legitimate and called us in," the officer replied.

With Rick's and Carol's gazes fixed on him, Caleb said, "I wrote that check to Georgie and counted myself lucky that she'd take it. She has a lot of pride, you know. She's the widow of a distant family member and we knew she needed help, but she wouldn't stay with us. Is there a law against cashing a check?" he added calmly.

"No, sir!" the officer exclaimed.

Rick told his parents, "The stress of the situation took its toll on Georgie. She had tremendous pains and so this officer called an ambulance. Dr. Wilson was on call and he's in with Georgie right now."

The other deputy looked at Caleb. "Sir, we're real sorry about this situation. We hope Ms. Brown and her baby will be all right."

Caleb nodded and the two officers said their goodbyes and left the hospital.

Rick fell into a chair and buried his face in his hands. "I can't believe this is happening."

Carol sat beside him and patted his back. "Patrick will do his best, Rick."

"What if his best isn't good enough? Georgie will be devastated if something happens to the baby."

"Why does it matter so much to you?" Caleb asked.

Rick stared in horror at his father. "Are you a monster? Georgie is a sweet person who's worked hard to try to make it on her own. Without any help. And that baby is your grandson. Don't you care anything for him?''

''I didn't mean I don't care. But I wondered why you care so much. It would be sad if the baby died, but it sounds like this is all so personal to you.''

''It is personal. I've spent time with Georgie. I saw where she was living. I met that stepfather of Cal's. I...I showed her the stars away from the city lights. Of course I care about her.''

''That's fine, but don't let it go any further. She's not our kind of people,'' Caleb warned, feeling he was being perfectly reasonable.

Rick didn't respond, but glared at his father as he stood and began pacing back and forth. Finally he sat down, but not with his parents. When Dr. Wilson came out, Rick was the first to reach his side. ''Patrick? Is she okay? How's the baby?''

Patrick rubbed his face, not answering immediately. ''I'm sorry. It was touch and go for a while, but we got the labor stopped, at least for now.''

Rick let out a big sigh.

''I've got to keep her for at least twenty-four hours, and she's going to need lots of bed rest for the remainder of her pregnancy. I understand she was at the bus station when all this occurred. Will she be staying with you?''

Both Carol and Rick assured him that they would take care of Georgie. Caleb remained silent.

Patrick looked at Caleb. ''Is there a problem with providing for Georgie and her baby?''

''No, of course not. Carol takes on these charity cases all the time.''

"I thought she was some kind of kin?" Patrick asked.

"Yes, she is," Carol said softly. "Actually, to be perfectly honest, her baby is kin. As his mother, Georgie is family, even if she's not a blood relation."

Caleb nodded but said nothing.

"Okay. Go home and get some rest. She probably won't be released for a few days." Patrick said good-bye and walked back into the treatment rooms.

Rick put his arm around his mother. "Don't worry, Mom. I'll be in to check on her in the morning, bright and early."

"You've been neglecting that horse you're training," Caleb complained.

"Want me to drive you home, Mom?" Rick asked, ignoring his father.

"Your mother came with me!" Caleb snapped, his patience wearing thin.

"Yes, thank you, dear. I'm returning with Rick," she said to her husband, and walked out without another word.

Caleb didn't like the way things were going one bit. His wife was angry with him and his routine had been totally disrupted. His children weren't too happy with him, either. What was he going to do?

Two weeks later, nothing much had changed.

"What are we going to do?" Joe asked his brothers, sister and their spouses. At Rick's request, they had all gathered at Joe's house to discuss their parents' situation. "Mom and Dad are further apart than ever. I guess Georgie is doing better, but our parents' marriage is almost DOA."

"Do we know for sure Georgie is doing better?"

Michael asked. "I mean, has anyone seen her beside Mom?"

Kelly, Anna and Lindsay assured him they had visited with Georgie a bit now that she was back at the Crawford ranch. Then Rick added that he had, too.

His brothers stared at him.

"Why so interested?" Michael asked.

Rick appeared embarrassed, but Lindsay answered for him.

"Because he's a thoughtful guy, that's why. Georgie's carrying our nephew."

Joe added, "And ignoring her isn't going to make her go away. Dad's tried that."

Pete cleared his throat. "Just how bad are things with Mom and Dad? I mean, I know they aren't sharing a bedroom but—"

Rick interrupted tersely. "They won't be in the same room with each other."

"But how can they work things out if they won't even talk?" Lindsay asked.

"That's why I thought we should get together," Rick said. "And while Georgie is doing better, it's hard on her, feeling the tension in the house and knowing she's the cause. She asks me about it every once in a while, but I can't reassure her."

"You seem awfully concerned about this woman," Michael pointed out.

Rick whirled around to glare at his younger brother. "I live there, so it affects me. Besides, Georgie doesn't deserve to be treated like someone with a communicable disease."

Anna spoke softly. "This isn't helping to solve our dilemma. First of all, does Caleb want to make up with Carol?"

"Yeah," Rick answered. "You should see his expression when Mom walks out of a room when he enters. He's miserable. But he's too proud to admit it."

"And Mom?" Lindsay asked.

"I'm not sure. She's not as easy to read as Dad."

"Okay," Pete said decisively. "We work on Dad. After all, it's been forty years since he courted a woman. We're going to have to give him lessons."

Joe stared at him, his mouth agape.

"Come on, Joe, don't play dumb. You managed to convince Anna to marry you," Pete pointed out. "The only two who may get off the hook are Michael and Rick. After all, they're not married. But the ladies can give us a lot of insight."

"And Christmas is coming," Kelly added. They stared at her as if she'd made an irrelevant statement. But Lindsay nodded.

"That's right. We all know how Mom likes Christmas to be special, a family time."

"You're right," Michael said slowly. "Dad may try to hide it, but he loves Christmas, too."

They all nodded in agreement.

"So we'll call this Operation Christmas," Kelly said with a smile. "In hope that the family will be back together in time for the holiday."

"Georgie's baby will be born by then," Rick said, as if thinking out loud. "I hope she'll stay for Christmas."

"Where is she going to go?" Michael asked. "From what I can tell, she has no home other than that back bedroom."

Without a word, Rick walked out of their little meeting.

"What's wrong with him?" Michael demanded.

"Rick is a bit more sympathetic to Georgie than some of you," Lindsay said.

"I think he needs to get out more," Michael replied.

"You mean live his life like you, dating a different woman every week?" Pete teased.

Lindsay ignored her brothers' discussion. "I think the three of us," she said, waving at Kelly, Anna and herself, "should offer to have Thanksgiving at one of our houses."

She'd certainly caught everyone's attention. Joe said, "Mom won't go for that, Lindsay, and you know it."

"Of course I do. But we should offer, forcing her to make a conscious decision. She could drift along for months with a grudge against Dad."

"She's got a point there," Joe said, grinning.

"Okay, you three do that and we'll talk to Dad," Michael said.

"Who is 'we'?" Joe asked. "It seems to me that it's easier on you because you can just drive away. The rest of us have to face him most days."

"Well, I'll talk to him, then. If you three are cowards, I don't mind doing it alone."

Michael's taunt of cowardice roused his brothers and their discussion grew louder. The ladies slipped out of the room. "Do you think this is going to work?" Anna asked.

"I don't think we can make it worse," Lindsay responded. "And I think something has to be done. Thank you both for pitching in. Although Mom may not take us seriously, since you're due at Thanksgiving."

"I can tell her I'm volunteering for Christmas, and leaving Thanksgiving to one of you," Anna said.

"That's good," Lindsay agreed. "Well, let's get Operation Christmas underway."

Chapter 9

Caleb strode into his house, his jaw set. He used to turn up fairly regular for a coffee break and a chat with Carol during the afternoon. Now, he could be assured there would be no chat. But he needed a cup of coffee.

To his surprise, Georgie was sitting at the table with Carol, having a cup of cocoa. "I thought you couldn't get out of bed!" he said.

Georgie immediately tried to rise, but Carol caught hold of her arm. "Patrick said she was doing so much better, she could get up for a little while each day."

"Glad you're doing better," Caleb said calmly. "Sorry to disturb, but we've had a cold front come through and I need some coffee to warm me up."

In the past, those words would have sent Carol rushing to the counter where the coffeepot was plugged in. Now she said, "There's coffee made. Help yourself."

Caleb got his own coffee and sat down at the table. Both women seemed surprised.

"Where's Rick?" he asked.

"Isn't he out in the barn?" Carol queried.

Georgie bent her head over her warm mug, hoping no one would think to ask her. Rick had explained to her last night what he was going to do to try to bring his parents back together.

"No, he's not in the barn," Caleb told his wife. "He fed his horses this morning, then he disappeared. I'm wondering if I need to remind him that there's a lot to do on the ranch."

Carol answered stiffly. "I think he knows that."

"Yeah," Caleb said glumly.

The conversation didn't seem to be going anywhere. Georgie decided to help it along. "Do you think it will get very cold?"

Caleb answered. "The weatherman this morning said by nightfall, it would be close to freezing."

"Maybe we should get you a coffeepot for the barn," Carol suggested.

Georgie wanted to jump in and stop that from happening, since the only time Carol and Caleb seemed to cross paths was in the kitchen, but Caleb responded by telling Carol, "Nope. A change of scenery helps as much as the coffee."

Georgie sipped her chocolate, happy with Caleb's answer.

Rick came rushing in at that moment and she couldn't hold back a smile. He'd been so good to her, keeping her company each evening, checking on her through the day. She looked forward to each visit.

"Brrr, it's cold out there," he announced, as if it would be a surprise.

"Yeah. There's hot coffee in the pot. Get yourself a

cup." Caleb didn't seem to think his wife should wait on Rick when she refused to wait on him.

Rick didn't hesitate to wait on himself. He sat down at the table with his coffee and smiled at Georgie. "How's it going? No pains?"

"No pains," Georgie said, smiling back. In some ways he reminded her of Cal, but he was much more attentive than Cal had been. Sometimes, late at night, she questioned her devotion to Cal. She was afraid she'd believed herself in love with him because of the family he could give her. Helen had treated her like a daughter, and Georgie had been so grateful to them both. But would gratitude have been enough to build a lasting relationship on? If she hadn't gotten pregnant, would she and Cal have become engaged? Cal had deserved better. But she'd been faithful. And would continue to be, she told herself staunchly.

"Mr. Crawford says it might freeze tonight," Georgie said.

Apparently he thought her formality was out of place. "Call me Caleb," the rancher said.

Georgie's cheeks turned a little red, but she did as he asked. "Thank you, Caleb. With all your sons, I guess using 'Mr. Crawford' could get confusing."

"Yeah. Has anyone talked to Joe or Anna?" he asked. "Seems to me it's about time for that baby to come."

Rick met Georgie's gaze and then looked away.

Carol answered his question. "I talked to her last night. She saw Patrick yesterday and he thinks it will be within a week or two."

"They aren't too exact, are they?" Caleb said with a slight smile.

Some special feeling seemed to flow between Carol

and him. She smiled and said, "We know about that, don't we?"

Rick, looking back and forth between his parents, asked, "What do you mean?"

"Joe came early, taking us by surprise," Caleb replied.

Rick stared at them. "He was a preemie? But he's such a big lug."

"You were no little potato yourself, Son," Carol said. She looked at Georgie. "You should be prepared, dear. The Crawford men are big."

"Dr. Wilson said my baby was gaining weight, with your good cooking, Carol. He said I should thank you, and I do."

"She's the best cook in the county. She used to enter the cooking contests at the state fair, but she finally had to quit. She didn't have anyplace else to display blue ribbons," Caleb said with a real smile.

Caleb's words took Georgie by surprise. Now she saw why Carol had fallen in love with him. He could be a handsome man when he smiled.

She also noticed the smile on Rick's face. She was going to have to watch herself. She needed to concentrate on her baby, not on the feelings Rick was arousing in her.

"I guess it's time to get back to work. Rick, can you help me put out some extra hay before lunch?" Caleb asked.

"Sure, Dad. I need to talk to you, anyway." Then he looked guilty, as if he'd said the wrong thing.

"Something wrong?" Carol asked.

"No, Mom. I wanted to ask Dad about the horse I'm training, that's all."

His father gave him a steady look, but didn't say anything.

With a nod to the ladies, the two men walked back out into the cold together. Caleb waited until they were out of hearing. "Since when do you want to ask me about your horses? You know I've never been as good as you."

"Aw, Dad." Rick quickly glanced over his shoulder. Then he said, "I really wanted to talk to you about Mom."

"About your mother? What about her? She seems to be doing okay."

"I don't think she is. I think she misses you."

"I haven't gone anywhere!"

"Dad, we're all worried about you."

"About me? I thought you said you wanted to talk about your mother."

Rick started walking faster. "I mean—I mean both of you."

Caleb caught up with his son. "Who do you mean by 'we'? Who is worried and what are you worried about?"

Rick stepped inside the barn, out of the sharp wind. When his father joined him he said, "All of us kids. We're worried about you and Mom getting a divorce."

Caleb stared at him, his mouth hanging open. Then he straightened and said gruffly, "No one is talking about divorce. That's not going to happen."

"Have you talked to Mom about it?"

"Of course not, Son. There's no reason to. We're…going through a difficult time, I admit, but—"

"Mom mentioned it."

As if someone had pricked a hole in a balloon, Caleb seemed to shrink before his son's eyes. He sank back against a stack of hay bales. "What did you say?" he whispered.

"Mom...well, it was Lindsay who asked, and Mom said she didn't know." Rick sat down beside his father. "That's why we're all worried. I know what you did was a long time ago, but, well, Mom's gonna need some encouragement and...well, we figured you may have forgotten how to—to court a woman."

Caleb stared at him for several minutes before he rose to his feet. "Are you out of your mind, boy? She's my wife!"

"I know that," Rick retorted, irritated.

"Well, I don't need any advice about courting your mother. I've lived with her for almost forty years."

"So when's the last time you sent her flowers?" Rick challenged.

"Sent her flowers? Why would I do that?" Caleb growled.

"It's a nice thing to do, to tell her you're thinking of her. You know."

"No, I don't. Your mother would think I was guilty of something if I did that!"

"Well, you are, aren't you?"

That accusation left Caleb with nothing to say. He rose, hoping to drown his misery in hard work.

"Wait, Dad!" Rick called. "I wanted to help, so I sent her some flowers...from you. I sent some to Georgie, too."

"Why her? It's all her fault, anyway."

"No, it's not, Dad. She deserves better treatment than that."

"Okay, fine. Just don't do anything else for me. I can argue my own case." He stomped away, clearly not interested in discussing how he would take care of his problem.

Carol decided to bake another cake while Georgie was there in the kitchen with her. "I'm used to company while I work," she said, a wistful note in her voice.

"I guess Caleb likes to come in for a cup of coffee," Georgie said softly. "He's very handsome when he smiles."

"Yes," Carol agreed, and quickly began taking out her mixing bowl and gathering the ingredients.

"Is there anything I can do to help?"

"Yes, there is. I need these pecan halves broken up. Can you do that?"

"I think so, if you don't mind if I occasionally eat one. I love pecans."

"Good. We all like them, especially Rick."

Georgie felt her cheeks turning pink and she kept her head down to concentrate on the nuts.

A knock on the front door startled both women. Carol wiped her hands and hurried to see who had called. She wasn't expecting anyone.

When she appeared in the kitchen doorway a couple of minutes later, she carried a beautiful arrangement of red roses.

"Oh, my!" Georgie exclaimed. "Those are beautiful flowers."

"Yes, they are, aren't they?"

"Who sent them to you?"

"I haven't read the card yet." Carol put down the vase of flowers. She reached for the small card tucked among the leaves and opened it.

Georgie watched her face as she read the card. She

didn't appear pleased, rather, more quizzical than anything.

"Flowers from Caleb?" Carol murmured with a frown.

"Didn't the card say?"

"It says Caleb, but…but it's not like him. I mean, he always sent flowers to me when I had a new baby, but…"

"It's certainly charming of him."

"I suppose…" Another knock sounded and she frowned. "This is an unusual day." She waved a hand toward Georgie and went to the door again.

This time she reappeared with two baskets, each holding a beautiful mixed bouquets.

"Two? My goodness, this must be an eventful day," Georgie said, smiling.

"One of them is for you," Carol announced, shocking Georgie.

"Oh, my, I've never received flowers before."

"Never?" Carol asked as she set both baskets down. "Surely, your parents—" She broke off as Georgie's expression closed. "I'm sorry, I didn't mean to intrude."

Georgie gave a small smile and pulled the card out of the envelope. "Oh! How nice! Rick sent them to brighten my room."

She beamed at Carol. "Isn't that sweet?"

"Very." She opened her own envelope and read the card. "My flowers are from Caleb."

Even Georgie thought that was unusual. "Two in one day?"

"Yes. Strange, isn't it?"

Another knock sounded on the door.

Carol and she exchanged a laugh. "It couldn't be, could it?" Georgie asked.

"I do have more than two children." When Carol reappeared, she did indeed hold a third delivery, a nice flower arrangement. "I can't believe—" Another knock.

She put those on the table and returned to the door for another bunch of flowers. "I have six children. Lindsay wouldn't send flowers for her father, and Logan lives in Texas, too far away to know exactly what's going on. So I think this should be the end of the barrage of flowers. Amazing. I wonder if any of them told their dad what they were going to do."

As if on cue, the phone rang. While Carol answered the phone, Georgie took her bouquet into her bedroom. The flowers did brighten the space. And they brightened her heart, as well.

By the time lunch rolled around, Carol had received three calls, from Michael, from Pete and from Joe, asking that their father return their calls. Carol arranged the flowers on the china cupboard, which cheered up the kitchen.

Georgie decided to join them for lunch. She wouldn't stay up long, but she didn't want to miss anything.

Rick and his father came in together and washed up in the workroom. When they entered the kitchen, Caleb acted as if everything was normal. Rick, however, came to an abrupt halt. Then he nudged his father and cleared his throat.

"Huh?" Caleb said with a frown. His gaze swept the room, becoming riveted on the four flower arrangements. He looked a little flustered, especially since

Carol was watching him. He opened his mouth but nothing came out.

"Thank you for the flowers, Caleb," Carol said calmly.

After a moment, he answered, "You know I didn't send them, Carol. I didn't think our kids were that dumb, but it appears I was wrong."

"Thank you for being honest, Caleb," she said, bringing a bowl of mashed potatoes to the table.

"I'm sorry I didn't think of it. They brighten up the room so."

Georgie said, "Rick, thank you for sending me some flowers. It was my first time to receive any."

"I'm glad you liked them. Where are they?"

"I put them in my room, and you're right. They do brighten it up."

"You've never gotten flowers before?" Caleb asked.

"Caleb…" Carol said in a warning voice.

"What?"

"It was very thoughtful of Rick," Carol said.

"I'm not saying it wasn't. I just wondered why she'd never gotten flowers before. Haven't you ever been sick?"

"No," Georgie said. Then she asked Carol if she could fill her plate and eat in her room.

"Don't leave on my account. I won't ask any more questions, I promise," Caleb said.

"Caleb, you're embarrassing her!" Carol exclaimed.

"What the hell did I do? I told her I wasn't asking her to leave."

"You pointed out the fact that she was embarrassed by your question."

Rick stood. "Fill your plate, Georgie. You and I can go eat in the dining room and leave these two alone."

Georgie wasn't sure what she should do. She looked at Carol, who nodded in the direction of the dining room.

Carol got up and fixed them tea, and Georgie found herself seated at the beautiful cherry-wood table.

"Georgie," Rick began, "You're not seeing him in his best light. I told him this morning that Mom was thinking about divorce, and it took the wind out of his sails. And…and I told him about sending the flowers, but it seems my brothers had the same idea. I guess Mom didn't believe Dad had sent the flowers after four bouquets arrived for her."

Georgie bubbled with laughter. "It got to be real funny, as one after the other was delivered. But she didn't believe it even when the first was delivered. She said it wasn't like Caleb."

"That's true. They've never—that is, since I can remember—spent any time apart. We never even tried to pull the wool over their eyes because they kept track of us pretty good and told each other what was going on."

"How lucky for you."

"Yeah. Your parents didn't do that?"

"No."

They ate silently for several minutes. Then Rick asked again, "Does it upset you to talk about your parents?"

"Yes."

"Why?"

"Because I don't come from a caring family. The contrast is painful. But it doesn't matter, anyway. After my baby is born, I'll be out of here."

Meanwhile, in the kitchen, Caleb and Carol ate their lunch silently, avoiding each other's eyes. Finally,

Caleb said, "I really wasn't trying to embarrass Georgie. It's unusual for someone to refuse to talk about their family. It would've been rude not to ask."

"I shouldn't have jumped on you, but I'd already discovered she didn't want to talk about them," Carol replied.

"Why?"

"I don't know. I guess she's not close to her parents. She always speaks highly of...of Helen."

"Helen was a nice woman. She didn't deserve the way I behaved."

"No."

"Neither did you."

"No."

"I've said I'm sorry, Carol. What else do you want? Blood?"

Carol's features grew cold. "Do you think it's that simple? You say you're sorry and all's well?"

Caleb dropped his head. "I guess not. You'll let me know when I've suffered enough, won't you?" He rose from the table and left the kitchen, his meal unfinished.

Carol stared after him. Then she dropped her face into her hands and sobbed.

Chapter 10

Carol was surprised to have company that afternoon. Lindsay, Kelly and a very pregnant Anna dropped by for a cup of tea—to warm themselves, they said, smiling innocently.

She invited them in, but she warned them to keep their voices down. Georgie was sleeping in the bedroom beside the kitchen.

"How's she doing?" Lindsay asked.

"Much better. I've been feeding her well. The baby has gained weight and the doctor is letting her get out of bed a little bit each day."

"Oh, that's wonderful," Anna said. She lifted a bag into her lap. "I brought along some of the books Joe bought for me to read. Just lying in bed can get very boring."

"That's so sweet of you, Anna," Carol said, smiling. "Caleb was asking this morning if it wasn't time for you to have your baby."

"I keep thinking it's time, but Patrick tells me to be patient."

"We're glad you and Caleb are talking," Kelly said. "We know things have been difficult for you. That's why we're here."

Carol's eyes widened, but she waited for their explanation.

"Mom," Lindsay began with quick glances at her co-conspirators, "you've always made holidays special for us. And we think it's our turn to do that for you."

Carol leaned back against her chair. "What do you mean?"

"Well, we thought instead of you providing Thanksgiving and Christmas for us, we should host the holiday celebrations this year. Kelly wants to do Thanksgiving, and I'll handle Christmas."

Carol stared at them. Then she said carefully, "And why would you do that when I'm not ill and have no little children underfoot?"

"Because you might not be in the holiday mood," Kelly said softly.

"I don't think a dead turkey and an oven need to worry about my mood before they combine for a good meal."

"But Carol—" Anna began.

"I also have the most room, plenty of china and more experience than the three of you put together," Carol finished with her chin in the air.

"Shh, not so loud, Mom, or you'll wake Georgie," Lindsay said.

Carol's temper rose, along with the color in her cheeks.

But it was the opening of a door that brought her

under control. Georgie appeared in the door of the kitchen.

"Is everything all right?" she asked.

"Come sit down at once, Georgie," Anna said. "You shouldn't be on your feet."

"Is my presence causing more trouble for Carol? I am doing better. I could probably manage on my own," she suggested, eyeing the three young women. She'd met Lindsay, Kelly and Anna while she was in the hospital, but she didn't really know them. But she was determined not to cause Carol any more grief.

"Carol?" she asked, waiting for the answer to her question.

Carol smiled slightly. "Just consider them three more baskets of flowers."

Georgie sat down beside Anna. "But they wouldn't—"

"No, but they're trying to push me, to make me make up with Caleb so everything can be normal again. My inability to forgive and forget is disturbing them."

"Mom!" Lindsay exclaimed.

"Carol!" the other two cried.

"I don't blame them," Georgie said, startling Carol.

"What? What did you say?"

"It's your fault, Carol," Georgie said, again shocking her. "You've raised your children to care, to reach out to people who are suffering. Why wouldn't they reach out to you and Caleb? Wouldn't you do the same if one of them was suffering?"

"Well, yes, of course, but we're older. We have experience. We know what we're doing," she finished, but they all saw her listening to her own words, beginning to question them.

After the silence lengthened, Lindsay said softly, "What can we do to help, Mom?"

Carol sighed. "I don't know. Your father wanted to know what he could do. I can't give him an answer. I need time. I'll adjust, I'm sure. I can't imagine life without your father. But...maybe he's right. Maybe I want him to suffer a little. I want us both to learn something from this—this experience. It can't be so simple as to say 'I'm sorry,' and Helen and Cal are magically forgotten."

"You're right," Lindsay agreed. "There are things to be learned. Our husbands should learn. We, their wives, should learn. We'll give you time, Mom. That's really what we were trying to let you do."

"No, you were trying to make me realize how disruptive a divorce would be. I know that."

Anna reached over to squeeze Carol's hand as it lay on the table. "You've given us magnificent husbands. Anything we can do to help, you have only to ask."

"Thank you," Carol said, sniffing a little.

"I still think I should leave. You don't need my constant reminder of what went wrong," Georgie insisted.

"Yes, we do," Carol said. "Otherwise, it's like sweeping everything that happened under the rug. I think I instinctively knew that when I insisted you stay here. Besides being the right thing to do, it's the one thing that will force us to face our problem."

Georgie rubbed her hand over her bulging stomach. "Then you and Caleb had better work on it, because once Cal, Jr. arrives, I'll be moving on."

"Where will you go?" Lindsay asked. "It would be better for you to stay around here, where you have family to help you. Raising a kid on your own is difficult."

"But you're not my family. I'll go back to Dallas. Maybe by then I'll be able to find a better job and a place to care for the baby. A lot of women make it like that. And maybe I'll have the trust fund to help me."

"Don't you have any family, Georgie?" Lindsay asked.

Carol spoke before Georgie could. "You're the third person to ask about Georgie's family. She says she has no one and she would prefer not to talk about it. But she's a part of our family whether she thinks she is or not. You have a couple of months to think about what you're going to do, Georgie. I hope you change your mind."

Georgie smiled at Carol but said nothing.

Anna arrived home feeling better about her mother and father-in-law. Joe's family was so wonderful. Like Georgie, she'd had no family, no assistance, and worst of all, no love. Not even from her first husband. Her hand absentmindedly stroked her big stomach as she thought about Joe, her new husband. He'd thought he was too ugly to find a wife and have children. But he was beautiful to her.

She sighed and made a cup of decaffeinated tea. The children were watching television and Joe had gone out to the barn for a few minutes. She heard the back door open and knew he had returned.

"Honey?" he called.

"In the kitchen."

"But I told you I'd take care of dinner tonight," Joe said as he came through the door. When he saw her drinking her tea, he relaxed. "Good. You need to rest more."

She smiled at his mothering. He thought he was so tough, but he was just like a mother hen, protecting his little family, ever diligent. "Joe, I don't think your mom is thinking about divorce. I think she just needs time to…to think, to accept what happened."

"And I'd like to give her time, all she wants. But I'm not sure Dad can hang in there that long. He doesn't realize how often he consulted Mom. They shared everything and told each other everything."

Anna raised one brow.

"Okay, okay, everything except about Cal. Anyway, do we know anything about Georgie? Or Cal, for that matter?"

Anna shook her head.

"I think I'd better call Michael. He mentioned to me that maybe we should hire a private eye. We need more information."

"Surely you don't have to investigate Georgie?"

"Has she told you about herself?"

"No, but I've hardly spent any time with her." Anna remembered the conversation in Carol's kitchen this afternoon. "Your mom said today that she didn't want to talk her family, that she doesn't have any."

"Everyone came from somewhere."

He crossed the kitchen to the phone. Michael's number was on speed dial, and his brother soon answered.

"You still at work?" Joe joked.

"Sure. I'm a lawyer. We work around the clock," Michael said in a teasing voice. His brothers, working from dawn to dusk and then doing the paperwork of farming and ranching, teased him about his easy lifestyle.

But Joe didn't take the bait. "Listen, Mike, I've been thinking. Do you know any good private eyes?"

"Sure. Why?"

"Well, Georgie seems okay. It seems like she's telling the truth, but she's never given us any information about herself. Says she has no family. I just keep getting an uneasy feeling about everything. I don't want anything to explode in our faces."

"I'm glad someone is thinking straight," Michael said with a sigh of relief. "Oh, by the way, I sent flowers in Dad's name. I called to tell him, but he never called me back."

"No," Joe said wryly. "There's no doubt you're a Crawford, little brother. Pete, Rick and I also sent Mom flowers with Dad's name on them. She didn't believe it and he was unhappy. It wasn't our finest day."

"Yikes! I guess not." There was a pause, then Michael said, "What are we going to do, Joe? You're the oldest. Can't you think of anything?"

Joe accepted that mantle, as he always had, trying to make sure his family was safe. "Anna said she doesn't think Mom is considering divorce anymore. She just needs time. The only thing is, they need to spend time together. Right now, Dad stays in the barn as much as possible, and Mom is always in the kitchen."

"I have an idea!" Anna said from behind Joe, pounding on his back.

"Wait a minute, Mike. My wife is trying to beat me up. What idea, honey?"

"We'll arrange for someone to give them tickets to the town's Thanksgiving dedication service, and they'll have to go. They'll spend an entire evening together."

Joe didn't explode with happiness. Finally he sighed. "Well, it's better than nothing."

"You ungrateful person!" Anna said, sticking out her tongue.

Joe laughed and pulled her into his arms. "My mother always said to be careful. It might freeze that way."

She giggled, loving having his arms around her. As big as she was, he always made her feel loved and beautiful. He was a special man.

"Mike, did you hear Anna's idea?"

"Yeah," Michael said dryly. "Yeah, and it might work, but I was wondering when you were going to remember I was on the line."

"Anna easily distracts me. Someday, you'll understand, little brother."

Michael snorted in irritation. His brothers had always teased him and said he wasn't old enough for anything. "Yeah, right."

"Okay, we'll set that up. The girls offered to do the holidays for Mom, and she didn't take that well. But they are doing what they can."

"Good for them. The problem is that both Mom and Dad are stubborn." There was a pause. Then Michael asked, "Are you going to the Borman auction tomorrow? They're hoping for a good turnout, but with the economy down, I don't know. I think some of their equipment is in good shape."

"I hadn't intended to. I don't want to leave Anna alone all day."

"Oops, I forgot about Anna's 'condition.'"

Joe could hear a smile in Michael's voice. "It's not something I would forget." He grinned at his wife.

"I think you should go," Anna said to her husband. "You'll have your beeper, and Patrick said it would be another week or two."

Rather than answer her, he pulled her against him and returned to their earlier subject. "Michael, do you think we should put a P.I. on the case? Will it upset everyone?"

"Maybe. Or at least Mom. But I think we need to do this. We should have from the first. It's up to us to protect our family."

"Yeah. Okay. You'll take care of it? I'll contribute to the cost. And I'll try to make the Borman auction at least for part of the day tomorrow."

After hanging up the phone, he said to Anna, "That's a secret I want you to keep. No telling the others. We're hiring a P.I. to look into Georgie's background."

"But she's so nice. Are you sure it's necessary?"

"No, I'm not. But better safe than sorry."

"Okay, I'll keep quiet."

Georgie shifted on her bed, trying to find a comfortable position. Carol had moved a television into her room to help entertain her. But there wasn't much to watch during the day except the soap operas.

The women on those shows had multiple problems, but they strolled about in designer clothes and always had a hunk handy to help them out. They had no grasp of reality.

Then Georgie chuckled. She had Rick and his brothers handy, and they were certainly hunks. Only...they didn't really want to fight her battles. And their presence was only temporary. When she'd been a child, there had been no one to champion her.

Certainly not her mother. Rita Brown had been a bitter woman. She'd had an affair with a married man and gotten pregnant, much as Helen had done. But the man had gone away when he learned about her pregnancy, leaving her in dire straits.

She'd always blamed Georgie for her difficulties. Rita had become an alcoholic by the time Georgie was ten. She didn't often work, and collected money from the government. The only good Georgie was to her, Rita frequently said, was that, because she had a child, she collected more money.

Georgie never saw any of it. She was lucky if she got one decent meal a day. Early on, she'd learned to do odd jobs for their neighbors, baby-sitting, running errands or doing chores.

Whatever she made, she usually spent at the grocery store, carefully comparing prices to get the most for her money. She often tried to fix something for her mother, too, hoping to substitute food for her mother's booze.

It hadn't worked, needless to say. Georgie had quit school when she was sixteen and taken a full-time job, working extra hours whenever possible. She always saved a little, putting it in a bank account she'd opened, but if she didn't intercept the welfare check, she'd have to pay the rent as well as for their food each month.

It was a relief when her mother finally died, when Georgie was eighteen. She felt guilty about being so relieved, but her mother had been a shell of a woman, with no concern for anyone, including her daughter. About six months later, Georgie met Helen.

She and Georgie worked together, and for months, she'd heard Helen rave about her son. When Georgie finally met him, she was already prepared to like Cal just because he was Helen's boy.

To her amazement, he seemed attracted to her. They grew close in no time. Helen treated her like a daughter, and Georgie was thrilled. It was something she'd never experienced. When Helen and Cal had been killed, she'd mourned, of course, but sometimes she thought she mourned more for Helen than she did for Cal.

The baby beat a tattoo on Georgie's side, and she rubbed her stomach. "Don't worry, baby, I'll love you always," she whispered.

The phone rang, but Georgie didn't move. Carol had had an unexpected meeting in town. She'd turned on the answering machine so Georgie wouldn't be bothered. Instead of answering the phone, Georgie reached over and turned off the television, deciding to read one of the books Anna had brought her.

"Where are you? I've got the children with me. I don't have anyone to keep them. I'm trying to make it to the hospital, but I thought maybe you could drive me. Oh!" The voice broke off with a sob.

Georgie swung her legs off the bed and sat up. That was Anna's voice. She ran to the kitchen and the phone, but Anna had already hung up. Then Georgie looked out the kitchen window and saw Anna's car. She hurried outside, grateful she'd dressed in the maternity jeans Carol had bought her and one of Anna's tops.

"Anna? Are you all right?" she asked, pulling open the door on the driver's side.

"No! I'm in labor and—ooh!"

Obviously she was having another pain. They seemed to be coming close together.

Georgie realized there was no time to dawdle. As soon as Anna finished that contraction, she said. "Scoot over so I can drive. I'll have us at the hospital in no time."

"What about the kids?" Anna asked in panic.

"I'll take care of them once we get you there."

Julie was calling out "Mommy!" with fear in her voice every time her mother had a pain, and Hank was crying. Georgie didn't waste time trying to soothe the children. The first thing she had to do was get Anna to the hospital.

Once she'd settled behind the wheel, she got the car moving and flew down the long drive to the county road. "Anna, between pains, try to call the hospital and tell them to get ready for your arrival."

Georgie drove carefully but fast. "Don't push, Anna, if you can help it," she cautioned at one point. When the hospital came into sight, she was greatly relieved, because the pains were coming faster and Anna was screaming with each one.

Pulling into the emergency area, Georgie stopped the car right by the doors. A nurse and two orderlies were waiting by the curb, obviously alerted to their arrival by Anna's phone call. They pulled open Georgie's door and reached for her.

"Not me," Georgie said. "Her!" She pointed to Anna, and everyone immediately recognized there wasn't a moment to spare. They hurried around the car and got Anna into a wheelchair, and the nurse and one of the orderlies disappeared with her through the emergency room doors.

The second orderly came back to Georgie. "Are you all right?"

It was hard to hear him because the children were both crying loudly.

"Yes. But I may need some help getting the children inside. And I have to park the car."

"I'll get the kids out of the car. You take them into

the waiting room and I'll park the car. Then I'll bring you the keys.''

''Thank you so much,'' Georgie said, amazed at such helpfulness. Once she got the children inside, she put Hank on her lap and held Julie to her side and began telling them that their mother was going to be all right, all the time praying she was right.

Chapter 11

The Borman auction had been underway for several hours when Joe found himself growing restless. He got up from the folding chair he'd been using just as the beeper in his pocket went off. Anna had told him she'd only use it in an emergency. He pulled his cellphone out and called the house at once, but she wasn't there, or at least didn't answer. He immediately tried her cellphone, but it was busy. What was going on?

"I've got to go! Something is wrong!" he announced to his father, Pete and Rick. He started running for his truck, the other three men close behind him.

"Did you talk to Anna?" Pete asked, sliding into the passenger seat just as Joe started the engine. Caleb and Rick were getting into Caleb's truck.

"No. But she said she wouldn't use the beeper unless it was an emergency. I keep getting a busy signal on the cellphone and she doesn't answer at home." The auction house was half an hour away from Lawton.

"Give me your phone. I'll call the hospital and see if Anna has contacted them," Pete ordered.

"Good thinking!" Joe agreed, holding out the device. Then he pressed down on the accelerator, anxious to reach his wife's side.

Pete discovered that Anna had called the hospital and was due there any minute. He relayed that information to Joe, who drove even faster. "Hey, bro, let's be careful. We want to get there in one piece."

Joe ignored him. He and Anna had two children, both from her first marriage, and he loved them dearly. But he'd never been at the birth of his own child. He'd promised her he'd be there.

When they reached the hospital, Joe stopped the truck by the emergency entrance and leaped out. "Park it!" he ordered his brother, then took off running.

Pete sighed with relief and did as he'd asked. A moment later their father and Rick pulled up behind.

Caleb got out of his truck. "Is she here?"

"Should be. She'd called ahead to say she was on her way."

"Come on, let's go find out what's happening. I imagine Carol drove her. She'll know what's going on."

They went in the emergency room, to find several people sitting near the nurse's desk, obviously waiting. They had almost passed through when Rick stopped in his tracks. "Look!" He pointed to a white-faced Georgie with two small children pressed against her, sleeping.

Caleb strode over to her. "Georgie, what are you doing here? Where's Carol?"

"She had to go to a meeting in town. I don't know how to reach her."

Rick sat down and lifted Hank into his arms. "Where is Anna?"

"They took her away as soon as we got here, and the children were upset, so I haven't had a chance to ask anything." Her gaze, as well as her quivering lips, revealed her fears.

Rick wrapped an arm around her shoulders. "How are you doing?"

"F-fine."

Even Caleb realized she'd about reached her limit. "I'll try to call Carol. Pete, you get Kelly or Lindsay to come take the kids. Rick, when someone else arrives, you get Georgie back home and in her bed." With those orders, he headed for the nearest phone.

"I can—"

Rick interrupted Georgie. "Do as Dad says. You got Anna here, didn't you? That was the important thing. Now you need to take care of yourself. We've got enough family to share the jobs."

Georgie closed her eyes and said nothing else.

Pete used Joe's cellphone to call the store, knowing both Lindsay and Kelly were there doing inventory this morning. When Kelly answered, he explained the situation and she said both women would be there in five minutes.

Caleb had apparently found Carol, because he was now harassing the nurse on duty for information.

"Mr. Crawford, I personally took your son to his wife. He got there before the baby was born. That's all I can tell you. You and your family need to go to the maternity waiting room. It's just down the hall to the right."

"Send my wife there when she gets here."

"Yes, sir, but I'm sure she knows where to go."

He returned to their little group and told them to move down the hall.

Rick, however, was concerned about Georgie. "Dad, I think I should take Georgie on home. You and Pete can take care of the children, can't you?"

"Sure we can," Caleb agreed.

Georgie protested, but she had no choice. Wishing she could do more for this family who'd been so good to her, she walked with Rick's arm supporting her. She'd almost reached the door when Caleb called her name.

"Georgie, you did good today, just like part of the family. Thank you."

Tears spurted into her eyes and she buried her face against Rick's chest. Rick nodded at his father and got her into the truck without wasting any time.

When Joe reached the maternity ward, a nurse put him in a room and handed him a pair of scrubs, insisting he change before he saw his wife. In lightning time he reappeared, leaving his boots and clothes scattered on the floor behind him.

"Anna!" Joe called as soon as he saw her, reaching for her hands and cradling her face, covering it with kisses. Anna immediately seemed to relax.

Before she could say anything, Dr. Wilson said, "Anna, it's time to push hard. The baby's head is crowning. On three, okay?" He counted, and when he reached three, Anna half sat up, with Joe's help, and pushed with all her might. In no time, Joe saw his son, lustily yelling, a big baby compared to most but small in Joe's eyes.

"Hello, Son," he said softly.

Patrick wrapped the baby in a soft towel and handed him to Joe. "Show him to your wife."

"Anna?" Joe said, awe in his voice, "Look. He's beautiful!"

"Yes," she agreed, her eyes full of tears.

"Are you still in pain?" he asked, tucking the baby in his arm so he could touch her, too.

"No, Joe. Now that you're here, everything's fine. Is someone looking after the other children?"

Joe looked blank. "I don't know. I haven't seen them. Isn't Mother here?"

"No, Georgie said she had a meeting in town. Georgie drove me here and took care of everything, but I know she's supposed to be in bed."

"Don't worry, honey. Dad, Pete and Rick came with me. They'll take care of everything," he assured her. Anna accepted that and closed her eyes.

"Are you going to take a nap?" he whispered.

"Maybe a quick one. It was a hectic morning."

"I should've been there," Joe said, feeling guilty.

"No, Joe. We made it. There was no way to know he would come today. Have we settled on a name?"

They'd discussed several names, but hadn't been able to make a final decision. Joe looked down at his son, now resting calmly in his arms, sucking on his fists, and he nodded. "Yeah. I'd like him to be called Jonathan Caleb Crawford. Is that okay with you?"

"I think it's perfect."

Joe bent over and kissed his wife. Johnny Crawford gave a loud yell, demanding his father's attention, an event that would occur more than once in the next twenty years.

* * *

Rick was in trouble. He looked down at Georgie's blond head tucked firmly against his chest as he escorted her to the truck. The realization that he was more worried about her well-being than seeing Anna and the new baby was an eye-opener.

Georgie looked up. "Is something wrong?"

"Why would you ask that?" he demanded in an almost belligerent tone.

"Your heart rate changed. Like you thought we were in danger or something." She tried to step away from him, but Rick held on tight. "Do you need to stay here?" she asked.

"Nope. But it suddenly occurred to me that I missed lunch. How about you? Did you eat lunch before you did your rescue thing?"

She blinked those big blue eyes several times before she said, "No, I didn't. I'd forgotten all about lunch."

"Then it looks like we'll have to stop for lunch on the way home."

"I'm sure your mom has something I can fix when we get home, so you won't have to spend your money—"

"Are you implying I'm too broke to buy lunch?" he asked, pretending outrage.

Georgie blushed a bright red. "No, of course not, but there's no need for you to spend your money on me. I'll wait until I get home. I'll find something."

He opened the door to his father's truck and lifted her into the seat without commenting. Then he circled the vehicle and got in behind the wheel. He drove half a block and parked. "Sweetheart, you are about to eat the best chicken-fried steak in the whole state of Oklahoma, maybe the whole United States."

"But I said—"

"Yeah, but I didn't agree." Rick came around the truck again and opened her door. "You can either walk in, or I'll carry you. Makes no difference to me."

She quickly scrambled down out of the truck, afraid he wouldn't wait for her to decide. "I'll walk. I have some money at home. I can pay you back as soon as we get there."

"Uh-uh." That was what made her so irresistible. The wonder that anyone would want to do something nice for her. All the girls he'd dated expected to be treated like princesses. Georgie expected to be ignored or mistreated. Life had certainly taught her some ugly lessons.

And he'd discovered he wanted to be the one to spoil her, to protect her, to share in her awakening. He cared for Georgie Brown more than he'd thought possible.

And his father would be furious with him.

He wondered how Georgie felt about him. She seemed to like him, but she had loved Cal. She would probably mourn for him for a while. But Rick could be patient.

"Hey, Rick, what are you doing here in the middle of the week?" a large woman wrapped in an old, faded apron shouted from across the restaurant.

"Howdy, Alice. Another Crawford baby is being born today, so we missed lunch. Thought maybe you could bring us two of your chicken-fried steak dinners."

"Comin' right up. Find a place to sit."

Rick led Georgie to a table. She'd have more room for the baby there than in a booth. "Don't we need to see a menu?" she asked in a whisper, as she sat down.

"Nope. You gotta taste her chicken-fried steak.

She's famous for it. And afterward, her coconut cream pie is to die for.''

"I don't think I should have pie. That would be too much.''

"Georgie, you have to have pie. We'll share a piece if you're full.''

Rick looked at Georgie, realizing that he'd started spending time with her because he felt sorry for her, trapped in that bedroom with a family she didn't even know. He'd started bringing in copies of movies to watch with her. All his favorites. That had been so much fun, sharing with her. When she didn't like one, they would argue about its worth, contents and plot.

She was a very intelligent woman. In fact, it wasn't her beauty that intrigued him—it was her mind. How his brothers would howl with laughter when they heard that! Rick wasn't crazy. He wouldn't purposely choose a woman who was almost seven months pregnant with another man's child as the girl of his dreams. But it wasn't as if he had a choice.

Damn it, he couldn't even kiss her. He couldn't take her on a date. When he had sent her the flowers, she'd insisted she'd pay him back, until he got angry with her.

Alice came out with two big platters and set them down before them. ''Y'all want tea?'' she asked.

"No, I'll have water,'' Georgie said.

"I don't reckon it's you who's having a baby today. Not if you're about to eat all this food,'' Alice said.

Georgie blushed again. "Oh, no, my baby's not due until December. Anna Crawford had her baby today.''

"Oh! Well, good for Anna.'' The woman gave a happy nod and headed back toward the kitchen.

"Hey, Alice, don't forget the pie,'' Rick called after

her. Then he turned to Georgie. "Okay, try the steak," he ordered, keeping his eye on her sweet face.

She cut off a piece of the steak, buried underneath cream gravy, and put it in her mouth. Slowly, she chewed. Then she smiled at him. "It's delicious. I love it!"

Rick let out the breath he'd been holding and began his own feast, satisfied with her reaction.

Half an hour later, when Alice brought out the pie, she put two large pieces on the table. "But Rick said we could share a piece. I can't eat much more," Georgie protested.

"But you're going to need the energy. I have a surprise for you tonight," Rick told her.

That remark distracted her, and Alice hurried away.

"What do you mean?" Georgie asked.

"I'm going to teach you something new. We can't let your brain turn to mush just because you're pregnant, can we?" He grinned at her.

"No, but—"

"Taste the pie," he urged. When she put the first bite in her mouth, she closed her eyes and sighed.

"There should be a law against this. I'm going to weigh as much as a house after eating this."

"Nope. You're going to be just about perfect, Georgie. And tonight, I'm going to teach you to play chess."

He waited for her reaction. If he'd told any other woman that he was going to teach her that, she wouldn't have been happy. But Georgie's expression changed from surprise to absolute joy.

"Really? Rick, are you serious? I've always wanted to learn. Do you think I can?"

"Of course you can. I'm an expert teacher. Of

course, I won't teach you too much. I'll need to still be able to beat you. But I'm sure you'll catch on quickly."

She plied him with questions while she ate her pie, not even noticing that she swallowed every bite until there was nothing left. "Oh, Rick, I ate the entire thing. You tricked me by talking about chess."

"Yep! And not another word about it until you've had a good long nap. We have to give Junior his rest or he'll complain."

"He'll probably complain about me eating so much. It doesn't leave him much room, you know."

"I think he loved all that good food. He probably grew a foot from this meal."

She groaned, but she was laughing, too, and Rick loved it.

They were getting ready to go when the door opened and Joe, Pete and Caleb came in.

"What are you doing here?" Caleb demanded, surprise in his voice. "I thought you were taking Georgie home."

"Neither of us had eaten lunch. I thought she should taste Alice's food."

Caleb's face broke into a smile. "She's the only woman who can outcook Carol." Then he hurriedly added, "But if you tell Carol I said that, I'll deny every word of it."

His sons laughed at him, Joe slapping him on the shoulder. Then Georgie noticed Joe's attire—a green scrub shirt with two blobs of black ink on it. "You're wearing the baby's footprints? Oh, that's wonderful. How is he?"

Though normally silent, Joe gushed at her question.

"He's wonderful! Eight pounds twelve ounces, twenty-three inches long and hungry as a bear."

Rick reached out to touch the footprints on Joe's hospital garb. "Hey, that's pretty neat, Joe."

"And how's Anna?" Georgie asked.

"She's fine. I got there just as the baby was ready to come out. She's taking a nap right now. But I'm sure she'll soon be feeling up to having visitors if you want to go back—"

"We can't do that. Georgie has to have her own nap. Maybe I'll take her in to see Anna tomorrow." Rick put his arm around Georgie's shoulders and guided her past the other three Crawford men. He caught his father's curious expression and figured Caleb would have a warning about not getting too close to Georgie. But he was just going to have to get used to it. Rick had made up his mind.

Chapter 12

Caleb waited at the hospital until Carol was ready to go home. Since Rick had used his truck to take Georgie home, Caleb could use needing a ride back to the ranch as his excuse for catching a lift with Carol.

Finally his wife said goodbye to Anna and Joe and gathered Julie and Hank, promising to bring them to see their mommy in the morning. Caleb picked up Hank and extended his other hand to Julie. "Come on, Julie."

"I'll take them," Carol said sharply.

"I know you will. But I'm hoping you'll take me, too, since Rick drove my truck."

He knew Carol would have no choice. Joe and Anna would be upset if she ignored his request. When she nodded, not giving in gracefully, he sighed. He was so damn tired of being estranged from his wife. He missed her in so many ways.

They didn't speak until they reached Carol's car and

he put Hank in the car seat she kept in the rear. "Will Julie be all right in a regular seat belt?" he asked.

"Yes. She's a big girl, aren't you, Julie? We'll need to go to Joe's house and get some clothes for the children."

"Grandma, can I bring my dolly?" Julie asked.

"Of course you can, sweetie. And Hank can bring— what does he call that dog?" Carol asked, distracted by her faulty memory. "I hate it when I forget something."

Caleb chuckled. "At least I won't be alone when that happens to me."

She wasn't amused. Before she could speak, Hank himself provided the stuffed dog's name. "Woof!"

They all turned to stare at the little boy. At two, he knew a few words, but he seldom spoke.

"That's right. How could I forget that? We're going to get Woof and Julie's dolly. And we're going to bake a cake for Mommy when she and your baby brother come home. Won't that be fun?"

Julie nodded. "Is Grandpa going to help us?"

Caleb could've kissed the little girl. She assumed everything was fine, so why wouldn't he help?

"I sure am," Caleb said before Carol could answer. "I'm a great helper when Grandma is baking a cake."

"You think it's a help to gobble down half of it? If so, then you're right, you're my best helper."

"Yes, ma'am," Caleb agreed with a wicked grin.

She didn't even smile, but she wanted to. He could see it in her eyes. And he felt closer to her than he had in weeks. He spent a happy afternoon, playing with the children under Carol's observant eye and helping her when he asked for it.

By dinnertime, he felt he'd made real progress. She

sent him to the bedroom where Hank had been napping. He got the boy up and changed his diaper and washed both their hands. "Time for dinner, Hank boy. Grandma's done a lot of cooking."

"Hungry." Hank's one-word conversation left no doubt about his meaning.

"Me, too."

When he got back to the kitchen, Caleb discovered Georgie was sitting at the table. Anxious to keep the ground he'd covered that afternoon, he spoke calmly to her. "Feeling better after your escapade this morning?"

"Yes, thank you."

Caleb turned to Carol. "Did you call the hospital and talk to Joe or Anna?"

Before she started to answer, Rick came in and sat down beside Georgie. "Evenin', everyone."

"Evening, Son," Carol said before she answered Caleb's question. "Yes, I talked to both of them. They're doing fine and expect to come home tomorrow. I hired Betty to go over and give the house a good cleaning in the morning, and the girls and I are going to take over some food tomorrow."

Caleb smiled. "You're a good woman, Carol Crawford."

She took his compliment calmly, but Caleb noticed the other two adults exchanging significant glances.

"What've you got planned for tonight, Son?" Caleb asked abruptly. It was Friday night. Usually Rick went to town. Sometimes he even drove to Oklahoma City to hang out with Michael.

Rick smiled at Georgie before he looked at his father. "I'm teaching Georgie to play chess. Just because she can't move around a lot doesn't mean we shouldn't exercise her mind.''

Caleb gave Rick a sharp look. "On Friday night? I thought you usually went into town."

"Sometimes," Rick responded. He didn't look at Georgie, but she was staring at him, a question in her gaze. Good. Caleb didn't want his son spending too much time with her. Their lives were too complicated as it was.

"Well, if you want to go, I can teach Georgie to play chess."

"No, thanks, Dad." Rick took another bite of his dinner, not appearing to be disturbed by his father's offer.

Carol, with her gaze on Caleb, said, "That's nice of you, Son, if Georgie wants to learn chess."

"I'd like to, Carol, but I don't want to disrupt Rick's normal activities," Georgie said, as if Carol had asked her a question.

"Don't try to weasel your way out," Rick said with a teasing tone. "You're just afraid I'll beat you."

Georgie laughed—an unusual occurrence, Caleb realized, noting how pretty she looked when she was happy.

"I *know* I'll lose, silly. I just don't want to be stomped into the ground."

"Ah, Georgie, you know I won't do that...often," he added with a grin.

Caleb thought the two of them seemed to be in their own little world, a fact that bothered him a lot. "I saw Holly in town today," he said, trying to sound casual. "She asked about you."

"Really?" Rick responded, but he didn't sound even mildly interested.

"Yeah. She's already home for Thanksgiving. I didn't realize she'd get here so early." He nodded to Georgie. "She's an old friend of Rick's. She's working on her master's in business."

"How wonderful. Rick, we can wait for another time if you want to see Holly tonight," Georgie told him.

Caleb was pleased. The girl wasn't dumb. She knew what he was trying to accomplish.

"No, thanks." Rick took another bite. "Hey, eat your dinner, Georgie. I don't want you using weakness as an excuse to not do your best."

She laughed again and Caleb realized he hadn't accomplished anything, because his son wasn't taking the hint. Caleb shifted his gaze to Carol and realized he'd made a mistake. Georgie wasn't the only one who'd figured out what he was doing. Carol was furious with him. Any progress he'd made this afternoon was lost now. Damn it.

Georgie studied Rick's face as he sat on her bed, the chess set in hand.

"Are you sure you want to spend your evening doing this?" she asked softly.

His head jerked up and he stared at her. "Why wouldn't I?"

"Because most young men like to spend their free time with women who might be a little less…" She looked down at her belly "…pregnant?"

"You listened to Dad. Don't do that."

"Why not?"

"Dad doesn't understand you. Hell, he's hardly spoken to you. But you've become…my friend, Georgie. I like spending time with you."

"I like it, too. You've been great to me, Rick, in

difficult circumstances. But I don't want you to upset your father.''

Rick laughed. "It wouldn't be the first time. Dad thinks he can control our lives. He's tried ever since Joe turned twelve. And he's been frustrated. But with the parents we have, we're all bound to be stubborn and hardheaded. Just like them.''

"I guess we all inherit things from our parents," she said solemnly, a touch of sadness in her voice.

Rick went about setting up the chessboard, but he'd heard the doubt, as well. "What did you inherit from your family?''

She gave him a brief smile and touched the horse figure he'd set on the board. "I didn't know chess had a horse.''

"That's the knight. He's an interesting piece,'' he assured her, but all the time he was wondering why Georgie always refused to talk about her family.

"Why did your father teach all of you to play chess?''

"He said we should use logic in dealing with problems, and chess would teach us that. When it was Lindsay's turn, he wasn't going to teach her because she was a girl.'' Rick held up a hand as Georgie opened her mouth to protest. "I know, I know. You should've heard Mom. She convinced him, of course. Lindsay became a good player, sometimes beating us.''

"Good for her.''

"You would think that. But I'm teaching you because you'll need to teach your son. Unless you marry someone who can play chess.''

"Let me get a piece of paper and write down that requirement for when I'm looking for a husband.''

"Are you being sarcastic?''

"Do you think it's possible?" she asked, again being sarcastic.

"Yes, I do, and I think it's a good idea. If you figure out what you want, then you'll know him when you meet him."

"I've already got that figured out."

"Someone like Cal, I suppose? What was he like?"

"I'll tell you what you want to know, but no, I'm not looking for a carbon copy of Cal."

"Why? Wasn't he good to you?" Rick hoped he hadn't sounded too anxious. But he wanted to know Cal had treated her well.

"What I'm trying to say is that I don't intend to marry."

"Why not?"

"We'd better get on with the lesson. I go to bed early these days, you know."

He wanted to push her to talk to him about his half brother, but he thought better of it. He could draw her out while they played chess in the evenings to come. If he tried to force the issue, she'd clam up for good.

"All right. We'll start with the two most important pieces, the king and the queen."

While he wanted her to learn, her intense concentration alarmed him. "Hey! I'm not giving you a test or anything. Don't work so hard at it. It's supposed to be fun."

"It is, but I don't want you to have to explain over and over again. You'd get bored with our lessons."

He laughed and touched her cheek. "I don't think so."

His words didn't soothe her. She seemed more intent than ever after that. Then, after another half hour, she told him she was tired and wanted to go to bed now.

"You might even have time to give Holly a call, since most women don't go to bed so early," she said.

"Who said I wanted to call Holly?"

"I just said you could if you wanted to." She was putting the chess pieces away and not looking at him.

He reached over and caught her chin, raising it so that she had to meet his eyes. "Georgie, don't pay any attention to my father. I can take care of myself."

"Of course you can, unless you're too intent on being a do-gooder to do what you want."

He chuckled. "No one's ever called me that before."

"You've been a do-gooder to me. And I appreciate it, but I don't want to be a burden. And I don't want your father hating me, either."

"You worry too much," Rick said, and bent down to kiss her forehead.

She jerked back, her eyes wide. "Why did you do that?"

"Because I wanted to. Now kiss me good-night and I'll tuck you in." He pointed to his cheek and bent down. She hesitated and he thought she was going to refuse. But she finally leaned forward and dropped a light kiss on his cheek.

"There. And you don't need to tuck me in. I have to go brush my teeth first."

"Need any help?"

"No! No, I just need to be alone."

"Okay. I can take a hint. I'll go and dream about beating you at chess. How's that?"

"I think you need to get a life. You should be dreaming of Holly, not about winning a chess game."

"You've got Holly on the brain. You've never even met her."

"I know she's smart and pretty."

"How do you know that?"

"Your father has good taste in women. Look at your mom. And he said Holly's working on her master's."

"Maybe you're logical enough already."

"Maybe so. But thanks for teaching me chess," she said, finality in her voice.

He pushed up from the mattress and stood staring at her, his hands on his hips. Then, with a casual "See you tomorrow," he sauntered out of her bedroom. He had a lot to think about.

Chapter 13

Georgie awoke to hear raised voices coming from the kitchen. It didn't take long to realize she was part of the argument, but she wasn't going to interfere. What could she say?

She'd heard another argument between Rick and his father yesterday. When she'd tried to discuss it with Rick, he refused, pulling out the chessboard and encouraging her to make the first move.

She knew the family—or at least Caleb—was worried she was after Rick. She wanted to assure Caleb she wasn't going to marry Rick. Not that she didn't care for him, because she did. But she understood the differences between her and Rick. She knew there was no place for her in the Crawford family.

She thought again about leaving, but she was too comfortable here. She intended to relieve Caleb's worries as soon as she could, but if she did so in front of Rick and Carol, they would argue with her.

But she would leave paradise when her baby was born. She'd have to carry in her heart the happiness she'd enjoyed here. And the love. She hoped Carol and Caleb would work out their problems. If Georgie could leave anything behind, she wished it could be peace and love for the two of them. Then she could tell her little boy about his grandparents, even if he never met them.

Carol rapped on her door and stuck her head in. "Did we wake you, Georgie? Sorry. Caleb was in a bad mood this morning."

Georgie didn't let on that she knew what the argument was about. It was easier that way. "Did I hear Pete's voice? Was Kelly here, too?"

"No, just Pete. Don't forget we have your doctor's appointment this morning at ten. I did some of your laundry last night, so you should have something to wear."

"Of course, Carol. I'm going to have a shower and dress."

"But you haven't had breakfast. There's no one in the kitchen. Put on your robe and come out and I'll fix you something."

Georgie was just finishing a good breakfast when she heard the back door open. She feared it was Caleb coming in for a cup of coffee, but it wasn't. It was Rick.

"Morning, sunshine," he said, greeting her with a smile. He bent over and kissed her cheek.

She protested. "Rick, you're going to give people the wrong idea."

"Maybe it isn't the wrong idea." He went to the counter and poured himself a cup of coffee. "When will you be ready?"

Georgie immediately looked at Carol and saw puzzlement on her face. "To do what?"

"Isn't your doctor's appointment today?"

"How did you know?" Carol asked. "Did Georgie tell you?"

"No. I asked Patrick. He didn't think it was a secret," Rick said, raising an eyebrow.

"I didn't mean...it wasn't a secret," Carol said. "Anyway, Georgie and I will leave in half an hour, so we'll be there on time."

"I'll take her, Mom. I know you're busy."

"Nonsense! You're the one with work to do. I'm taking Georgie."

"No, I am. Tell her, Georgie."

"Rick," Georgie said, "I appreciate your thoughtfulness, but people are already talking. I don't think—"

"Who's talking? What are they saying?" he asked.

Carol took over. "There's been some gossip around town. Pete told us people are saying you got Georgie pregnant and won't marry her."

Instead of getting angry, Rick turned to face Georgie, a warm smile on his face. "We can take care of that. We'll just get married."

Carol gasped.

Georgie stared at him. Then she stood, quietly said no and left the room.

Rick called after her and started to follow, but Carol stopped him. "Rick, you can't go around saying things like that. You'll upset Georgie."

"But I meant it. I'll marry her tomorrow if she wants to."

"Rick! Your father would never speak to you again."

"I would regret that, Mom, but it wouldn't stop me from marrying Georgie."

She stared at her son, who was calmly sitting there sipping his coffee. "Rick, are you serious?"

"Oh, yeah."

"But Georgie said no."

"I know she did. But I haven't had a chance to plead my case. She only lost Cal about six months ago. I don't expect her to fall for me. We've become friends. I'm hoping it will turn to love over time. But that doesn't mean we can't go ahead and marry if it's what would be best for her and the baby."

"You…you're serious?"

"Yeah, I'm serious. Georgie is wonderful. She's had a tough life, but she hasn't given up. I want to protect her and her baby. Even if she won't marry me, he'll be my nephew. He deserves our protection. But Georgie…I want to always be there for her."

"Okay, but taking her to the doctor today isn't a good idea, Rick. There's already talk. You'll make things worse if you insist."

Rick stood and paced about the kitchen, running his fingers through his thick dark hair. "I don't know what to do, Mom. I want Georgie to know how I feel. But I need to give her time to get over Cal. And I need to protect her from gossip. They cancel each other out."

"I don't know, Son. Have you talked to your father? Because I can tell you he won't be happy with you."

"But you are, aren't you, Mom? You like Georgie."

"Of course I like her, what I know of her. But she won't say anything about her family. We don't know much about her."

"I know she has a big heart. I know she loves her unborn baby. I know she's not looking to hurt you or

Dad, even though he hasn't been very nice to her. I know she's smart and willing to work. What else do I need to know?''

''Maybe you're right, but I don't see how you can convince her of your feelings right now.''

''I want to be there for her. That's why I need to take her to the doctor.''

''No,'' Carol said firmly. ''I will take her. Patrick won't let you in for the examination unless Georgie asks you to come in. I'll let you know what the doctor says.''

The door opened and Georgie, her long hair pulled back in a ponytail, still a little damp from her shower, entered the kitchen. ''I'm ready, Carol.''

''All right, dear. I'll get my purse and keys. Rick, will you escort Georgie out to the car?''

As his mother left the kitchen, he walked over to Georgie. Her blue eyes met his and she stared at him solemnly. Then she stepped around him and headed for the back door.

''Georgie!'' he called, hurrying after her. He caught up with her as she reached the porch, and took her arm in his hand. ''Are you mad at me?''

''No, of course not. But I won't allow you to upset your parents or cause even more gossip. I've already done a lot of harm to your family. I won't do more.''

''Who told you about the gossip? Who told you that you'd done our family harm?'' he demanded, pulling her closer.

Georgie shook her head. ''I hear a lot from my bedroom, Rick. You know that.''

''All right, if you think it would cause more gossip, I won't take you to the doctor today. But I want to know what he says.''

Carol came out of the house and called Georgie to get in the car. She did so, ignoring Rick's demand. Carol backed the car toward the barn and then pulled forward out of the driveway.

Rick stood staring after his mother's car. He wanted to hold Georgie in his arms and refuse to let her go. He wanted her to cling to him, to want to be with him. Neither of those things seemed possible.

"What are you doing, Rick?" Caleb called from the entrance to the barn.

"I was making sure Mom and Georgie got off to her doctor's appointment on time."

Caleb snorted. "You know your mother is always prompt. She doesn't need your help."

Rick started toward the barn without answering.

"Have you talked to Holly?" Caleb asked.

"No."

"I thought you two were friendly."

"We are friends. But that's all. She knows it and so do I. I'll call her when I have a little free time."

"So, who do you have your eye on? It's time for you to be settling down."

"I think I've still got time. But I've found the woman."

"You have? Who is it?"

"Georgie."

"Don't tell me that!" Caleb roared.

"Too late. I already have."

"Son, think. She's having another man's baby!"

"She's having my nephew, a member of our family. And she's not married to the father because he's dead."

"Son, don't ruin your life because you feel sorry for this girl. That's not a good reason to marry someone.

We don't know anything about her. She's kept her private life secret. She must have something to hide.''

"I'm not listening to you, Dad. I know what I'm doing.''

And he walked away.

"Young woman, I want to talk to you!''

Georgie who had been napping on her bed, blinked her eyes several times, trying to awaken. "Yes?''

"I'm telling you I won't stand for it. I understand why you think it would be a good idea, but I'm telling you it won't work,'' Caleb said from her open doorway.

"Mr. Crawford, what are you talking about?''

"Your plan to make sure your baby is a Crawford.''

Georgie wondered if she was dreaming or having a nightmare. So far, nothing made sense.

"Are you talking about the DNA test? You think I lied about my baby being Cal's?''

"No! I'm talking about your plan to marry Rick!''

"Mr. Crawford, now I really don't know what you're talking about! Rick is teaching me to play chess. That's all.'' She remembered the kiss he'd given her, but it had been friendly, not passionate.

"Chess! Bah! That's just an excuse.''

Georgie realized her agitation was upsetting her baby. She put a hand on her stomach and drew a deep breath. Breathing slowly, she muttered to her child, hoping to calm him.

"What is it? What are you doing?''

"I'm sorry. The baby is kicking. I'm trying to calm him.''

The man stared at her stomach. "Did he kick hard? He's strong, isn't he?''

"Yes. Cal was, too."

"He was? Do...do you have a picture of him?"

"Yes." She slowly pushed herself upright and pointed to a photo album she'd brought from the apartment. "I'm sorry you never met him. He would've loved to be a part of your family."

Caleb brought over the album to her, waiting for her to open it.

She turned to the first page. There had been few pictures in her life until she met Helen and Cal. It was as if her life began when she'd met them. One of her favorite photos was on the first page. She turned the album around so Caleb could see it clearly. Cal was dressed in jeans and a plaid shirt, holding her hand. They, along with Helen, had gone to the Texas State Fair in Dallas. In another photo, one Helen had taken of them, Georgie was holding a teddy bear Cal had won for her.

"You look happy," Caleb told her.

"I was. Cal and Helen were wonderful. You would've been proud of him. He was a kind man, a good man, like your other sons."

"What did he do for a living?"

"He graduated from college with a degree in accounting and he was studying for his CPA license."

"He was good with numbers? Huh! Rick is good with numbers. Is that why you're drawn to him? Or is it just that he's available?"

"Mr. Crawford, I'm here until my baby is born so I can give him a healthy start. I'll leave as soon as he arrives. You won't have to deal with me, your grandchild or any guilt you feel about Cal. It will be as if nothing ever happened. Okay?"

With those final words, she turned on her side, her

back to Caleb Crawford. If she hadn't turned, he might've seen the tears in her eyes.

Caleb left Georgie's bedroom feeling vaguely guilty. Partly because he didn't return her photo album to the shelf where she'd found it, because he wanted to look through it.

He went to the kitchen, putting the album on the table, and filled a cup of coffee to drink while he perused it. He sat down at the table and took a sip of coffee to gather his courage. Then he slowly turned the first page.

Half an hour later, he turned back to the start and began again. He'd seen that Cal appeared to be a happy young man, always smiling and genial, a great deal like Caleb's other sons.

He'd noticed something else in those pictures. He didn't quite know what to call it, but he'd seen a difference in Georgie. Toward the end of the album, he'd seen a confident, happy young woman. As if she knew she was loved and wanted. The opposite of how she appeared around him.

Just then, Carol came into the kitchen carrying two bags of groceries. Caleb jumped up to take the bags out of her arms. "You been shopping?" he asked.

"Yes. What are you doing in here at this time of the day? No work to do?"

"I was talking to Georgie."

"Did you upset her?" Carol asked, anger in her voice.

"I didn't mean to. Anyway, she showed me some pictures of Cal. She was...was tired, so I brought the album out here."

Carol took a step toward the album. She stopped. "Do you think she'd mind if I looked?" she asked.

Caleb shrugged his shoulders. "She didn't seem to mind me looking, and she likes you a lot better than she does me."

Carol opened to the first page of the album and took her first look at his illegitimate son.

"Oh. He looks so much like *our* boys."

"Yeah." Caleb said that word heavily.

"Would you feel better if he looked more like Helen?" Carol asked.

"I don't know. I expect I'd feel guilty no matter how he looked. But he seemed to be happy in those pictures. He and Georgie both. Helen doesn't look so happy. I think her husband may not have been good to her. It seems to me Georgie may have said something about that. And he's not in the album even once."

"That's odd. But Helen is?"

"Yeah. You can tell Georgie loved her, too." He turned a few more pages, showing Carol the pictures.

"How sad that Cal and Helen died so young. How sad that Georgie was left alone."

The bedroom door opened and Georgie came into the kitchen. "I couldn't find my album," she said, staring at Caleb in an accusing way.

"I hoped you wouldn't mind if I looked at the pictures," he said hurriedly. "And Carol came in and wanted to look, too."

"I'm sorry, Georgie. If I'd known you would object, I wouldn't have looked," Carol said apologetically.

"It's all right, Carol. I just—I wanted to be sure it was safe."

Carol handed the album to Georgie. "I understand. I've heard people say that if there was a fire, the first thing they would save, after their family, of course, was their photo albums.''

"Yes." Georgie pressed hers to her chest.

"Do you have other albums? You know, ones with pictures of you as a baby, or with your parents?" Caleb asked.

Georgie shook her head and changed the subject. "Carol, would you mind if I fix a sandwich now and not come to dinner this evening? I'm not feeling well."

Carol's forehead wrinkled with concern. "Should I call Patrick?"

"No. I just don't feel social this evening. Rick will feel he has to entertain me if I come to supper. I thought maybe you might want to invite someone to dinner and I'd be in the way."

Carol looked confused, but Caleb sat up straight, realizing at once what Georgie meant. "You're right, Georgie. We could invite Holly and hear all her news. You wouldn't be interested in hearing her go on about life at university. Can we do that, Carol?"

"Even if we invited Holly, it doesn't mean you'd have to eat in your bedroom," Carol said sharply. Her words were for Georgie, but her hard stare was directed at her husband.

"I'm tired, Carol. The sooner I eat, the sooner I can go to bed. I think that would be best."

"I'll fix your dinner at once, child."

"Tell Rick I don't feel up to company tonight," Georgie added, looking directly at Caleb.

"Right." He didn't say anything else, but he nodded in Georgie's direction, letting her know he appreciated what she was doing.

She backed into her bedroom. "Just a sandwich or

GET 2

HOW TO GET YOUR
2 FREE BOOKS AND FREE GIFT!

1. Peel off the MIRA® sticker on the front cover. Place it in the space provided at right. This automatically entitles you to receive two free books and an exciting surprise gift.

2. Send back this card and you'll get 2 "The Best of the Best™" books. These books have a combined cover price of $11.98 or more in the U.S. and $13.98 or more in Canada, but they are yours to keep absolutely FREE!

3. There's <u>no</u> catch. You're under <u>no</u> obligation to buy anything. We charge nothing – ZERO – for your first shipment. And you don't have to make any minimum number of purchases – not even one!

4. We call this line "The Best of the Best" because each month you'll receive the best books by some of today's most popular authors. These authors show up time and time again on all the major bestseller lists and their books sell out as soon as they hit the stores. You'll like the convenience of getting them delivered to your home at our special discount prices . . . and you'll love your *Heart to Heart* subscriber newsletter featuring author news, horoscopes, recipes, book reviews and much more!

5. We hope that after receiving your free books you'll want to remain a subscriber. But the choice is yours – to continue or cancel, anytime at all! So why not take us up on our invitation, with no risk of any kind. You'll be glad you did!

6. And remember...we'll send you a surprise gift ABSOLUTELY FREE just for giving THE BEST OF THE BEST a try.

SPECIAL FREE GIFT!
We'll send you a fabulous surprise gift, absolutely FREE, simply for accepting our no-risk offer!

Visit us online at
www.mirabooks.com

® and TM are registered trademark of Harlequin Enterprises Limited.

BOOKS FREE!

THE BEST OF THE BEST™ — Here's How it Works:

Accepting your 2 free books and gift places you under no obligation to buy anything. You may keep the books and gift and return the shipping statement marked "cancel." If you do not cancel, about a month later we will send you 4 additional books and bill you just $4.74 each in the U.S., or $5.24 each in Canada, plus 25¢ shipping & handling per book and applicable taxes if any.* That's the complete price and — compared to cover prices starting from $5.99 each in the U.S. and $6.99 each in Canada — it's quite a bargain! You may cancel at any time, but if you choose to continue, every month we'll send you 4 more books, which you may either purchase at the discount price or return to us and cancel your subscription.

*Terms and prices subject to change without notice. Sales tax applicable in N.Y. Canadian residents will be charged applicable provincial taxes and GST. Credit or Debit balances in a customer's account(s) may be offset by any other outstanding balance owed by or to the customer.

If offer card is missing write to: The Best of the Best, 3010 Walden Ave., P.O. Box 1867, Buffalo, NY 14240-1867

BUSINESS REPLY MAIL
FIRST-CLASS MAIL   PERMIT NO. 717-003   BUFFALO, NY

POSTAGE WILL BE PAID BY ADDRESSEE

THE BEST OF THE BEST
3010 WALDEN AVE
PO BOX 1867
BUFFALO NY 14240-9952

NO POSTAGE
NECESSARY
IF MAILED
IN THE
UNITED STATES

something, Carol. Don't go to a lot of trouble.'' And she closed the door.

''Did you talk to her about Rick's feelings?'' Carol demanded.

Caleb knew he looked guilty. ''Maybe.''

''Damn you, Caleb. Don't you see what a good person she is? Did you see how sad she looked?''

''We have to keep Rick from ruining his life,'' Caleb told her adamantly.

With a deep sigh, Carol began making dinner for Georgie but not before she said to her husband, ''And you're the perfect person to know just how to ruin a life, aren't you?''

Chapter 14

Rick was running late for dinner. He'd been trying to catch up on his routine to make up for the time he'd lost these last few weeks. But he was anxious to see Georgie and hear what the doctor had to say.

He came inside, washed up, then went into the kitchen, a smile on his face.

Suddenly a woman's arms were around his neck. And it certainly wasn't Georgie. "Uh, hi, Holly. I didn't know you were here," he said, pulling her arms down and stepping back.

"Well, I guess not. I had to accept an invitation from your folks to have a chance to see you," Holly pointed out, frowning.

"Well, we've been busy, what with…everything," he said lamely. "Mom and Dad invited you to dinner? That's nice. I bet you've got a lot to tell us."

"Oh, I do. I finish next spring. Then I'll be back here, or in Oklahoma City, like Michael."

"That's nice. Uh, Mom, where's Georgie?"

"She ate early so she could go to sleep. She said she was really tired."

Rick turned to go to her bedroom and his mother stopped him. "She said she'd see you tomorrow."

"What did the doctor say today? Is everything okay?"

"He thinks the baby may still come early—as soon as a week or two instead of around Christmas. But now that she's been taking care of herself, the baby has grown a good deal."

Rick frowned. "Georgie was okay with that?"

"Of course. There's not much she can do if she's not. Nature has its own schedule."

"Who is Georgie?" Holly asked, an innocent expression on her face.

"She's the widow of Caleb's cousin and is expecting his baby in a week or two," Carol told the young woman. Then she changed the subject by asking, "So, how's school going?"

Holly talked about her experiences at Oklahoma University. When Caleb entered a few minutes later, she jumped to her feet and gave him a big hug. Rick compared his father's greeting of Holly to the way he had greeted Georgie and had a suspicion his father was behind Georgie's early bedtime.

Two hours later, Rick had eaten dinner and heard every detail of Holly's life in Oklahoma City. And was bored to tears. He imagined Georgie's beautiful smile and longed for her to open her door.

When he walked Holly to her car, she stunned him by asking, "Have you heard anything I've said?"

He gave her a sharp look. "Of course I have."

"Really? So the gossips are wrong? You're not in love with Georgie?"

"I thought you didn't know who she was?"

"I'd heard. I also heard the rumor that the baby is yours, but I didn't believe that. If it was your baby, you would have already married her."

"Thank you for that at least," he said grudgingly.

"You're a good man, Rick. I should've married you a long time ago, when I had the chance."

"No, Holly. You were right. We were a habit with each other. Now I know what being in love is like. And I wish the same for you."

She leaned forward and kissed his cheek. "Then I wish you luck, Rick. If you need a character reference, send her to me."

"Thanks, Holly. I hope that won't be necessary."

She smiled and slipped into her car. Rick watched as she drove away. He'd meant what he said. He was very glad she'd turned down his marriage proposal. He'd dated her for four years. He knew she'd expected him to declare himself.

But when he'd asked her to marry him two years ago, she'd turned him down, saying they were a habit. That she wasn't ready to be tied down. At first his feelings had been hurt. Then he'd realized she was right.

His mind flashed to Georgie's smiling face, and he began to worry again.

When Rick returned to the kitchen he found his father drying the dishes his mom had washed.

"What happened to the dishwasher? Did it break?" Rick asked.

"No. But it makes a lot of noise and I didn't want to wake Georgie," Carol said.

"What's wrong, Mom? Did Patrick tell her something that upset her?"

"No, Rick, other than moving up her due date. He wants to see her every week, too. The doctor always does that for the last month."

"Is she scared about the delivery?"

"She seemed excited about the baby coming early. She did mention something about not intruding in our lives after the baby came, but I assured her she'd need a few weeks to recover after his birth."

Rick switched his steady gaze from his mother to his father. "And did you tell her she'd have to leave at once?"

"I did not! We talked a little and she showed me pictures of Cal. He...looked a lot like you and your brothers."

"Did he treat her well?"

Caleb nodded slowly. "He must've. She looked very happy in all the pictures."

"What about the pictures of when she was younger?"

Caleb looked at Carol, waiting for her to answer that question.

"There weren't any," she said. "The album began with pictures of her and Cal, and some included Helen. No one else."

Rick frowned. "No baby pictures? None of her parents?"

Caleb sighed. "No, none. When I asked about other albums, she changed the subject and decided to eat in her room."

Rick shook his head. "I'm worried about her."

Carol hesitated before she confessed, "It was Georgie who suggested we invite Holly to dinner."

"Why would she do such a thing?" he demanded, glaring at his parents.

They both stared at him but said nothing.

Rick turned and headed for the stairs. He'd find no answers until he talked to Georgie in the morning.

Life was good. Joe leaned against his tractor, smiling at the rich land that surrounded him. Over his shoulder, he could see his house, where Anna and the children awaited his return.

For so long he'd thought he'd never have a family. But once he'd met Anna, things had certainly changed.

Now he had a wife and kids, and tomorrow they were going to his parents' place to celebrate Thanksgiving. He would have much to be grateful for.

"Joe!"

He turned around, saw Rick loping toward him, and went to meet him. "What is it?"

"I have a problem."

"Ah. You've heard the gossip about you and Georgie?"

"Yeah, but I don't care about that."

"It might make it hard to get a date, Rick. You'd better keep that in mind."

"The only woman I want to date is Georgie."

Joe rubbed the back of his head. "Mercy. I suppose you informed Dad of that fact."

"Yeah."

"He didn't threaten to send you to your room?" Joe teased.

Rick squared his shoulders and stared at his brother. "I'm not a child, Joe. I'm twenty-eight. More than old enough to figure out who I want to marry."

"Sorry, Rick. You're right. I shouldn't have teased you."

Rick shrugged his shoulders. "I need some help, though. I want to ask you and Anna some questions."

"Both of us?"

"Yeah."

"Okay. Let's go have some coffee."

Since he'd left Anna in their big bed, feeding little Johnny, Joe parked Rick in the kitchen with coffee and a sweet roll to keep him occupied. He found Hank and Julie in the den watching *Sesame Street* while they finished their cereal. "Julie, you'd better get dressed. Aunt Kelly will be here in a few minutes to take you to school."

"Okay, Daddy," she said, never moving her gaze from the television.

"Julie," he prompted. "Now."

"Okay, Daddy," she repeated, but this time she actually got up, moving slowly to the stairs.

Joe walked over and patted Hank on the shoulders. "You doing okay, Son?"

Hank nodded. "Mommy?"

"She's feeding the baby. Then she'll be down to say hi. Okay?"

Hank nodded again. A man of few words, Joe thought with a grin. Julie always made up for her brother's silence.

When Joe climbed the stairs, he found Anna staring at their sleeping son.

"You feeling okay?" he asked.

"Of course. Is Julie ready to go with Kelly?"

"I sent her up to dress. You want to check on her?"

"I'd better. And Hank?"

"He's finishing his cereal and watching *Sesame Street*."

"Oh, dear, Kelly's dropping him off at the Mother's Day Out day care. He has to be dressed, too."

"I'll get him. We have company. Rick is downstairs and wants to talk to both of us."

"Why?" Anna asked.

"My guess would be about his feelings for Georgie."

"Okay," Anna said slowly. She'd been briefed on the rumors going around. Her husband kept nothing from her.

"I'll go get Hank."

Joe also stuck his head in the kitchen to tell Rick they had to get the children ready and then Anna would be down. Five minutes later, Kelly pulled up and honked. Julie came running down the stairs—dressed with her hair brushed—and Joe carried Hank to Kelly's car. He made sure they were both buckled in, and thanked Kelly before he headed back to the house. He passed Rick again and met Anna as she slowly started down the stairs. "I told you to wait on me," he scolded his beloved wife as he swept her into his arms and carried her to the bottom.

"How will I get any stronger if you always carry me?"

He kissed her in answer and then walked with her to the kitchen.

"Good morning, Rick," Anna said, smiling. "Did Joe give you something to eat? I can scramble eggs if you want."

"No thanks, Anna. I didn't mean to cause trouble."

"You haven't. We're just not used to getting both kids off at the same time. But next year Hank will start preschool, so we might as well get used to it." She smiled at her husband, knowing he would never complain about doing things for the kids.

Joe put out more sweet rolls and poured a glass of milk for Anna. She looked longingly at Rick's cup of coffee and then dutifully picked up her milk.

When Joe joined them with a cup of coffee, he looked at his brother. "Okay, ask away."

Rick set down his coffee. "Uh, I wanted to know how—how you courted Anna when she had kids. I mean...I've never dated anyone who was responsible for a child, and I don't want to mess up."

Anna reached over and patted his arm. "I gather we're speaking about Georgie?"

Rick nodded, studying his coffee cup.

"Why?" Joe asked.

"You object? You think I just feel sorry for her? That's Dad's theory."

"I don't know if you do or not. I haven't seen the two of you together except at Alice's, and you disappeared quick enough."

"I had to get Georgie home so she could have a nap. The morning had been hard on her."

"I don't know what I would've done without her when I went into labor," Anna said, smiling again. "She was wonderful. Julie said she told the children I would be all right and hugged them."

"Yeah. She's going to be a great mama," Rick said.

"I'm sure you're right. But Rick, it's only been six months since Cal died. Don't you think you may be rushing things?"

Rick didn't respond right away, but Joe said, "Anna's got a point, Rick."

"Of course she does. But Georgie swears she's leaving as soon as the baby's born. And Dad's not going to beg her to stay.''

Anna, ever the comforter, said, ''It's been difficult for him, Rick. His wife is hardly speaking to him and the woman who gave away his secret is living in his house.''

''It's not Georgie's fault. She never complains. She apologizes for causing problems. She disappears into that room, all alone, most of the time.''

''Your mother bought a small television to entertain her,'' Anna pointed out.

''Yeah, and she watches it occasionally, but she doesn't know any of the shows. She apparently watched a couple of shows with Cal and Helen, but she's never had a television of her own.''

''Why?'' Joe asked. ''They're cheap these days.''

''When I asked her that, she shrugged her shoulders and said she'd gotten used to doing without. She said she read a lot.''

''That's better for you,'' Joe said.

''I don't think anyone ever pampered her or took care of her. I want to be the man who does that. But she's the one who suggested Mom and Dad invite Holly to dinner last night. That's what's got me worried.''

''How did she know about Holly?'' Joe asked.

''Who is Holly?'' Anna queried.

''She's a local girl I used to date. She's going to OU and working on her master's in business. Dad was pushing Holly on me one day when Georgie was in the kitchen with us.''

''I suppose it could mean she's not interested in you,'' Joe said, trying to be gentle.

"No, that's not what it means," Anna said. Both men stared at her.

"It's not?" Rick asked eagerly. "How do you know?"

"Because I'm a woman. At this point Georgie may not be thinking of getting a man for herself, but she could be worried about you. Has your father expressed an opinion about you and Georgie?"

"Several times," Rick said with a heavy tone. No one had any doubt about how Caleb felt.

"Ah. Then I think Georgie is trying to make up for some of the difficulty her presence has caused. I know she's upset, but at this point there's not much she can do."

"So I should keep on spending time with her? And show interest in her baby? Joe showed interest in Julie and Hank, didn't he?"

"You could say that," Anna said, with a big smile and a flirtatious look at her husband.

"Okay, Anna, you've helped me a lot. I appreciate it." Rick stood, obviously ready to go.

"What does Mom say about you and Georgie? Is she supportive?" Joe asked.

It was clear Rick didn't want to answer that question. After a moment, he said, "She's worried. It's because Georgie avoids mentioning her family at all. They saw a photo album yesterday that began with her meeting Cal and his mother. They appeared in most of the pictures. Georgie is there, of course. Dad said she looked happy, which I guess means Cal treated her well."

"Mom has a point, though, Rick. She's hiding something."

"Maybe. But Georgie is a good person. Otherwise she wouldn't be concerned about Dad and Mom's happiness. She doesn't blame Dad for his behavior. And he hasn't exactly been friendly.''

"You're right about that," Joe agreed with a sigh.

"I think Georgie is a good person," Anna said.

Rick squeezed his sister-in-law's hand. "Me, too, Anna." Then he bent and kissed her cheek. "Thanks," he said, and left the house, looking happier than he had when he'd arrived.

Joe watched his brother until he drove off in his truck? Then turned to his wife when she asked, "Joe? Did I say the wrong thing?"

"No, honey. You said what you felt."

"Yes. Georgie reminds me of how I felt when you came into my life."

"Then I wish Rick good luck. But you have to admit we don't know much about Georgie."

"That's true." Anna seemed to remember something. "What about the private investigator Michael wanted to hire?"

"I don't know. Mike hasn't called since we talked that day. Maybe he'll come for Thanksgiving and I can ask him. Surely he'll have some information then. Unless Georgie is a secret spy." He laughed, but Anna didn't. "Hey, I wasn't serious, sweetheart."

"I know you weren't. But how will Rick take it if he finds out about the P.I.?"

"I hadn't thought of that," Joe said, rubbing his chin. "I suppose he won't be too happy, but he'll get over it if it clears up the mystery. I don't think Mom will object if it does."

"And if Georgie has a secret she thought she could keep hidden? A secret that doesn't hurt anyone but her?"

Joe thought for a minute. "Well, Anna, I would

think that honesty is the best policy. You see, that's exactly what Dad thought about his illegitimate son. And it hurt lots of people, including my mother. So I'm for honesty. And Rick won't stop loving her, no matter what he learns about her.''

"I hope you're right," Anna said softly.

Chapter 15

The day before Thanksgiving, Georgie awoke to more stirring in the house than she'd ever noticed before. When she entered the kitchen, she found Kelly and Lindsay there with Carol.

"Morning, Georgie. How are you feeling?" Lindsay asked.

"Fine."

"There's scrambled eggs and bacon on the back of the stove, Georgie. Or if they're too cold, I can—"

"They'll be fine," Georgie assured Carol. She took down a plate and transferred several pieces of bacon and a little scrambled eggs onto it. Then she put a piece of bread in the toaster. When her plate was full, she picked it up and headed for the bedroom again.

"Where are you going, Georgie?" Kelly asked in surprise.

"I thought you might want privacy," Georgie explained. She knew some of the family felt she intruded too much.

Lindsay laughed. "The only secret we've got is what kind of pies I'm making."

"You didn't forget tomorrow is Thanksgiving, did you?" Carol asked. "We're planning the meal. Usually Anna would be here, too, but we're excusing her from the work because of little Johnny."

Georgie asked, "Do you all have a big dinner? With a turkey and all the trimmings? The whole family?"

Kelly looked at her thoughtfully, but Lindsay laughed. "Sure, just like millions of other families. You know, a big feast followed by men watching football and women doing dishes. About the time we finish, the men are ready for leftovers."

Georgie looked at all three women. "Then why do you do it?"

Carol answered her question. "Well, dear, it's a time to give thanks for the food, the household, the new babies and each other. We all enjoy it, even those of us who cook and clean. And not all the men get to watch football. They also have to take care of the children, you know."

"Haven't you celebrated Thanksgiving before?" Kelly asked.

"Well, Helen made a nice dinner last Thanksgiving, but there was just three of us, so it was quiet."

"Ah," Carol said, letting out a sigh, "then I'm glad you're going to share Thanksgiving with us."

"No! I'll stay in my bedroom. I don't want to disrupt your family gathering."

"Oh, no, you won't!" Kelly exclaimed. "You'll enjoy the day. But you have to put in an order for which part of the turkey you want, 'cause it goes fast. And I insist you eat some of the pie so there won't be too much left over. I haven't lost all my weight from Alexandra's birth.''

"We don't want to talk about things like that," Lindsay protested, rubbing her tummy. "My baby is six months older than yours." Both women laughed and Georgie looked at them with big eyes.

"Do your husbands fuss about it?" she asked.

"Nope," Kelly said.

"They wouldn't dare," Lindsay added. "They both gained some weight, too, and they didn't have nearly as good a reason."

Carol stood and crossed the kitchen. She opened a box, pulled out a card, brought it to the table and handed it to Georgie. "Can I count on your help? This is the recipe for green beans that everyone likes. I've bought all the ingredients, but the closer to dinner we get, the more things I have to do."

Georgie looked at Carol, amazed at how the woman knew exactly what to do to make her feel at home. "I'd be glad to help, Carol, if you think I won't mess it up."

"Of course not, silly. And these happen to be a favorite of Rick's."

All three watched the change in Georgie. The pleasure that had shone in her face for a moment disappeared. "I—I'd better not. I'll stay in my room." She stood and abandoned her breakfast and left the kitchen.

"Mom?" Lindsay said. "What just happened?"

"Rick is showing some interest in Georgie. I thought maybe by mentioning his name, I'd get an idea of how she feels about him. Instead, I made her withdraw."

"Do you want us to go talk with her?" Kelly asked.

"No. I'll talk to her later. Let's finish up before

lunchtime. I'll just take the rest of Georgie's breakfast to her.''

Carol went into the bedroom and came right back out. When the other two questioned her, she said Georgie was fine.

But after Kelly and Lindsay had gone, Carol knocked on her door. ''Georgie?'' She opened the door and found Georgie staring at her. ''Did you finish your breakfast?''

''Yes, thank you, but I'll bring the plate back to the kitchen. You don't have to wait on me.''

''I know I don't. You're a very considerate guest. Your mother would be proud of you.'' She noticed that Georgie didn't seem to appreciate her remark. ''Georgie, I didn't mean to embarrass you when I mentioned Rick liking the green beans. I thought the two of you had become friends. I thought you'd like to make a dish that he enjoys.''

''Carol, we both know how Caleb feels about Rick spending time with me. I enjoy his company and he's always a gentleman, but Caleb thinks—I don't want to make things worse for you than I already have. If I made a dish that Rick particularly likes, it would ruin your holiday. I don't need that on my hands, as well. I've already done enough damage to your family.''

Carol saw the tears the girl tried to hide by turning her face away.

''Dear, I'd like to tell you that Caleb would welcome you tomorrow, since it's a holiday. But we both know he's…concerned about the implications of your visit. But even Caleb wouldn't want you hiding in your bedroom. And you have done nothing wrong. You need to remember that.''

''Thank you, but we—''

"I want you at our Thanksgiving table tomorrow. If it will make you feel any better, I should tell you that we frequently have visitors at Thanksgiving and sometimes Christmas, too. The children would often bring a friend from the dorm who couldn't go home for the holidays. They were always welcomed as much as the family. But you *are* family. And you will share a real Thanksgiving dinner with us, if I have to drag you out by your heels," she said, a big smile on her face.

"But Rick—"

"I'm not going to plead Rick's case for him. He's quite capable of doing so on his own. But you're going to be the mother of Caleb's grandchild. And tomorrow, we want to share our traditions with you." Carol leaned forward to hug her, and Georgie dissolved into tears on her shoulder.

"What's going on in here?" Caleb asked from the open doorway. "Did somebody die?"

Georgie pulled away to hide her face in a tissue.

Carol stood and stared at her husband. "No. We were discussing Thanksgiving, that's all. Georgie has volunteered to help with some things tomorrow. Is that all right with you?"

"I suppose so, as long as she can cook," Caleb said, still staring at Georgie.

"I think Georgie would like to be left alone," Carol said as she swept past Caleb and into the kitchen.

He continued to stand in the doorway, frowning at Georgie until she looked up. "Why are you crying?" he asked her.

"Carol asked me to join you for Thanksgiving. I told her I would stay in my bedroom."

"Of course not. You'll join us."

She nodded.

"Oh. We enjoyed looking at your photo album," he added.

"Thank you."

"Was Cal good to you?"

Georgie raised her head and straightened her shoulders. "Yes, he was wonderful to me. He and Helen both."

"What did you two...I mean, other than what you did..." He waved toward her stomach. "I mean, did you go to movies, go bowling?"

"No. We took walks and went to the library. Sometimes I helped do the grocery shopping. Helen invited me to dinner a lot. She was wonderful."

"Did Cal have any hobbies?"

Georgie slowly shook her head. "He took good care of his mom and me. He read a lot. He liked cars." She shrugged her shoulders.

"Well, we have a good meal on Thanksgiving. And—and we watch football."

"Yes, Lindsay said."

"Okay, well, you're not going to cry anymore, are you?" he asked, as if he thought she would break out in tears at any moment.

"No, and I apologize for having done so. Please ask Carol to forgive me."

"Right. I'll see you later."

He returned to the kitchen, where Carol was preparing lunch.

"Why was she bawling like a newborn calf?" he asked.

"I don't think she's had many hugs. And she's never been to a real Thanksgiving celebration before."

He stared at her. "What? Never?"

"No, Caleb, never. So I want you to be extra nice to her—well, as nice as you can be, tomorrow."

Caleb scratched his head. "I didn't mean to be rude. But can't you understand why I didn't want her to stay here? I mean, it's causing a lot of gossip."

"Try thinking of how she felt, all alone, with no money, no insurance, no family. She must have been so scared."

"I didn't realize...I thought maybe she was making up the story."

"Oh, Caleb," Carol said with a sigh as she put a bowl of salad on the table.

"Where's Rick?" Caleb asked as he sat down at his place.

"I don't know. He didn't say anything about missing lunch."

"And her? Is she going to eat lunch?"

"She just had breakfast an hour ago. And I think she's embarrassed about crying. I'll have lunch with her in a little while."

Rick entered Oklahoma Chic, looking for Kelly or Lindsay. When the saleslady approached him he asked her where his sister and sister-in-law were.

"They're on their lunch break right now. I believe they're across the street."

Rick headed for the pizza place where they usually had lunch. Sure enough, he found them at a table by the window.

"Rick!" Lindsay exclaimed. "What are you doing in town?"

"I need to talk to you two. Where do you buy maternity clothes?"

"You're pregnant?" Kelly asked teasingly.

"Yeah, right! I want to buy Georgie something pretty to wear tomorrow. All she's got are a couple of things Mom bought her—jeans, a few shirts. Y'all always dress up for Thanksgiving. I don't want her to feel bad."

"That's very thoughtful," Kelly said, smiling at him. "We bought most of our maternity clothes in Dallas."

"Oh. I don't have time to go to Dallas."

"No, you don't," Lindsay agreed. "Besides, will Georgie accept a new dress from you?"

Rick pulled out a chair and slumped down in it. "Probably not. But I don't want her Thanksgiving celebration ruined because she feels bad about what she's wearing."

"You are a very thoughtful person, Rick Crawford," Kelly exclaimed. "I have a very nice maternity dress that's perfect for the occasion. How about I loan it to Georgie? She might not mind that so much."

"You think you can talk her into it?" Rick asked, a frown on his brow. "She's very stubborn."

"That's why she fits in well with our family," Lindsay said with a grin.

"She does, doesn't she?" Rick agreed, pleased with his sister's statement.

"Yes, she does," Kelly declared. "Are you going to do something about that? Make it permanent?"

"Yeah, but..." He stopped himself. "How did you know?"

Both ladies laughed. Kelly said, "You've been mooning around her for a while now."

"Why doesn't she recognize it?" he complained.

Lindsay looked at her brother with sympathy. "I think she does, but she can't believe it's real. I think she'd like to believe it, but she doesn't believe in Cinderella stories.''

"Yeah," he agreed sadly. "I think she's had a very difficult past. But she won't tell me anything. She'll talk about almost any subject except herself."

"I'll go home and get the dress after work and take it over to show her. Maybe she'll agree to wear it."

"Thanks, Kelly. I really appreciate it. You've both been really good to her." He kissed their cheeks and hurried to his truck.

"He's really got it bad, doesn't he?" Lindsay asked.

"Yeah. They'll be a terrific couple, I think. Especially once Georgie realizes he's serious."

"I hope she doesn't break his heart," Lindsay said, her voice worried.

When Georgie awoke the next morning, the fragrant smell of cooking turkey filled the house. She dressed in her maternity jeans and a large shirt. The dress Kelly had brought her to wear for dinner was hanging in the closet. But Georgie wouldn't put it on until she'd done her work. She didn't want to take the chance of spilling something on it.

How sweet of Kelly to offer. All the Crawford women were kind to her. Probably because they'd all been pregnant recently.

It wouldn't be long before her pregnancy would be in the past, also. Her baby gave a big kick. "Be patient, little one," she whispered. He was getting stronger. According to the doctor, it wouldn't be long now.

She almost bumped into Carol as she came out of her bedroom. "Carol! Did I oversleep?"

"No, of course not. But I was going to see if you

wanted to get up for breakfast now. I want to get it cleared up so I'll have room for everything else.''

''Of course.''

Carol took a step back. ''I thought you were going to wear Kelly's dress?''

''I am. But I want to help you first, and I was afraid I'd get it dirty. I'll change before dinner.''

''Good thinking.'' Carol was completely encased in an apron, though Georgie could see the hem of a purple dress peeking out below. ''I've tried that before but I never have the time.''

She escorted Georgie to the kitchen table, where her breakfast was set out.

''And be sure you eat it all because we won't have dinner until two. You'll be starving by then.''

''Yes, ma'am,'' Georgie said with a warm smile.

''I know,'' Carol said, ''I sound like a drill sergeant, don't I? The boys used to tease me all the time.''

''I bet you had to, with five sons. Was raising Lindsay easier?''

''In some ways. In others, she was more difficult. But she had to work hard to become her own person. She actually went to Chicago after college and worked there for a while so she could learn to make her own decisions.''

''She met Gil in Chicago?'' Georgie asked in surprise. She'd met Lindsay's husband, who, to her mind, seemed a lot like Lindsay's brothers.

''Sort of. His sister lived in Chicago. Lindsay was coming home for Thanksgiving and an early snowstorm hit Chicago, closing the airport. She decided to drive, and his sister, a friend of Lindsay's, asked if her brother could have a ride.''

''Aha! That must've been an interesting ride.''

"True. You just never know when love will strike."

"How did you and Caleb meet?"

Carol grew dreamy-eyed as she remembered. "We met at a church social. My parents had just moved to the area and they wanted to meet some of their neighbors. I didn't want to go, but they insisted. When we walked in the door, the conversations stopped. The people of Lawton weren't used to having strangers around. Then suddenly, Caleb took my hand and introduced himself. He was a handsome devil," she said with a shake of her head.

"He still is," Georgie said softly. "And he passed his looks down to his sons, all of them."

"He certainly did," Carol agreed with a smile.

Caleb entered the kitchen. The expressions on their faces made him stop and look behind him. "What are you two talking about?"

Carol laughed and winked at Georgie. "Nothing that need concern you," she assured her husband, chuckling.

He frowned at the two of them, but let the question go. "Anything you need me to do?"

"Yes, I need the extra table put up in the dining room. After Georgie finishes her breakfast, we'll get the tables set. It's easier to do them early."

"Okay. When will Logan and Abby and their two be here?"

"Abby said about ten."

"Is Logan your other son?" Georgie asked.

"Yeah. Our grandkids are Texans like you," Caleb said, smiling.

"And you still claim them? Amazing," Georgie said, teasing Caleb for the first time.

It took him by surprise, but he roared with laughter as he left the kitchen.

Carol watched him leave with a soft smile. "Irresistible, isn't he?" she said softly.

Chapter 16

After breakfast, Georgie helped Carol set the two large tables that had been squeezed into the generous-size dining room. As she finished, she saw Carol arrange something at each place setting. "What is that?"

"These? They're place cards. I assign everyone a seat. If I didn't, all the guys would sit together so they could talk sports. I won't have that at Thanksgiving dinner."

Georgie had never eaten a meal where she had a place card. She followed Carol around the table, reading each name. When she found her own it made her feel so much a part of the celebration.

Then she realized that she was to sit next to Rick. She figured Carol didn't realize what she'd done. Georgie wanted to say something to her about it, but was afraid to. She knew Caleb would be very unhappy.

She worried about it all during the morning, as she put together the green beans, cut up fruit for the fruit salad, made a pitcher of iced tea. When Kelly and Lindsay got there, she pulled them aside and asked about the place cards. "I need to change where I'm sitting. Will Carol get upset?"

"No, of course not," Lindsay said. "Want me to change it for you? Where do you want to sit?"

"Um, I'll change it, if you don't think she'll mind."

Georgie slipped out of the kitchen and picked up her place card, moved it to the other table and placed Julie next to Rick. She knew the little girl liked her uncle, and didn't think Julie would object.

Then she went to her bedroom and slipped into the beautiful maternity dress Kelly had loaned her. She'd even brought knee-high stockings, telling Georgie that they were better for her than panty hose. She had only her tennis shoes to wear with it, but with the long skirt, they didn't show that much. She still felt large and awkward, but the blue dress made her feel elegant.

A knock on her door interrupted her thoughts and she swung it open.

Rick stood there, taking in her appearance. "You look beautiful, Georgie," he said. Before she could respond, he bent over and kissed her lips gently.

"Rick! You—you shouldn't do that. What if someone saw you?"

"Then they might figure out I'm courting you," he said with a smile.

"You shouldn't tease like that," she said, and pushed past him, frowning.

Rick watched her go, pleased with her appearance. He followed her into the kitchen and then through to the dining room when Carol ordered him out of her kitchen. Lindsay was on her way into the kitchen and she grabbed his sleeve. Leaning over, she said, "Someone rearranged the place cards. You might want to check them.''

Rick followed his sister's gaze to Georgie, who had returned to the kitchen to stir the fruit salad with whipped cream.

"Thanks, sis," he whispered, and started checking the place cards. When he found Georgie's on the second table, he moved it back beside his.

When his father came in, Rick faced him and said, "Don't move the name cards, okay?"

"Why would I? That's your mom's job."

"Okay."

"Everything all right?"

"Yeah. Is Logan here yet?"

"I think I just heard them pull in. Let's go see."

Rick followed his father out, sure the name cards would stay the way he'd fixed them.

Georgie put the fruit salad in the refrigerator when she'd finished it. When she asked Carol for another job, she was told to put the condiments on the buffet. As she walked by the first table, she automatically looked at the name cards. When she discovered her name next to Rick's again, she came to an abrupt halt. Then she grabbed her name card and returned it to the other table, moving Julie's back beside her uncle.

Georgie placed everything on the buffet, then stood watching for a moment, as if expecting the name card to move itself. Since she was the only one in the room, however, she decided she was being silly. With a sigh, she went back to the kitchen.

Logan, Abby and their six-year-old daughter, Michelle, and three-and-a-half-year-old son, Lee, came into the kitchen from the back door. They met up with

Georgie just as she entered the kitchen from the dining room.

"Hello, you must be Georgie," Abby said, extending her hand, a smile on her lips. "We're glad to finally meet you."

"Yes, I've heard so much about you and your husband and your children," she answered.

Abby introduced her little ones, who were charmingly shy, and her husband. Logan was obviously like his brothers, and deeply in love with his wife. Crawford men were special.

Caleb had followed them in, and Carol gave him a bowl to put on the buffet. He was happy to be included. He'd felt ostracized from his family quite a bit the past few weeks.

As he turned away from the buffet, Caleb glanced at the nearest table and automatically read the place cards. Suddenly he stopped and stared. Rick had put Georgie's card next to his own, but it wasn't there now. Had he changed his mind?

Caleb looked toward the kitchen. No one was coming. He picked up Julie's name card and searched the two tables until he found Georgie's, switching the two. Rick would probably be surprised, but Caleb wanted Thanksgiving to be a happy affair.

He walked into the living room just as Joe announced that Michael was here. Joe seemed deeply interested in his youngest brother's arrival, and Caleb followed him with a frown.

"Michael!" Joe called out. When he reached his brother, he gave him a hug. Caleb did the same.

Michael reciprocated and then turned toward the house, eager to greet the rest of the family.

"Wait!" Joe called.

Both Caleb and Michael stopped and looked at him. "What for?" Michael asked.

"Did you hire the private eye?" Joe kept his voice low, but Caleb heard his question.

"What was he going to hire a P.I. for?" he asked.

"To check on Georgie," Michael said. "Yeah, I did. Everything's fine."

Joe caught his arm and headed for the barn, dragging his brother behind him, closely followed by Caleb.

"Hey, I'm starving," Michael protested.

"You always are. This won't take long," Joe assured him.

When they reached the barn, Joe had Michael sit on a bale of hay, as if it were the witness chair. "What did you find out?"

Michael shrugged his shoulders. "Not much. Sad stuff is all. Georgie's father was married to another woman and abandoned her mother as soon as he learned of her pregnancy. Her mother became an alcoholic. Georgie raised herself. She worked lots of jobs to pay for food because her mother spent any money she had on alcohol. She quit school at sixteen to support herself and mom. Never went back. The woman died when she was eighteen, and Georgie's been on her own ever since."

His succinct response didn't beg for sympathy, but Caleb was appalled. "Poor kid."

"Yeah," Joe agreed. "We sure had a better life."

"She probably wouldn't talk about her past because our lifestyle intimidated her," Caleb said slowly. "No wonder she's never celebrated Thanksgiving. She had nothing to be grateful for."

"It's good she came to us," Joe said, watching his father.

"Yeah. Too bad I wasn't more…friendly."

Michael clapped his hand on his father's shoulder. "You didn't know, Dad."

"Your mother didn't know, either, but she took her in. Your mother is a saint."

"Yeah," Michael agreed with a smile.

"Don't worry, Dad. None of the rest of us are," Joe assured him. "By the way, I wouldn't mention the investigation in front of Rick. I think he might be offended."

"But is it wise to keep another secret? It caused a lot of problems last time," Caleb asked.

Michael agreed with Joe. "I don't think this one will hurt anyone. Now can I go to the house and maybe sneak a few bites before dinner?"

"Yeah," Caleb agreed. "And the first game is on. Maybe your mom will have put chips and dip in the living room."

"All right!" Michael responded, leading the way to the house.

Georgie stayed in the kitchen until Carol announced that dinner was ready. She'd put out snacks on the kitchen table for the women who were busy cooking. She had also put snacks in the living room for the men busy watching a football game.

From the kitchen, the women would hear occasional cheers from the men.

"I wonder who's winning?" Anna asked. She was sitting at the table, holding Johnny.

"Why don't you go watch the game?" Georgie suggested. She, too, was seated, at Carol's insistence, resting until dinner was ready.

"Oh, I don't think so. That living room is the men's

territory today. Besides, I get to hear all the gossip in here.''

Even Georgie grinned at her answer, though she suspected there would be more gossip if she left the room. Johnny began crying and she offered to go change him.

"Are you sure? He looks little but he's heavy," Anna stated.

"I'm sure. It will be good practice," Georgie said, standing and reaching for the baby.

Once she was out of the kitchen, Abby said, "She seems nice."

"Yes, she is, and will soon be a member of the family if Rick has anything to say about it," Lindsay said.

"Really? It won't bother him that her baby isn't his?"

"No, not at all," Carol said. After a moment, she said, "She is carrying a Crawford, after all."

Georgie returned at that point with Johnny in a dry diaper, so there wasn't any further conversation on the subject. And a minute later Carol took off her apron and announced that it was time for dinner. Several of the women went to collect the children and alert the men. Georgie held back, not sure what she was supposed to do now.

Lindsay took her arm reassuringly. "We all form a circle and each of us says what we're grateful for. Then Dad says a final prayer. Then we sit down and eat."

Georgie looked up fearfully. "I have to speak?"

"Everyone does. Well, unless you're Johnny or Hank or Alexandra or Joey. They're excused."

Georgie still lingered in the kitchen as long as she could. Then Rick appeared in the doorway and stretched out his hand. "Come on, Georgie. You're holding things up."

She didn't take it, but pushed past him. Holding Rick's hand would undermine her control. She headed for the second table, but he caught her arm.

"You're over here, sweetheart."

"No, I'm not. I'm sitting by Anna."

"Nope. Here's your name." He grinned at her, letting her know he'd caught her switching the cards.

"But I changed it—twice!"

"Too bad." He took her hand, and she suddenly realized everyone was waiting on her and Rick so they could ask the blessing, so she bowed her head.

Caleb started them off. "Dear Lord, you have been so good to us this year. Each of us has much to thank you for. Joe?"

Joe thanked God for his wife and children. As Caleb went down the row of family members, each named something specific in his or her life. Georgie was so distracted by Rick's warm grasp, she found it hard trying to think of what to say when Caleb called on her.

When it was Rick's turn, he gave thanks for Georgie. It was a simple statement, but that was the first time she had ever heard anyone express gratitude for her. Her mother had always blamed Georgie for her own miserable life, saying she would've been much happier if her daughter hadn't been born.

Georgie had no time to compose herself before Caleb called on her. The words came to her at once. "Thank you for the Crawfords and their generosity to me."

There was a pause and Georgie wondered if anyone was upset by her response. Then Caleb called on the next person and the prayer continued. When all but Caleb had spoken, he paused again. Then he said,

"Thank you, God, for all these blessings. And thank you for my beloved wife and her wisdom. Amen."

Georgie looked up and her eyes met Caleb's to her surprise. He smiled at her.

Carol was on her other side, and she, too, gave Georgie a sweet smile. Then she began passing bowls of food. Soon everyone was filling plates and laughing and talking. Georgie reveled at the joy that flowed through the room. The babble of children's voices, babies cooing, and adult conversations reminded her of the pictures she'd always seen of Thanksgiving dinners. She'd never believed them real, but now she was in the middle of such a scene.

Rick leaned over and asked, "You okay?"

She nodded, not looking at him.

"Then why aren't you eating?"

"There's so much," she said softly.

"Sure. That's the fun of Thanksgiving," he said, assuming she was referring to the food.

She didn't correct him. With a smile, she reached for the bowl of fruit salad, part of her contribution, and became a part of a real family for the first time in her life.

After dinner, the women began cleaning dishes but insisted Georgie stay off her feet. Rick sat down beside her in the living room and whispered an invitation for them to play chess. She seemed about to respond when his brothers asked him to join them in a tag football game outside during half time.

"Sorry. I'm playing chess with Georgie," he told them.

"We can play another time, Rick. Go join your brothers," Georgie insisted.

"Yeah, go ahead, Son," Caleb said. "I'll play chess with Georgie. It will give me a chance to see if you taught her anything. About chess, I mean," he added with a big grin.

Georgie couldn't believe her ears. With red cheeks, she accepted his offer. She wasn't going to turn down a friendly overture from Caleb.

Rick looked from Georgie to his dad and finally nodded in agreement. "But be nice, Dad," he added.

Caleb nodded and offered Georgie a hand to help her up from the easy chair where she'd been sitting.

"Thank you. It's become ridiculously difficult to get up," she confessed.

"It was the same for Carol...and all the girls, for that matter. Shall we play in your room? Otherwise, some of the little ones may come over and grab some of the chess pieces."

"That will be fine," she agreed.

Once they were seated and had the chessboard set up, Georgie, at Caleb's offer, made her first move. He frowned and raised an eyebrow.

"Just what did my son teach you?"

"Perhaps I should tell you that Carol gave me a book on how to play chess. I was planning to surprise Rick the next time we played."

"Well, you're a sharp little cookie, aren't you? I bet you did well in school."

Georgie stiffened. Then she consciously relaxed and shook her head. "Not particularly."

They each made several moves before Caleb cleared his throat and said, "I want to tell you that I appreciate the kind words you spoke in there." He nodded his head in the general direction of the dining room.

Georgie blushed and kept her gaze on the chessboard. "I meant them."

"I know you did. But I also know I wasn't very nice to you in the beginning. I regret that now."

"That's very kind of you. When I first came, I didn't realize I was going to cause you and Carol so many problems. I'm sorry."

"Honey, any problems created were my fault. You didn't do anything wrong."

She drew a deep breath and clenched her shaking fingers in her lap. "That's very nice of you, but—"

Caleb held up a hand. "No, young lady. I'll have no argument about this. Besides, it's your move."

Georgie took another deep breath before she pulled her thoughts together and picked up her knight.

About ten minutes later, she moved her queen and quietly said, "Checkmate."

Caleb looked at her and then the chessboard. Then he reached across the board to shake her hand. "I hope you'll give me another game soon, after I've brushed up on my skills. I'm impressed."

"Beginner's luck. Thank you for playing me."

"How'd she do?" Rick asked from the door. The touch football game had him breathing hard, but he looked pleased at the calm scene before him.

Caleb winked at Georgie. "She did okay. I'll let you take over now and play her. I think she has a little surprise in store for you."

Chapter 17

"Hey, what did Dad mean?" Rick asked as he seated himself on the bed across from Georgie.

"I think he was surprised at how well I played chess," Georgie said demurely.

"Ha! He didn't think I'd done a good job teaching you," Rick concluded.

She arranged the pieces on the chessboard again. "Do you want to go first?"

"Of course not. You begin."

She made the same move she'd used with Caleb, a move she'd learned from the book on chess. Like his father, Rick was surprised and looked at her suspiciously. "Did Dad teach you that?"

"No. Your mother gave me a book so I could learn by myself and not take up so much of your time."

"Oh, really? I think I'll have to have a talk with her." He decided on his strategy and moved his bishop.

Several moves later, he said, "That must've been some book. Maybe I need to borrow it."

Five minutes later, he accepted defeat. "Where is that book?"

She pulled it off the small bookshelf in the corner of the room. "Here it is."

He opened it and flipped through the pages. "I think I underestimated you. If you can make sense out of this, you must be brilliant. You must've breezed through school."

Her face looked sad and she shook her head.

"Georgie, why won't you talk about your past? Have you done something horrible?"

"Yes," she said after a minute, knowing she'd shock Rick. She'd dropped out of high school, gotten pregnant and never married the father of her baby. Because he'd died, of course, but she knew she'd made her share of bad decisions.

She hadn't been able to resist Cal. He'd loved her, which had seemed so strange…but wonderful. She hadn't been able to resist his allure. Now, just as she was trying to make wise decisions, she was again tempted by a man. And his family. It would be so wonderful to be a member of the Crawford family. But she was going to make the right decision this time. For her child's sake, she was going to be able to hold her head high and know she'd done the right thing…for everyone.

"I'm tired, Rick. If you don't mind, I think I'll take a nap."

"Georgie, what did you mean? What are you hiding?"

She stood and waited for him to retreat.

"Georgie, I want to know what you meant. You can't—"

"Is everything all right?" Carol asked, looking in the door.

"I think I'll take a nap if you can convince Rick to go watch football," Georgie said with a wan smile.

"Well, of course he'll let you rest. Run along, Rick. You can see Georgie later, after she's had some sleep."

Rick seemed to recognize defeat when he saw it. Reluctantly, he headed for the living room.

When Carol turned to go, Georgie stopped her. "Carol, Caleb apologized to me for his earlier behavior. He was very sincere."

Carol froze, a hopeful expression on her face.

Georgie crossed the room and hugged her hostess. "He's a good man, Carol."

Blinking rapidly, the older woman hugged her back. "Yes, he is." After another squeeze, she released Georgie and left the room.

Georgie closed the door, hoping that Carol and Caleb would get back together. She'd feel much better when she left if they had made up.

When she left. Georgie shook her head. She wasn't going to think about it now. She'd cry if she did.

Lying down on her bed, she closed her eyes and shut out the future. It would be hard enough to face what she must do when the time arrived without thinking about it in advance.

Carol found the house extremely quiet the next morning. Logan and Abby had gone back to Texas, extending an invitation to Georgie to visit them any time—as if she was really family—which had made

Carol very proud. The others had all returned to their own homes after a late dinner of leftovers.

The day after Thanksgiving was traditionally reserved for Carol's Christmas shopping—she usually left her family to make lunch from the leftovers while she went to Oklahoma City.

But today she was standing at the sink, stirring a pitcher of iced tea, when Caleb came in for lunch.

"What are you doing here?" he asked in surprise.

"You object?" she asked, arching one eyebrow.

"Don't be silly," he said gruffly. "You know I never object to your presence."

She made him a piece of Texas toast covered with slices of fresh turkey topped with gravy and placed it in front of him. "Is Rick coming to lunch?"

"Yeah, he'll be right along," Caleb responded.

He asked a blessing and began eating. "That sharp wind sure does stir my appetite," he said after he chewed his first bite.

"Yes, it does, doesn't it? Save some room, though, because I saved the last piece of coconut pie for you."

He looked up in surprise. It had been a while since he'd been spoiled by his wife.

"Georgie told me you apologized to her," Carol said, answering Caleb's unspoken question.

"Oh, yeah. I told the girl I was wrong."

"It means a lot to me that you would do so. You know, take her on faith."

Caleb raised his head and met her gaze. "Take her on faith?"

"We don't know anything about her."

Caleb put down his utensils and stared at his wife. He was facing a test and he knew it. "I wish I could say that was true. But I've learned my lesson."

"What are you talking about?" Carol asked, staring at him.

"I'm not going to lie to you. Michael and Joe hired a private investigator. He filled us in on Georgie's past. I didn't ask what he'd found, but I was relieved to hear it. She's had a bad life, but not because of anything she did. And it touched me when she told everyone how grateful she was for our kindness especially when I'd been so rotten to her. But I didn't take her on faith."

"I see," Carol said, her voice distant.

Caleb was no fool. He knew she was upset with him again. This time because he'd been honest; last time because he hadn't. "Didn't you want me to tell the truth?"

"Yes, but I wish...I wish you'd realized what a good person she is without a report."

"Me, too, Carol. But I'm not as wise or as trusting as you."

Carol turned back to the stove and prepared a second open-faced sandwich for Rick. But she looked over her shoulder as she was doing so and asked, "So what did the private investigator say about Georgie?"

"Private investigator?" Rick repeated, staring at his mother from the doorway. "You hired someone to look into Georgie's background?" he asked, outrage on his face.

Carol spun around, concern in her gaze. "Rick! I didn't know you'd come in."

"I guess you didn't," he exclaimed, "or you'd never have asked that question."

"It's not your mother's fault, boy, so don't harass her," Caleb said. "Sit down and I'll tell both of you what was said."

"I don't want to know!" Rick exclaimed. "I trust Georgie." He plopped down in his chair and stared at his father, as if daring him to continue.

Caleb shrugged his shoulders and took another bite of his hot sandwich.

They all ate in silence. Finally Rick said, "Where's Georgie?"

"She had an appointment with the doctor, and Anna was going in today, too. She offered to take Georgie with her."

More silence.

Finally, Rick said, "Okay, what did the P.I. say?"

"You sure you want to know?" Caleb asked.

"Yeah."

"Her father was married, but not to her mother. He left her when he found out her mother was pregnant, and she became an alcoholic. I think Georgie began working when she was twelve. She dropped out of school when she was sixteen and worked full-time to take care of herself and her mother. She's pretty much told us everything else."

"She hasn't been in prison? Broken the law?"

"Not that I know of," Caleb said, staring at Rick curiously. "Why would you think she had?"

"Because I asked her if she'd done something very bad and she answered yes. It's been driving me crazy!"

"Surely you couldn't think Georgie could do something illegal!" Carol exclaimed. "She's too sweet."

"Not everyone is as wise as you, Carol," Caleb said softly.

"Maybe you'd better tell her we know about her past," Carol said. "It might clear up any misunderstandings."

"I can't do that. She'll know I didn't trust her. Nor the rest of the family, either," Rick said.

"But—" Carol began, but Caleb stopped her with a wave of his hand.

"I think it has to be Rick's decision, sweetheart."

"But isn't he making the same mistake you made? Not being honest?" Carol asked.

"But, Mom, knowing something isn't like lying," Rick said. "I don't want to hurt Georgie's feelings."

"I think you're wrong," Carol said. "Oh, I hear Anna's car. I told her I'd have lunch ready for the two of them. You men had better scoot back to work and leave the kitchen to us womenfolk. We're going to talk about their health."

"But I want to say hi to Georgie," Rick protested.

"And I want my piece of coconut pie," Caleb complained.

"Take a coffee break about three. I'll give it to you then," Carol promised Caleb. She looked at Rick. "You can say a quick hello. That's all."

Caleb promptly left, greeting the ladies as they entered. Rick was less satisfied, but he greeted Georgie and asked if the doctor had said everything was okay.

"Yes, except I gained a lot of weight—no doubt, all of it from yesterday," she said with a chuckle. "Imagine that!"

"I'm sure it won't hurt anything," he said as he backed out of the kitchen.

Anna hooted with laughter. "That's just like a man. 'Everything will be all right, dear.'"

Rick quickly disappeared.

"I've almost got your lunch ready. Sit down. Want some juice or tea?" Carol asked.

"I think I'd better have water," Georgie said. "But I'll get it. How about you, Anna?"

"I'll take some skim milk. I'm not sure how much longer I can nurse Johnny. I don't seem to have enough milk to satisfy him. The pediatrician suggested I supplement my milk with a bottle."

"That happened to me after the fourth one," Carol said as she made up some sandwiches. "I worried myself to death, afraid Michael would suffer great harm if I didn't breast-feed him. But somehow I don't think it stunted his growth."

Since Michael was six feet three inches, both ladies laughed.

"I know," Anna agreed. "I asked the doctor about that, and he said Johnny is off the charts already." They all laughed again, and Anna added, "I sound a little bit proud, don't I?"

"With good reason," Georgie assured her. "Johnny is a happy baby. I hope mine is as healthy and happy."

"I'm sure he will be," Anna said with confidence.

"Did the doctor have any more ideas about when your baby would arrive?" Carol asked as she brought two plates to the table.

"He said soon, but not a definite time. If the baby's not here by the twentieth, however, he said he might consider inducing." Georgie rubbed her stomach. "I hope he comes earlier than that. It would mess up Christmas for y'all if I'm still hanging around then."

Both Carol and Anna objected to her statement.

"It's nice having someone pregnant about the same time as me. And our children can play together," Anna pointed out. "It was so much better for Julie when she had Drew around. They play together all the time. And

Alexandra is a little younger than Hank, but they're good friends, too.''

Carol squeezed Anna's shoulder. ''Your marriage to Joe added a lot of happy things to our family, dear. I was so pleased for him.''

Georgie watched the camaraderie between the two women and knew she was going to miss their company. She and Anna found it easy to talk, and Carol was as supportive as any mother could be.

''Lunch is delicious, Carol,'' Georgie said, bringing the topic of conversation to more commonplace things. ''I thought I wouldn't want turkey today, but this is irresistible.''

Anna giggled. ''Carol is famous for her different turkey recipes.''

''I threatened to do a cookbook about leftovers, but if anyone took one look at my five sons, they wouldn't believe I ever had leftovers!''

Georgie and Anna laughed again, picturing the robust Crawford clan.

''Well, if you ever do write a cookbook, let me know, because I'll be the first in line to buy it,'' Georgie said, knowing she wouldn't be around to learn the recipes firsthand. ''In fact, I wish you would.''

''You know, I could put something together just for my daughters-in-law. When Rick and Michael marry, our family will be complete until the next generation grows up. Hmm, I just might do that.''

''And would you sell it to me? I'm a distant connection, you know,'' Georgie asked.

''Sell? No, but you'll definitely get a copy. In fact, I may dedicate it to you, Georgie.''

Before Georgie could respond, Johnny let out a rous-

ing howl of hunger from his car seat on the kitchen
table.

Anna looked at her watch. "It's been less than an
hour since I fed him. That's why I think I'm not sat-
isfying him."

"Do you have the formula with you?" Carol asked.

"Yes, we bought formula and several bottles, on the
way from the doctor. They're all in the car." She
started to get up.

"Finish your lunch. I'll go get everything and fix
him a bottle. Then I can feed him while you eat," Carol
assured her, already halfway out the door.

Anna sighed. "She's so wonderful."

"Yes, she is," Georgie agreed.

"You know what the best thing is about her? She
doesn't realize how special she is." Anna took a bite
of her sandwich. "And I think that cookbook is a good
idea."

Caleb kept checking his watch. It seemed the hands
were creeping along at a slower than usual speed.
When his watch read five minutes to three, he headed
for the house. But he didn't hurry. He didn't want
Caleb to think he expected anything but coconut pie.

"You're right on time," she said as he came in.

"Am I?" he asked, as if he didn't know the time to
the second.

Carol took a piece of pie covered with clear plastic
out of the fridge. She unwrapped it and put it in front
of him along with a fork. "Want a cup of coffee?"

"Yes, please."

"Guess what the girls and I were talking about earlier?" she asked, her mind obviously on something
other than him.

"What?"

She set the cup of coffee in front of him and sat down at the table before she answered. "Georgie encouraged me to write a cookbook for the family, and then she asked if she could buy a copy."

"Ah. So you're going to start your own business?" He was teasing, of course, but he also felt a niggling worry that if Carol ever did so, she might not need him.

She smiled. "No. I'd give one to her, of course. But I think I'll do it. I think all the girls would like to have a cookbook, and when the next generation gets to the cooking age, I'd like to know that some of them would carry on making things my way."

"I'm hoping you'll be around long enough to teach them yourself."

"I hope so, too, Caleb, but you never know how long you have on earth."

"That's a melancholy thought," he said. He'd yet to take a bite of his favorite pie. But he wasn't there for pie.

Carol twisted her hands on the table, staring at them. "I've hated the time we've spent apart."

Caleb snapped his head up, staring at her. "Not as much as me. I've been sleeping on the guest bed. It's six inches too short and I hang off the end. I—"

"Oh!" Carol exclaimed. "I hadn't thought of that. Do you want to exchange beds?"

"Yes!" Caleb said, unable to believe it was this easy.

"Well, I can move my things in there this afternoon and you can sleep in the big bed tonight."

He'd been so eager, so sure his sentence had ended, he could hardly think. But something was wrong with what she'd said. "I can…" Then, of course, he realized she wasn't joining him. "No! No, I'll stay where I am until you invite me to *join* you. And not because you think I'm falling off the shorter bed."

"I never told you to *move* to the shorter bed," she pointed out softly, watching him.

He raised his eyes to hers again. "You didn't?"

"No. You decided to leave me."

"Stupidest thing I ever did! I've missed you, Carol."

She blinked her eyes rapidly. "Me, too. I haven't been warm since you left."

"Will you let me move back in? You know I won't lie to you again, don't you?"

"Yes, Caleb, I do. But maybe I was asking too much of you. There aren't many people who would condemn themselves."

"No, Carol, I was wrong. I caused both of us pain, and I caused Georgie pain. I learned a lesson."

"Then yes, please, you can move back in this evening."

"Do I have to wait that long?"

"Well, I am a little chilled with that north wind blowing," she said demurely.

Caleb rose and swung her into his arms, heading for the stairs. "I'll never gripe about the north wind again!"

The coconut pie remained on the kitchen table and the cup of coffee soon grew cold.

Chapter 18

The following Monday, Anna, Kelly and Lindsay put their children—all except Johnny—in school or day care, in order to join Carol on her revised shopping trip to Oklahoma City.

Georgie refused their invitation to join them. Instead, she offered to watch over Johnny while they were gone.

"Are you sure it won't be too hard for you?" Anna asked.

"We'll be fine. I'll feed him a bottle and then we'll both take a nap. Everything will be fine." Georgie smiled at Anna.

"Okay. But I'll call and check on you."

"Of course. And if I have a problem, I'll call Joe."

Georgie stood on the front porch, waving goodbye. Georgie went back into the kitchen and, after putting Johnny down, washed her breakfast dishes. Then she made several bottles with formula for Johnny so she'd have them ready.

Carol had offered to pick up anything she wanted to buy for Christmas presents, but she'd asked for nothing. She didn't have much money and she needed to save it until she proved her baby was a Crawford and she could get him the trust fund. Who knew how long it would take to get the testing done?

Besides, she wouldn't be here for Christmas.

She shoved that thought away. The end was coming soon, faster than she wanted.

Carol had left lunch in the fridge, so all she had to do was heat it up when Rick and his dad came in. Everything was ready. She picked up a magazine Carol had left lying on the kitchen counter and went into her bedroom to rest until either Johnny or Rick and Caleb needed her.

While reading the magazine, Georgie drifted into a light sleep. When a knock on the front door awakened her, she hurried to greet the visitor—and wondered if she was having a nightmare.

Leon Dipp, Helen's husband, stood there.

"So, you're still living the easy life, are you?" he asked with a sneer. "I should've known. I figured the letter came from you!"

"What are you talking about? What letter?" Georgie asked, confused by his words.

"The letter the police got asking them to reopen the investigation of Helen and Cal's deaths. The insurance refused to pay me my money. Life hasn't been easy for me, while you live a life of luxury. That's not fair."

Georgie didn't like the threat in his voice. "I didn't write a letter to anyone about their deaths."

"The police said it came from Oklahoma."

"I'm not the only person in Oklahoma."

He glared at her, but she straightened her shoulders and lifted her chin. "Why are you here?"

"Because I didn't get any money. That means I need Cal's trust fund even worse than before. I've got a paper here for you to sign, giving me the money. You sign it and I'll go away without making a fuss."

"No! I won't. That money belongs to my baby."

"If you don't cooperate, I'll go to Crawford and tell him all about your past. These are classy folks. They won't like it that you're a little slut who didn't even finish high school." He grinned evilly at her.

Georgie wrapped her arms around her swollen body, hoping he wouldn't notice her hands trembling. "You can tell Mr. Crawford anything you want about me. But I'm not going to help you steal my baby's money!"

"You're making a mistake, thinking you can take me on. Helen thought the same thing and look what it got her!"

Georgie stared at him in horror. Had this man actually planned Helen's death? "Go away! And don't ever come back!" she shouted, hoping to get rid of him before she fell to pieces.

"Georgie?" Rick called from the kitchen.

Before she could pull herself together to answer, Rick appeared beside her.

"I've seen you before," he said. "You're the creep who threatened Georgie and destroyed her things."

Leon glared at him. "I'm here to see your father. I have some information he'll want."

"No!" Georgie protested.

Rick took one look at her color and led her to the

sofa in the living room. "Sit down, Georgie. I'll take him to see Dad. I'm sure everything will be all right."

Rick didn't know what the man wanted, but was pretty sure he was up to no good. Rick didn't care. He just wanted Leon to get away from Georgie.

"If you'll come with me, my father is in the barn." He went through the front door and waved for the man to follow him. Rick looked over his shoulder to be sure Georgie was still on the sofa. He would come back as soon as he made sure his father understood the situation.

"Dad?" he called as he entered the barn. Caleb, who took a moment to appear, asked, "What's up, Rick? I thought you—oh. I didn't know we had company."

"We don't. This man is Leon Dipp, Helen's husband. The man who was threatening Georgie."

Caleb's gaze shifted to Leon. "I see. Mr. Dipp, how may I help you?"

Rick recognized his father's caution, but suspected their guest did not. Caleb sounded pleasant if formal. The man immediately launched into a rant about Georgie's past, telling them she was not going to be a proper mother to her baby. Dipp felt he should be made guardian of the child. "I will, of course, care for the baby in Helen's memory."

"How kind of you," Caleb said. "Most men wouldn't want to be tied down by a baby who isn't kin to them."

"Well, I couldn't sleep at night if I didn't offer. I loved Helen, you know. She was a good woman."

"Yes, she was. My son mentioned something about some questions in regard to the wreck."

Leon Dipp stiffened. "Georgie wrote a letter to the

police. The insurance is holding back payment because of her.''

"Georgie didn't write that letter," Rick said calmly. "I did."

Leon's gaze narrowed, but he appeared to realize his enemy wasn't weak or slow. He decided his best victim would be Georgie.

"Well, you were wrong to do so, but I suspect you were misled by Georgie. That's understandable. She misled Helen and Cal, too. You see, she never graduated from high school. She made a living the old-fashioned way."

When neither man moved or made a comment, he went on. "You know, she made her money on her back. I certainly had her a few times. She won't care anything about her baby. She just wants the cash."

Rick, his fists clenched, tried to step forward, but his father stopped him.

Caleb moved closer to Dipp and said calmly, "It wouldn't be healthy for you to continue to malign Georgie. We know her past. She's a part of our family now, and she and her baby are welcome here. You're not. If you bother us again, I'll file charges against you. And I've got enough money to ensure that you never see the light of day again. Do you understand me?''

"You're making a mistake!" Leon screamed as he took a step backward. "She's trash, I tell you!"

Rick pulled free from his father's hold. "You're the one who's trash. You'd better get off our place. If you come back, you'll be met with a shotgun."

"No violence, Son…unless he does come back. And shoot low. We don't want his death on our hands." Caleb took a shotgun he'd had leaning in a corner and handed it to Rick.

Terror swept Leon's face and he turned and ran. Rick stepped to the door of the barn and watched him jump into his sports car and back out of the driveway. "He's gone."

"Good," Caleb said. "You didn't mention that you'd written that letter."

Rick leaned the shotgun against the wall and faced his father. "It all sounded too convenient to me. The detectives told me that they'd had their suspicions. I got a letter last week saying they had discovered a connection between the driver of the other car that hit Helen's vehicle and Leon Dipp. The insurance company has decided to withhold payment until they've satisfied their doubts. I guess that's why the man came here. He's desperate for money."

"Yeah. Was Georgie okay?"

"She was pale, but I had her sit down."

"Well, if you'll help me with this hay, we'll both get to the house faster."

They both loaded the hay bales into the back of Caleb's truck before they headed to the house.

As soon as Rick had left the house to take Leon Dipp to the barn, Georgie believed she was doomed. Leon could be persuasive. And even if they didn't believe him, he could very well come back and try to do her harm, especially if he had done something to Helen and Cal.

All she could think of doing was to run and hide. She went to her bedroom and quickly gathered her essential belongings, only enough to fill a small duffel bag. This time she made sure she took her billfold with enough money to buy a bus ticket.

The phone rang. She answered it and found it to be

a neighbor going into town who wanted to know if Carol needed her to get anything for her.

Georgie quickly asked for a ride. The neighbor promised to be there in five minutes. Georgie checked on little Johnny, then wrote a note about the bottles ready in the fridge. She knew Caleb would be in for lunch soon and would take care of his grandson.

Fifteen minutes later, she was on a bus headed for Dallas. The time had come to leave, and she hated it as much as she'd thought she would.

"Georgie?" Rick called as he entered the kitchen. He opened the door to her bedroom and discovered his nephew sleeping soundly in the middle of Georgie's bed. "Johnny's in there," he told his father as he moved through the house, calling for Georgie.

Caleb found the message about Johnny's bottles. It said nothing about Georgie's departure, but it had a note of finality to it. He waited in the kitchen until Rick returned, panic on his face.

"She's not here!" Rick announced. "I should've stayed with her, but I wanted to make sure—" He stopped abruptly, his cheeks turning red.

"You wanted to make sure I'd do the right thing?" Caleb asked wryly. He couldn't blame his son for not trusting him. "Don't worry, Son, she'll understand."

"But where is she? Surely she hasn't run off again. She's too pregnant to be walking to town."

"Probably, but you'd better drive along the road a little ways. I'll make some calls."

An hour later, neither of them had had any success in finding Georgie. Caleb had spent part of his time holding Johnny. They were trying to figure out whether to call the police when the phone rang. Rick snatched it up, since his father was holding Johnny.

"Hi, Mrs. Appleton," he said into the phone. "No, Mom's not here." He figured their neighbor would ask him to have his mother call when she returned.

Instead, Mrs. Appleton said, "I hope I did the right thing. I'm not sure that little girl should be traveling by herself, even if it was an emergency. She looked like she was ready to give birth any moment."

"Georgie? You're talking about Georgie?" Rick asked, gripping the phone tighter.

"Why, yes. When I called to offer to pick up anything from the store for Carol, Georgie asked if I'd give her a lift into town. I thought it strange that no one there could go if it was an emergency—"

"Mrs. Appleton, where did you leave her?" Rick asked, interrupting her explanation.

"The bus station, of course. She said she had to get to Dallas. And a bus just pulled up as I stopped. I waited until I saw her buy a ticket. Then I left when she got on the bus."

"Thank you," Rick said before he hung up the phone. He quickly filled his father in on the situation, got in his truck and headed to Lawton.

Georgie wondered if she'd been wise to run away, but she was so worried about what Leon Dipp might do to her. She didn't doubt that he'd harm her and her child if it meant he could get Cal's trust fund. And Leon wouldn't give up until he got what he wanted.

Once her baby was born, she could contact the lawyer and send him the DNA proof. Then she'd be all right. She'd need to find herself a place to live where Leon wouldn't find her. Maybe a suburb of Dallas.

But she couldn't go back to the Crawfords. If she did, she'd subject them to Leon's greediness and perhaps even bring them harm. At least she left knowing that Carol and Caleb had made up. Their refound happiness was evident.

With a sigh, Georgie admitted she'd miss the Crawford family the rest of her life. Rick in particular. But they would be better off without her. And if she could hide from Leon, she and her baby would be better off, too. She shifted in the bus seat, her back aching a little. Perhaps she'd pulled it, or maybe the seat was particularly uncomfortable.

She tried to doze a little, to pass the time as much as to keep up her strength…and to forget the pain of her departure. She suddenly felt lost, more than she ever had in her life. She must've grown soft, staying with the Crawfords, knowing every meal would be provided and her bed would be warm and comfortable each night.

She was on her own again, except this time she'd have her baby to protect and provide for. And she was scared.

When Rick reached the bus station, he found a line of people buying tickets. All he could do was wait his turn to speak to the man at the counter. When Rick inquired about a very pregnant woman buying a ticket to Dallas, the man nodded. "Yep. I sold her a ticket."

"For the bus to Dallas?" he asked.

"Yep. It was."

"Does it stop anywhere else?"

"It stops at Wichita Falls."

"When and for how long?"

"The schedule says two-fifteen," the ticket agent

told him. "He usually gets there a little early, but the driver won't leave until then."

It was a drive of almost two hours and the time was already twelve-fifteen. Rick figured he could make it to Wichita Falls faster than the bus by taking some back-road shortcuts. But if he couldn't beat the bus, he'd call Logan. It was only a half hour from his brother's ranch to Wichita Falls.

Rick raced for his truck. As he gunned the vehicle down the street, he berated himself for not letting Georgie know how he felt about her. Perhaps then she wouldn't have run away. But he'd been afraid to tell her while she was still pregnant. And why *had* she run away? Surely she knew he'd protect her from Leon Dipp. Didn't she trust him?

He was angry with Georgie, as well. Did she have to run away every time things got difficult? He'd done everything he could to convince her he cared about her. Was it impossible for her to stay in one place? Would she ever truly trust him?

Seventy miles outside of Lawton, Rick saw the red lights of the highway patrol in his rearview mirror. With a groan, he pulled over.

"Sir, may I see your license and registration papers?" the uniformed officer asked when he reached Rick's truck.

Rick silently produced them.

"Did you realize you were driving in excess of eighty miles an hour?"

"Yes, I did. But I'm in the middle of an emergency. I'm trying to get to Wichita Falls. The woman I love is on a bus bound for Dallas and I'm trying to catch up with her bus before it leaves so I can bring her back home."

"Well, sir, she has the right to go where she wants."

"I would never do anything to force her to return to Lawton. But she's nine months pregnant. And she's being threatened by a man who could do her harm. She needs to be at home, waiting for the birth of her child."

"You the father?" the officer asked.

"No...but I wish I was. The father is my illegitimate brother, who we just found out about. He's dead and we're taking care of Georgie until her baby's born." He noticed the stunned look on the officer's face. "Sorry. I know it's complicated, but just give me the ticket so I can go. I've got to get her off that bus."

"A bus went by about ten minutes ago. Would that be the one you're talking about?"

"Probably," Rick said, sitting up straighter and staring down the road.

"All right. Follow me, and we'll see if we can catch it before it crosses the state line."

The officer strode back to his patrol car as Rick stared after him. He couldn't believe the man was going to help. When the officer passed him, waving for him to follow, Rick made sure he stayed right behind him.

The bus was only traveling at fifty miles an hour. Still, it took almost half an hour before the patrol car pulled it to a halt.

Rick parked his truck behind the patrol car and raced to the door of the bus. He certainly had a lot to say to Georgie and he wasn't about to let her get away from him this time.

Chapter 19

Georgie sat frozen in her seat. She had a strange feeling the bus had stopped suddenly because of her. She could see the lights from the state trooper's car and was worried that Leon had thought up a story to get her. What was she going to do?

She held her breath, waiting to see who followed the trooper onto the bus. When she saw Rick's rugged features, his eyes scanning the passengers, she almost fainted with relief.

She needed him right now. Because she had an emergency that wouldn't wait. She stood and reached for her bag.

"There she is!" Rick yelled, trying to get past the trooper.

"Sir, if you'll just wait," the man said. When she reached the two of them, the officer said, "Ma'am, the gentleman wants to take you home. Is that okay with you?"

"Yes, please, Officer. I realized I made a mistake. I was going to catch the next bus back when we got to Wichita Falls."

Her words seemed to please the trooper—and shocked Rick. He would have another shock a few minutes later, Georgie knew.

The men backed down the steps and Rick took her arm to ensure she was safe, hugging her when she reached the ground. "I'm glad you realized you shouldn't have run. I'll take care of you."

"Yes," she said, keeping her voice even and hoping they'd get in his truck quickly. She couldn't stand much longer.

Rick helped her into his truck and then shook the trooper's hand and thanked him. He watched the officer pull away with a wave before he came back to his truck.

"I'm glad you didn't argue with me. We'll stop in the next little town and find us something for lunch. Then—"

"No!" she said emphatically. Then she gasped as the pain came again. "I'm in labor. I need to get to Lawton as soon as possible." She took a deep breath. "My water broke a while ago."

"Why didn't you tell me while the officer was still here? Man! He won't believe me this time." Rick put the truck in gear and made a fast U-turn, his tires spinning a little on the gravel on the edge of the road.

"Honey," he told her, "I don't think I can get to Lawton in under an hour. How long do we have? I can find another hospital."

"I don't know. The pains are about five minutes apart, I think. A first baby is supposed to take longer, but I don't know if it will because of my previous early labor.''

"Does that change things?''

Georgie tried to hold back the tears by squeezing her eyes shut. "I—I don't know.''

He reached out and caught her hand. "Don't worry. We'll make it. Everything is going to be fine.''

She was amazed at how comforting his touch was. But she was still worried about Leon. As soon as she got to the hospital, she'd write a will and leave her baby to Carol and Caleb Crawford if anything happened to her. Maybe that would ensure her son's safety.

A pain, more severe this time, had her tensing as she squeezed Rick's hand.

"Hey! Georgie, is that another contraction?'' he asked.

Almost before he stopped speaking, another pain struck her, even more severe. "Rick! I—I think the baby's coming!''

"No, Georgie, it—don't push!'' he ordered as he took a look at her. Immediately, he pulled the truck off the road, threw it into Park and opened his door.

Getting out, he ran around the front and opened Georgie's door.

"Lie down on your back and spread your legs,'' he told her.

"This is so embarrassing!'' she exclaimed. Even so, she did as he ordered.

He removed her panties and told her the baby was crowning.

"Sweetheart, Junior is impatient. Don't fight it anymore. Just wait until I say. Then push with all your might.''

After several pushes and what felt like hours to Georgie, he said, "This is the one, honey. Push all you can."

Georgie did as he ordered, the pain so intense she couldn't help but scream. Another shriek followed her own and she realized it had come from her child.

Slowly, she pushed up on her elbows. "Is he all right?"

"He's beautiful," Rick said.

He pawed through Georgie's duffel bag with one hand and drew out a soft towel. Wiping the newborn as clean as he could, he wrapped him in a baby blanket and gently laid him on her stomach. She reached out shaking fingers to cradle her child against her. "Baby? Oh, my baby, I'm so glad you're here."

The infant grew still as Georgie talked, and found his fists with his mouth. For the moment, he seemed satisfied.

"You'll have to keep your legs up so I can shut the door. Then I'll get both of you to the hospital as quick as I can."

Rick slid behind the wheel and lifted Georgie's head with one smooth move, placing her head on his thigh. "Okay, you two, hang on!"

Georgie cuddled her baby, awed by the miracle she held in her arms. When Rick stopped the truck, she asked, "What's wrong?"

"I'm being stopped by a state trooper. I think it's the same one as before." He got out of the truck. Moments later, she heard voices outside Rick's door. Then he opened the door and lifted her head again to put it back on his lap.

"What happened?" she asked.

"It *was* the same trooper. He says he can get us to Lawton in twenty minutes, and he'll radio ahead so Patrick will be waiting for us at the hospital."

"Oh, good."

During the drive, Georgie drifted off to sleep. When she woke, someone was lifting her baby from her stomach. "No!" she screamed, trying to stop them from taking the child.

She recognized Patrick's steady voice. "Georgie, it's just the nurse. We just need to check him out. Then she'll bring him back to you all cleaned up."

"Rick?" she called softly.

He immediately appeared in her line of vision. "Yes, honey?"

"Go with the baby. Don't let him out of your sight. Promise me!"

"But, Georgie, I don't understand why—"

Patrick interrupted him. "Just do as she asks. We'll work it out later."

Rick leaned down and kissed her lips before he promised, then disappeared from her view.

Things moved quickly. Georgie had a thorough examination, then after a sponge bath and a change into a hospital gown, was given a shot for her discomfort. She asked for her baby, but Patrick told her the child was still being examined. Later they would bring him to her room.

When she awoke, she saw Rick sleeping in a reclining chair by her bed. Her baby, wrapped in a clean blanket, was sleeping in a plastic bassinet on her other side. She leaned on one elbow and gently touched the rosy cheek of her child.

She pressed the buzzer to summon a nurse. Two

minutes later, one entered the room, saying, "I was about to come, anyway, to feed your baby. The doctor wanted you to get a full night's rest. Did you need anything else?"

"Yes, I need paper and pen. And *I* want to feed my baby," Georgie whispered.

The woman looked unsure, but shrugged her shoulders. "I'll be right back."

When she returned with pen and paper, Georgie took them and began writing. After she'd signed her name, she asked the nurse to sign as a witness. Then Georgie took the paper back, folded it and stuck it in Rick's shirt pocket. After that she held out her arms for her baby.

There was a smile on her face as she watched her son eagerly accept the bottle the nurse handed her next. "Look! He already knows how to suck."

"We fed him earlier. You know new babies have to eat frequently. Every two hours."

"How late is it?"

"It's almost 2:00 a.m. You had visitors while you were sleeping. Mr. and Mrs. Crawford came. They admired your little boy. What are you going to call him?"

"Richard Calvin Crawford. Richie for short. If no one objects," she added, looking anxiously at Rick as he slept.

"Oh, I like that. When you finish feeding him, I'll take him out to the nursery so he won't wake you again."

"No!" Rick stirred and Georgie lowered her voice. "I—I think he should stay here with me. I don't mind waking up."

"Well, that's not hospital policy, I'll ask my supervisor.'' She made sure Georgie knew how to burp her child, and then waited patiently until Georgie got the right results and laid the child in the bassinet.

"Has he been here all along?" Georgie asked the nurse, waving at Rick.

"Yes, he came in with the baby and hasn't left your side since."

Georgie nodded but said nothing else. Then she told the nurse good-night, assuming they'd leave the baby in the room with her.

She settled in her bed, with a very important man on each side of her. She fell right to sleep, certain she and her baby would be safe.

Rick woke her the next morning. "Sweetheart, they're bringing your breakfast. Do you want to wash your face and all that stuff before you eat?"

She stared at him. She'd been sleeping so hard, it took several minutes for her to remember what had happened. "Yes, uh, yes, I do." She pushed back the cover and swung her legs over the side, so quickly that she felt light-headed.

Rick raced to her side. "You should take it easy, sweetheart. I'll help you."

She accepted his assistance until they reached the bathroom door. "I can manage—where is Richie?"

"Richie?"

"My baby. Where's my baby?"

"The nurse took him to the nursery so you could sleep," he said with a smile.

"No! No, I asked her not to. Go see if he's there...I mean, see if he's okay."

"Georgie, you're getting too upset. It's normal, you

know. This is how they take care of newborns. Yours isn't the first one they've had here.''

His teasing smile didn't ease her fears. ''No! I need to know he's okay. Make them bring him back to my room. I want him to stay here all the time.''

''All right, I'll go talk to them. You, uh, take care of business so you can eat your breakfast. You need to build up your strength if you're going to keep the baby with you. What did you call him?''

''Richie...if you don't mind.''

Rick beamed. ''You named him after me?''

''I named him Richard Calvin Crawford.''

''Good name. I'm pleased.''

''Please go check on him,'' she asked again.

He nodded and left the room.

Rick stood in front of the large glass window and looked for Richie's bassinet. There it was, with the baby sleeping peacefully. If he was on schedule, he'd demand his bottle at eight. Rick checked his watch. That would be in fifteen minutes.

He caught the nurse's eye and motioned for her to come out of the nursery. When he asked that she bring the baby to Georgie's room when he awoke for a feeding, she agreed to do so if the mother had finished her own breakfast.

''She'll say she's through, even if she isn't, unless you bring the baby now. She wants him with her all the time.''

''She'll get over it. New mothers are always nervous.''

The nurse appeared to think her words would satisfy him.

"No. Something is bothering her and I don't want her upset. Please let the baby stay in her room."

"What's going on here?" Patrick asked, coming to stand by them.

Rick didn't hesitate to tell him about Georgie's reaction to the baby being gone.

"I think we must take the baby to her room." Patrick looked at the nurse. "Our mothers must be pampered. Please deliver the baby to Georgie."

Rick thanked Patrick and went back to Georgie's room, where he found her standing by the door, holding her hands pressed against her heart.

"Has your breakfast arrived?" he asked.

She ignored his question. "Where's my baby?"

"He's on his way. Why don't you eat some breakfast while you can?" He watched her carefully.

She said, "I'll eat after I feed Richie."

"Georgie, you've got to relax."

"No! You don't understand. I want my baby in my room. I insist."

"That's what I told Patrick. And he agreed. So the baby will be here in a few minutes."

She moved back inside the room, and Rick thought she intended to eat her breakfast. Instead, she paced the floor.

"Georgie, what's going on?" he asked, watching her.

She ignored him.

He grabbed her shoulders to bring her to a stop. "Something's wrong and you're not telling me."

She wouldn't meet his gaze, which told him he was right. "Honey, I'm here to protect you and Richie. But

I'll be better prepared if you'll tell me what's scaring you."

"Nothing. I just want to keep him close. It's because I'm a new mother."

Rick wasn't convinced, but he guided her back to her bed. Once he'd helped her into it, he pulled the rolling tray table over and encouraged her to eat.

She'd taken one reluctant bite of scrambled eggs when the nurse rolled the bassinet through the doorway. "The doctor said you could keep your baby in the room," she announced cheerfully.

Georgie beamed at her. "Thank you."

"Since he's not awake yet, you should eat your breakfast before he does wake up."

Georgie nodded and took another bite of eggs, but her gaze remained fastened on her son.

Rick was also fascinated with the baby. He'd like to unwrap him and examine every inch of his tiny body, but he didn't want to awaken him. "He's a good size, isn't he?"

The nurse nodded and said, "He weighed six pounds, fifteen ounces and was twenty-two inches long. That's very large considering he was born almost a month early."

Rick nodded. "Crawford babies are always larger than others."

"Even when they're grown, too," the nurse said, giving him a flirtatious look.

Rick laughed, enjoying her remark even more when he noticed irritation flash in Georgie's eyes.

"So he is a Crawford?" the nurse asked, suddenly realizing what Rick meant.

Georgie spoke up. "His father was a distant cousin to Caleb Crawford, but he died several months ago."

"Oh. So you're not the baby's father?" the nurse asked Rick, obviously pleased to learn that.

"Not yet," Rick said, smiling at Georgie. "I delivered him, though, so I'm as close to being his father as anyone could be."

Something he'd said brought a frown to Georgie's face. "Eat your breakfast before it gets cold," he told her.

The nurse said to call her if they needed anything else, and left the room.

"What's wrong? You remembered something, didn't you?" Rick asked.

"I need to tell you about…last night while you were sleeping, I wrote a—a will. It's in your shirt pocket. I made you and your parents guardians of Richie. If something happens to me, I want him to be safe. But I don't want you to be held back from marrying and having your own children. So if something happens, you should let your parents take care of Richie."

Rick found the paper in his pocket. Pulling it out, he scanned the words written there. As she'd said, it was a will giving guardianship of Richie to him and his parents. He was pleased that she'd thought of him in that capacity. He fully intended to be the baby's father in any case. But he didn't understand why making a will had been such a point to Georgie…unless there was something she wasn't telling him.

"Georgie, I'll be happy to care for Richie. But I need to know what's wrong. It's not normal for a woman to write a will as soon as she regains consciousness from having a baby."

"I'm not a normal woman with family all around her. There's only me. If something happens to me, I have no one I can count on, or at least, not legally. Leon might claim my little boy for the money, but he wouldn't take good care of him."

Rick knew the time had come for him to tell Georgie what he was feeling. Grabbing hold of her hand, he said, "No, he wouldn't. And he wouldn't love him as I already do, just like I love his mommy."

Chapter 20

Georgie had no idea how to respond to Rick's words. He loved her. But she wasn't sure what the future would bring. She stared at him.

"Don't you have anything to say?" he asked, frustration in his voice.

"It won't work, Rick," she said, her own voice low.

"I know it won't if you don't tell me what's wrong!" he snapped. When she said nothing, he continued. "Let's start with an easy question. Why did you run away?"

He thought that was easy? She sighed. "Leon said he was going to tell you all about me."

"So?"

"I don't stack up well against the women of the Crawford family."

"I think you do. Mom thinks you do."

"Rick, I didn't even finish high school."

"I know that. Look, Georgie, a couple of my brothers

were worried about the fact that you wouldn't talk about your past. They hired a private detective, and he told us all about your upbringing. We didn't tell you because we were afraid it would hurt your feelings. But your past doesn't mean anything to me except that you suffered a lot.''

If he'd told her all this a week ago, it would've made a difference to her. But now that Leon had threatened her, she didn't think she could ever live where Leon could find her. ''It doesn't matter.''

''What do you mean, it doesn't matter? I love you, Georgie. I want to marry you. I want to raise Richie as my own little boy. I want to have more children with you. What in hell do you mean, it doesn't matter? Are you trying to tell me you don't love me?''

That's what she should tell him. But even though she knew a future with Rick would be impossible, she couldn't bring herself to say those words.

''You won't answer me? Georgie, I love you! Can't you give me any encouragement?''

She shook her head.

''Then I won't take up your time!'' he exclaimed, and stalked out of the room.

She was alone with her baby, just as she would be when she left the hospital. She might as well get used to it.

Rick strode down the hospital corridor, so angry he could scarcely see. He'd poured his heart out to her and she'd given him no encouragement at all. She'd made it clear she didn't want his love!

Then he stopped. Hadn't she? She hadn't said anything that would make him think differently. But her eyes, those big blue eyes, had shown longing. Longing for what? For his love? But she had his love. So why had she looked as if she was in pain when he offered her his heart? All she had to do was take it.

Even more importantly, if she didn't have any feelings for him, why would she leave her child in his care? Yes, she'd put his parents second. He'd been her first choice.

Slowly, Rick turned around and moved back toward her room. He needed more answers. Like, why hadn't she said she didn't love him when he'd pressed her? Because she would be lying?

Was he groping for excuses? He stopped again and turned around, unsure of what to do.

"Rick!" his mother called out. "We're on our way to see Georgie…unless you think it's too early. Has she had breakfast?"

"Yes, she's just finishing. You should be in time to hear Richie when he wants his bottle. He has Crawford lungs."

"What did you call him?" Carol asked.

"Richie. She named him Richard Calvin Crawford. Richie for short."

"Where were you going?" Caleb asked, studying his son's face. "I thought her room was in that direction."

"It is. I was…I was angry. She wouldn't give me any encouragement at all. And she's acting weird about keeping the baby in her room."

"What do you mean, dear?" Carol asked, frowning.

"She insists on having Richie in her room, even when he's sleeping. She seems to think something is going to happen to him if he's not with her."

"Why would she think that?" Caleb asked. "Does she think the nurses aren't any good here?"

"No..." Rick said slowly, trying to think more clearly. "It's as if she's afraid someone might try to hurt the baby. Maybe she thinks Leon will come back. Maybe he threatened her. I never asked her what he said!" He whirled around and began walking quickly toward her room.

After exchanging a look, Caleb and Carol hurried after him. As they approached her room, they heard a baby crying loudly.

"That's Richie," Rick said with a wry grin. "I told you he was loud."

"Sounds very familiar," Caleb said. "Does he look like y'all did in your baby pictures? We couldn't see much last night."

"I think he does, but I haven't told Georgie that."

"By the way, Son," Caleb said, clapping Rick on his shoulder, "you did a damn fine job taking care of Georgie and her baby. I don't know that I would've done as good as you."

"Thanks, Dad, but I'm sure you could've done it. There wasn't a lot to do. She did most of the work. And he came so quickly, I didn't have time to think."

Carol said, "When Joe was born, I was in labor for fourteen hours. Be glad Richie came fast."

"I guess you're right." Rick couldn't stand the thought of Georgie being in labor that long.

His father said, "The first one usually takes the longest. If I were you, I'd build your house real close to the hospital, or you may deliver all your children."

Though his father's words brought pictures to Rick's mind that pleased him, he knew they meant nothing without Georgie. "She hasn't given me any encouragement, Dad."

"Of course she hasn't," Carol said in disgust. "A

woman isn't exactly feeling romantic just after child-birth. Wait until she comes home and has some time to recover.''

''I hope she'll agree to that,'' Rick said, his spirits rising again at the thought.

''She will, you'll see,'' Carol assured him before she went into Georgie's room.

Caleb caught his arm. ''Have you sent her flowers?''

''What?'' Rick asked, unprepared for his father's question. ''Uh, no, I hadn't thought of that.''

''Your mother and I sent her a dozen pink roses, like we did for all the girls. Red roses would be nice.''

Rick stared at his father. ''Does that mean you no longer object?''

''Yeah. I was the one at fault, not Georgie. If I'd listened to your mother, there wouldn't have been any problems. But I was too stubborn. I've changed my ways.''

''Good. Thanks, Dad. I'll go see to the roses while you and Mom visit with Georgie. Stay with her until I get back.'' Now that he'd thought through Georgie's behavior, he was sure she feared someone—probably Dipp—would hurt Richie. Rick vowed to protect her and the baby, as he'd promised.

Caleb entered the room to find the two ladies checking out the newest Crawford. Georgie had the bottle in her baby's mouth, while Carol was looking at his little toes and fingers.

''Look, Caleb,'' she declared as he came in, ''he has all his toes and fingers.''

''Well, that's a relief,'' Caleb said with a smile. He rounded the bed and leaned down to kiss Georgie on the forehead. ''Sounds like you did a good job, little girl.''

Georgie teared up. "Th-thank you, Caleb. Rick took care of us."

"And I'm proud of him."

"He left a few minutes ago," she said, nervously.

"Yeah, we ran into him. I'm sure he'll be back in a few minutes."

Georgie didn't say anything, but she looked doubtful.

"Has Patrick been by to see you?" Carol asked. "Do you know when you'll get to come home?"

"No, he hasn't. If it was up to me, I'd go home today. I'm afraid they'll take Richie back to the nursery at night, and I—I worry about him."

"Maybe we should ask Patrick if you can be discharged this evening. With me there to help you, I think we could manage."

Georgie's face glowed at Carol's suggestion. Then her smile faded. "No, Carol, that wouldn't be fair of me to ask that much. He wakes every two hours."

"That sounds about right," Carol said matter-of-factly.

"You need to get your sleep. I know all the work you do," Georgie said firmly.

"I'll go on vacation. Having you at home will give me an excuse to play with my latest grandchild more often. It will be wonderful!"

"But he's not—"

"My grandchild?" Carol interrupted, finishing Georgie's words. "Yes, he is. Helen isn't here. He's Caleb's grandson and that makes him my grandson. Oh, by the way, I like his name."

Georgie blushed. "I—I thought I should name him after Rick, since he delivered him," she said cautiously, glancing at Caleb from under her lashes. "That's all."

"Well, of course," Carol agreed without hesitation.

"I think it's a fine idea, too," Caleb said.

After looking more closely at Caleb, Georgie said, "I'm glad. I need to tell you that I wrote a will last night leaving my baby to you two if anything happens to me. Or Rick, if he wants. But I've told him I didn't want to keep him from marrying and having his own children."

Carol and Caleb exchanged a glance. Then Caleb asked, "Why are you worrying about that now?"

She answered as she had to Rick. "I'm alone in the world. I wouldn't want my child to have no one to turn to. And there's Leon, of course. He'd claim his connection gave him the right to keep Richie, but I know he wouldn't take care of him."

"True," Carol said, nodding. "That's good thinking, Georgie. And we promise we'd take good care of him."

"Thank you, Carol." Georgie again appeared teary-eyed, and Carol changed the subject. She asked to hold Richie while he finished his bottle. Georgie let her.

About that time there was a knock on the door. Caleb stepped back and opened it.

"Flowers for Georgie Crawford," a young man said. Caleb ushered him in and he appeared at Georgie's bedside with a dozen pink roses.

Georgie gasped. "Oh, how—how beautiful!"

"Clear off the dresser, Caleb, and put them over there. She'll be able to see them while she rests."

"Good idea." He did as Carol suggested, and the delivery man followed with the vase of flowers. When

Caleb tipped him, the man thanked him and hurried from the room. Caleb then handed the card to Georgie.

She slowly opened it, and when she read Carol and Caleb's names, with a sweet message, several tears escaped. "Thank you so much. It's so nice of you," she said, trying to smile.

"Nonsense. It's what we send to all our girls when they give us a new grandchild," Carol said.

"But I'm not—"

"Young lady, you've got to stop doubting us," Caleb said. "Just because I didn't act right in the beginning doesn't mean you're not one of us. You're the mother of our newest grandchild. That makes you part of the family."

Patrick knocked on the open door. "Well, looks like there's a party going on in here."

"Come in, Patrick," Caleb said, extending his hand to the doctor. "I'm waiting for you to tell me this is the best-looking baby in the hospital."

"I can't argue with that, Caleb. He's certainly big."

"Crawford babies always are," Carol said with a grin.

"Do you want us to step outside while you examine Georgie?" Caleb asked.

"That would be good. I've got a long list of patients this morning," Patrick agreed.

Just as Carol was going out the door, she said, "Oh, Patrick, could I see you for just a moment out here? I promise not to take much time."

"Of course, Carol." He excused himself to Georgie, saying the delay would give her time to finish feeding Richie. Then he, too, left the room.

"What's wrong, Carol?" Patrick asked, once he was in the hallway.

"We don't know. But Georgie is afraid someone will harm her baby if she doesn't keep him in the room with her all night, and she won't get any rest that way."

"She still thinks that?"

"Yes. We thought it would be a good idea if we took her home this evening. I would be there to help her and she'd feel safer."

Patrick frowned. "We have a very secure hospital. I don't know how someone would harm her child here."

Caleb said. "We know that, but Georgie has had a hard life. I think she's come to expect the worst."

Patrick nodded. "Maybe that's it. Yes, I'll release her at five today if you want to come take her home. But I'd like her to stay in bed another day or two."

"Of course," Carol assured him. "That just gives me more time to play with the baby."

Patrick returned her smile and then went back inside the room.

Georgie had the baby on her shoulder, burping him, when Patrick returned.

"I hope he's finished his bottle. We're getting complaints from your neighbors when he starts screaming."

She gave him a worried look before she realized he was teasing her. "I was afraid you'd throw us out."

"Not a chance until you earn your secret decoder ring."

"Oh, Patrick, I always feel better when I talk to you," Georgie said with a smile.

"That's quite a compliment, young lady. You might get anything you want if you keep talking like that." He smiled at her.

"Then…then could I go home today? Carol said she wouldn't mind helping me."

"Hmm. Well, if everything's okay with your exam, I might consider that. But you'd have to promise to stay in bed for a couple more days."

"I would, I promise," Georgie said eagerly, her cheeks flushed with excitement.

"You think it's that bad here?" Patrick asked, one eyebrow raised.

"No, of course not. But I'll sleep better in my own bed."

"Well, lie back and I'll see what's going on. Then I can make a decision."

The examination was quick, and he was just tucking the covers around her again when there was a knock on the door. Georgie was impatient to hear his opinion so she'd know she could keep her baby safe.

Rick stuck his head in. "Are you through?"

"Yes, I am. You can come in if Georgie doesn't mind."

Rick looked at her, and she felt awkward as she nodded. He'd been angry with her the last time she'd seen him.

Rick came in, followed by Carol and Caleb.

"How is she?" Carol immediately asked.

"She's doing well. And she can go home, if you'll take care of her."

"Of course. I'll take very good care of her," Carol promised, smiling at Georgie.

"Then I'll be back to check her out at five o'clock. Or as close to five as I can manage. Emergencies happen."

"Thank you so much, Patrick," Georgie said.

He took her hand. "Just remember your promise."

"I will."

"We'll need to have your baby examined before we release him, so don't give the nurses a hard time when they take him to the nursery for a few minutes, okay?"

Georgie didn't look as happy about that plan, but she agreed. Anything so that she wouldn't have to spend another night in the hospital. She and her baby could go back to Carol's, where Richie would be safe.

Chapter 21

Leon Dipp waited in the hospital cafeteria. After he'd left the Crawford ranch yesterday, he'd thought he had no options. He wasn't willing to risk his life by tangling with those Crawfords again. But in Lawton, near the hospital, he'd stopped for something to eat and found a solution to his predicament.

He'd seen a woman in a nurse's uniform, eating alone. A plan instantly started to form in his head and he proceeded to spin a sad story about his daughter who was expecting his first grandchild and refused to talk to him.

When he pretended to leave, the nurse, Agnes Bennet, begged him to give her his telephone number so she could call him when his grandbaby was born. After doing so, he started the drive back to Dallas, a satisfied smile on his lips.

When Agnes called that morning, he'd been surprised by how quickly everything was progressing. He stole a death certificate and forged information to say that Georgie had died. Then he wrote a will naming him guardian of her baby. He thought they looked professional. He also arranged for any money in his account to be transferred to an account he'd set up in the Bahamas. He was planning on living there while the money lasted.

He smacked his lips as he waited for Agnes to arrive. Soon he'd be able to afford the high life he loved. He'd dump the baby on the nearest church step. He certainly wasn't going to waste his time taking care of him.

When he saw Agnes's plain, chubby face, he gave her a soulful look, telling her how thrilled he was that she'd contacted him. That was true, of course, but not for the reason she thought.

The silly woman was almost moved to tears. However, when he urged her to take him to the hospital to see the baby, she hesitated. "Your daughter is...is very protective. She wants the baby in her room all the time. We've been ordered not to take him away until this afternoon, when he'll be examined before they take him home."

Leon was furious but managed to hide his disappointment, intent on the role he was playing. "Did you tell her I wanted to see her baby?" he asked.

"Oh, no! Leon, I'd never do that. I think she's wrong not to let you see your grandchild. But if you'll wait until a little before five, I'll take the baby from her room a bit early and let you hold him. Would that be all right?"

"Yes, of course. That would be wonderful." He leaned over and kissed her cheek, laughing silently as she flushed a bright red. He'd discovered long ago to make use of lonely old maids. While Helen had been prettier than Agnes, she, too, had been lonely and vulnerable. When he'd discovered she had a healthy savings account, he'd played her like an instrument. Just as he had Agnes.

"Five o'clock, dear Agnes. Thank you with all my heart."

"Oh, Leon, you are such a dear man," she gushed.

He backed away, blowing a kiss. Then he went to his car. He had some thinking to do.

He went to a pay phone and called Bill Taylor, the lawyer handling the trust fund. He introduced himself and explained that the mother of the baby had died, but the infant had survived. That he had the death certificate and her will naming him guardian. Was there anything else he'd need to bring to the lawyer's office tomorrow?

"Well, I'm quite surprised," Taylor said.

"Yes, it is sad when one dies so young, isn't it? Now the child won't even remember his mother."

"Yes. Who has the baby now?"

"I'm picking him up from the hospital today. I could bring him to see you this afternoon with the papers, if you wish."

"That might be a good idea," the lawyer said, much to Leon's dismay. He instantly berated himself for his own stupidity. He'd thought the offer to bring the baby to the lawyer would convince the man everything was on the up-and-up. He hadn't expected the man to agree.

"Fine. I'll be there at five-thirty," he managed to say calmly before hanging up the phone.

He'd better figure out what he'd need and where to dump the baby. He wasn't going to be stuck with the brat any longer than he had to.

* * *

Carol and Caleb left the hospital and returned home for lunch. Caleb checked on a couple of animals that were ill and talked to his ranch hands before returning to the house to eat. Life was so good now that he'd made peace with Carol. He hoped he hadn't caused any damage in Rick and Georgie's romance.

His cellphone disrupted his thoughts halfway to the house. He answered the phone but kept moving. "Hello?"

"Caleb? This is Bill Taylor. How are you?"

"Fine, Bill. How are you?"

"Well, I was sorry to hear about the young woman's death. I was surprised that she had someone to leave the baby to."

"What young woman?" he asked carefully.

"Georgie Brown. The one who wanted to claim the trust. I mean, I got the DNA proof from the hospital. I had asked Dr. Wilson to be sure and complete the test at once, and he did. I received it this morning. Then about half an hour ago, her father-in-law called me, saying she had died. He had the death certificate and a will naming him as guardian of the baby."

"What? Leon Dipp?"

When the lawyer said that was the man's name, Caleb ordered sternly, "Don't accept those papers. He's a con man. Georgie hasn't died. I just visited her in the hospital this morning."

"Caleb, this Mr. Dipp promised to bring the baby to my office this afternoon at five-thirty." Concern was evident in Bill Taylor's voice.

Caleb froze. Had Georgie guessed what Leon might do? Was this why she was frightened? "I'll get back to you, Bill." He turned off his phone and hurried to the kitchen, where Carol would be waiting.

* * *

Rick stood in Georgie's hospital room, watching as Lindsay and Kelly admire the new baby, declaring how he looked a great deal like their own children. Georgie seemed nearly overwhelmed by the attention and the gifts they'd brought.

When Rick's cellphone went off, he excused himself and went out to the hall so he wouldn't interrupt their constant chatter.

"Rick," his father said, "my lawyer just phoned me. Dipp called him and said he had a death certificate for Georgie and a will making him guardian of the baby. He wants the trust fund."

"Damn. We'll need to call the sheriff. Those will be false papers."

"True. But here's the worst part. He said he'd bring the baby with him at five-thirty."

"What? Is he crazy? Does he think he can just walk in and take the child from the hospital?"

"Would this be what Georgie was worried about?"

"I hadn't thought of that. But we're keeping Richie in the room with us. And I'm not about to let Leon Dipp get close to either Georgie or the baby."

"Of course not. I'll be there—your Mom and I, I mean—about four o'clock, as backups. We'll make sure they're both safe."

"Dad, I don't think we should tell Georgie. It will only make her more nervous."

"Okay. We'll keep it quiet."

Rick put his phone away and composed himself. He hoped he could get his hands on Leon this afternoon. He wanted to make sure the man never bothered Georgie again.

But he had to go back in and pretend nothing was wrong. It wasn't going to be easy.

"Well, are you ready to leave?" he asked his sister and sister-in-law as he came through the door.

"Oh, yes, we are. We'll bring lunch over tomorrow so we can visit with you and Carol, Georgie. Tell her we'll provide everything. And we'll call Anna and see if she and Johnny can come, too."

"That's so nice of you both," Georgie said, smiling broadly at them.

After they'd gone, Rick said, "You get along well with the ladies in our family, don't you?"

"Who wouldn't? They're all so wonderful."

"Yeah, they are, aren't they?" he teased.

"Who called just now?"

"My dad. He found a man who wants to see the horse I'm training. Dad thinks he'll be a good customer."

"Do you need to leave?" she asked. Her voice wasn't quite as calm as before.

"Nope. I'm not leaving you here alone. By the time I got back, Richie would have his mom wound around his little finger. We need to keep him in his place before he gets any bigger."

She laughed with relief. "You're teasing me."

"Yeah, I guess I am." He bent over and kissed her lips, hoping that would wipe any other thought out of her head.

"Rick, I told you—"

"I'll believe you when you tell me you don't love me, sweetheart," he said firmly. She sputtered but he ignored her. "I'm turning on the news channel. You can watch it with me or go back to sleep. You've got another half hour before the little general wants his next bottle.''

He slouched down in the chair beside her bed and used the remote to turn on the TV. Then he grabbed her hand, kissed it and stared at the television as if he'd forgotten all about her.

She was so convinced he had been teasing her, she didn't even try to pull her hand away.

Georgie spent the afternoon watching the florist come and go from her room, delivering flowers from all the Crawford couples, even Abby and Logan. But the prettiest arrangement was the long-stemmed red roses Rick had sent.

"How did your family all know?" she asked Rick, after thanking him for her roses.

"I imagine Mom called everyone. She tries to keep us up-to-date with all the family news.''

"Oh. Well, it's so nice of them all. I've never...well, I received the flowers you sent me weeks ago, but this room is filled with flowers.''

"Yeah. They all love you, too.''

She looked at him out of the corner of her eye but said nothing on that subject.

His parents came in and visited with them. When Carol checked her watch, she said, "I'd better go get a cart and load up all these flowers, so we can take them home with us.''

"I'll help you," Caleb said, jumping to his feet. He seemed restless.

Rick felt sure he could handle anything that might happen, but he'd be glad when they had Georgie and the baby safe at home.

When the door opened again five minutes later, he

figured it was his parents returning. Instead, it was an older nurse he'd seen earlier.

She nodded at both Rick and Georgie and then reached for Richie.

"What are you doing?" Rick demanded, reaching out to stop her.

"I'm taking the baby to Dr. Wilson. He has to give him a final checkup before he can be released."

"It's okay, Rick. Patrick explained it to me." Georgie took his hand, and he hesitated.

"Are you sure?" Rick demanded.

"Yes. It won't take but a few minutes."

Rick watched the nurse leave the room carrying Richie. Even though he remembered Patrick saying he would check the baby, Rick was uneasy about Richie being taken away. When his parents came in a couple of minutes later, he said he'd just go check on the baby.

His voice was calm, but Caleb stared at him closely. "Want me to come with you?"

"No. I don't want Georgie to be left alone. I'll be back with Richie." Once he got out of the room, he ran down the hall to the nurse's station. "Where's the Crawford baby?" he demanded.

Without even looking up, the nurse, a younger one, said, "He's in his mother's room."

"No, he's not! A nurse came and got him for Dr. Wilson to examine him."

"No, that's not scheduled for another ten minutes. Then I'm supposed to go get him." She looked up, and the expression of horror on Rick's face caught her attention. "What?"

"I told you someone came and got him. I think he's been kidnapped!"

"Don't be silly. That only happens in books."

"No, I—"

The elevator opened and the nurse who'd taken Richie stumbled out, blood oozing from her lip. "He— he tricked me. He's taken his grandchild."

"Who?" Rick demanded.

"Mr. Dipp. He told me he just wanted to see his grandson. I never would've helped him kidnap him. Please, you have to believe me."

Rick ignored her. Grabbing the phone, he called the sheriff's office. They'd been on alert about Dipp's intentions and promised to go to the lawyer's office, as they'd planned. They would send a deputy to the hospital right away, as well.

Rick threw down the phone and looked at the nurse behind the desk. "Keep her here. A deputy is coming." Then he ran down the hall.

When he got to Georgie's room, he didn't hesitate to say what had occurred. He no longer had any intention of keeping things from Georgie. "Dipp got the baby. He conned the nurse into helping him. I've called the sheriff's office."

"Richie? Leon has him? Oh, no!" Georgie shoved back the covers and started getting out of bed.

Carol went to her side. "No, dear, Rick and Caleb will get your baby."

Georgie couldn't stay in the hospital while her baby had been taken. "No. I have to go. You don't know Leon. He'll—he'll kill Richie if he's not of any use to him. He can have the money. I don't care. I'm strong. I can work. But I have to have my baby," she cried.

Rick and Caleb had already left the room. Carol told Georgie to get dressed and filled her in about where they suspected Dipp had taken the baby. Then she called one of her sons. "Pete, we have an emergency.

Can you pick up Georgie and me at the hospital? We'll be waiting outside. And hurry!"

Carol took Georgie outside to watch for Pete. When he pulled up, Gil and Joe, whom Pete had obviously informed about the situation, were right behind him. All three men circled Carol and Georgie, wanting to know what was wrong.

Carol quickly explained what had happened, and that she and Georgie wanted to go to the lawyer's office.

"We'll go, Mom," Pete said. "You and Georgie should go to the house, or back up to her room, so you'll be safe."

But Georgie wasn't having any of that. "I'm going, whether you take us or not. He has my child!"

Joe nodded. "Come on, Georgie. I'll take you."

Carol followed and both women got in Joe's truck. In no time, they were at the lawyer's office. But they didn't need anyone to tell them something had gone wrong. There were five sheriff's vehicles parked there, lights flashing.

"Oh, no," Georgie moaned. "What's happened?"

"You two stay here," Joe said. "I'll find out."

Georgie ignored him and got out of the car. Her son was in danger and she had to do what she could to save him.

Chapter 22

Rick remained crouched down near the door that led to Bill Taylor's office. Leon Dipp was alone in there with the baby; he'd released the lawyer a few minutes ago. The sheriff had tried negotiating with Dipp but so far he wasn't talking.

Through the blinds on the door, Rick could see that Dipp had put the baby on the office's sofa and was ignoring him. But the baby wasn't happy. His constant loud wailing only complicated the situation.

So far, no one had come up with a way to extract the baby from danger. Rick knew he had to do something, but he wasn't sure what.

"Leon!"

Rick heard Georgie scream as she got near the office.

He stood and spun around. "Georgie, what are you doing here?"

She ignored him and moved to the office window.

"Leon, I'm coming in. I can get the baby to stop screaming."

"I can shut him up, too, and I will if he doesn't stop that infernal noise," Leon replied from the other side of the door.

"I'm coming in," she said again. "Don't shoot."

Two police officers tried to stop her, but she surprised them with her strength and pulled away from them moving straight to the door of the office.

Rick tried to grab her, but she eluded him.

"I'll go with you," he insisted.

"No. He'll shoot you," Georgie told him.

"He may shoot you, too. That won't help Richie."

Before they could argue further, the door opened. Leon stood behind the half-open door, the crying baby in one arm. "You want this screaming thing? Here, Georgie. Have him."

Without waiting for Georgie to move closer, he tossed Richie in the air as if he were a piece of trash.

Georgie leaped to catch the baby and Rick was right behind her. They both fell to the floor as she caught the baby in her arms, but Rick's body took the brunt of the fall, shielding Georgie and the child.

When the police officers realized Leon was standing before them without a hostage, they ordered him to throw down his gun and come out.

Leon's response was to lift his gun and begin firing.

As the officers responded with their own guns, there was a rain of bullets. Rick hugged Georgie and the baby to him, trying to keep all of them as safe as he could.

Fortunately, the gunfire lasted only a few seconds. Leon fell to the floor only inches from them, and Rick pressed Georgie's face to his chest so she wouldn't see the blood splattered everywhere.

She pushed away from Rick so she could breathe and check on Richie. He'd been startled, but soon he began screaming again, though his little voice was hoarse.

"I need to take Richie—Rick, you're bleeding!" Georgie screamed. "Were you shot? Show me where and I'll—"

"Calm down, Georgie. I'm not hurt. I just need to clean up." In truth, he was pleased at her concern. She had to love him.

The deputies came over to help them to their feet and make certain no one was hurt. The rest of the Crawfords followed, equally concerned for everyone's safety. Joe offered to take Georgie and the baby back to the hospital.

Georgie looked at Rick. "I think you should come, too, and be checked out."

"Okay, I'll come, even though I'm fine." He had noticed that Georgie hadn't even glanced at Leon. He led her out into the parking lot so that she couldn't look even if she wanted to.

"We've called an ambulance for him. You can wait and ride in the ambulance," one of the deputies offered.

Rick felt Georgie shudder, the only acknowledgment he'd seen her make regarding what had happened to Leon. "No, thank you. We'll go ahead."

"Georgie, you have blood on your gown," Carol said. "Are you all right?"

"I think I pulled out my stitches," she whispered to Carol.

Rick heard her and lifted her in his arms. "You're the one who needs to see the doctor, not me."

Joe drove them all to the hospital, while Caleb decided to stay there with the police and make sure everything was taken care of. Pete and Gil remained with him.

Their arrival at the hospital, several of them blood-soaked, with a screaming baby, meant they got a lot of attention on a dull night.

After they were sure the baby hadn't been injured, Carol sat down in the waiting area and fed him a bottle. Patrick examined Georgie and repaired her stitches, warning her that her ordeal would require her to stay extra days in bed. He also gave her a shot to dull the pain.

He finally got around to Rick, who assured him he was dirty, not injured. Patrick was amazed when Rick told him all that had occurred.

An ambulance pulled to a halt and Patrick excused himself.

Rick could've told him there was no need to rush, but instead, he turned to his mother and Georgie. "Do we still get to take you home?"

"I think so," Georgie said, a little sleepy after her shot.

"I think we'd better check with Patrick," Carol cautioned.

Rick crossed to the doctor's side, knowing he was examining Leon. He declared the man dead and moved toward Rick. "Did you do that?"

"Not me. Fortunately, Georgie and I and the baby were on the floor. I need to know if Georgie can still go home tonight."

Patrick sighed. "I've never had someone so anxious to go home. Yes, she can go ahead, but I want her to definitely stay in bed for four days this time. And no field trips like today."

"Right," Rick agreed tiredly. "I'll tell her."

"And it wouldn't hurt you to take a day off. I suspect you're suffering a little from shock. I don't think this is the way your normal day goes."

Rick smiled and shook the doctor's hand.

Then he returned to Joe and the others. "Okay, we can go. We need your things from upstairs. Why don't we put you two in the truck and Joe and I will go get everything."

By that time, Georgie was too groggy to answer, but Carol agreed. Rick picked up Georgie and followed his mother and Joe. Once they got the women and baby situated, they went upstairs and gathered the flowers, supplies and Georgie's things.

"Interesting day," Joe commented as they headed for the truck.

"Yeah. How come you, Pete and Gil were there?"

"Mom called for a ride, saying it was an emergency. We all responded, thinking you might need help. But you took care of everything."

"Not exactly. I'm just glad I caught Georgie and she caught the baby."

"Yeah."

"We didn't intend for Mom and Georgie to show up there."

"And I thought you knew Georgie." Joe said. "A thousand of us couldn't have kept her away from her child."

"Yeah. I should've known."

They found Anna, Lindsay and Kelly waiting at the ranch house, a hot meal ready for everyone. Caleb, Gil and Pete came shortly afterward.

Rick carried Georgie into her bedroom, where his mother dressed her in a clean nightgown and tucked her in.

Rick sat by Georgie on the bed. "Is she asleep already?" he asked his mother.

"I think the doctor gave her a strong painkiller. She should sleep the night through."

"And Richie?"

"I'm putting him in our bedroom. I'll take care of the feedings tonight. You can take over in the morning."

"You've got it," he agreed. Then he leaned over to kiss Georgie's forehead.

He and his mother walked out of the room and turned off the light.

In the kitchen, they found everyone was sitting around the table. Kelly was holding Richie and Rick went right to her side.

"How's he doing?" he asked.

"As long as he's got his bottle, he's a perfect angel," Kelly said with a grin. "If you take it away, you'd better cover your ears."

Rick grinned. "I know. May I hold him?"

"Sure."

He took the baby from Kelly and kissed him, too. "Little guy, I'm so glad you're all right. I was worried about you. Mommy's going to sleep tonight, but I know she'll be taking care of you tomorrow. She loves you. And so do I."

He held the baby until he finished his bottle. Then he placed the quiet child against his chest and softly patted his back, humming under his breath. When the baby grew still, he knew he was asleep.

He crossed the room to his mother and asked if the bassinet was ready. She nodded. "And leave the door open so we can hear if he wakes up," she added.

Rick climbed the stairs and laid the baby down in the bassinet in his parents' room. After he'd settled the infant, he stood there, staring at Richie. He was so tiny, but Rick already loved him. He hoped he could convince Georgie to give him a place in their lives.

They'd been lucky today. He'd pray he'd be lucky again when he talked to her about their future.

His mother woke him at eight o'clock the next morning, the baby in her arms.

"He's all yours, Rick. I'm going back to bed. I'm exhausted," Carol said, looking very tired.

"Good idea, Mom," Rick said, reaching for the baby. "I'll take care of the general."

"That's a good nickname. But he's a sweetie." She bent down and kissed the baby and then her son. "Good night."

"Is Dad up?" Rick called.

"Yes. He's having coffee downstairs. He said he'd save a cup for you." Then she left his room.

Carol had made a bottle and started feeding Richie, so all Rick had to do was keep feeding. He carried the child downstairs, eager for a cup of coffee. He'd gone to bed about nine, unusual for him, and had slept like a log. But getting up and moving around this morning was tougher than usual.

"Morning, Dad," he said softly, sliding into a chair at the table. "Mom said you might pour me a cup of coffee."

Caleb chuckled. "You bet. Getting up with a baby

is harder than it looks. You don't have any time to pull yourself together. Your mother is good at it, but it takes a lot out of her.''

"Yeah. I'll do what I can to bear the burden.''

"You're going to find out that women are strong. It's an important lesson to learn. Offering them help is important. Even more important is to appreciate what they do.''

"You're right.''

"You'd better burp him now. You have to do that halfway through the bottle.''

"Right,'' Rick agreed with a grin. He'd been given a lot of advice by his father through the years, but this was the first time it was domestic advice.

His dad watched him for a few minutes. Then he got up and started frying bacon and eggs. Just smelling the food made Rick feel stronger.

After Richie finished his bottle, Rick spent some time talking to him, bonding with him. When it was time to put the baby down, he asked, "Dad, where shall I put the bassinet? I don't want him waking up Mom.''

"Let's put it in the den. If we start watching television, we'll move him to the dining room. That way we'll be sure to hear him.''

"I think we could hear him if we put him in the barn, Dad.''

"If you let Georgie hear you say such a thing, you'll be in real trouble,'' Caleb warned, grinning.

More domestic advice. But Rick knew his father was right. Right now, Georgie wouldn't tolerate any criticism of her son. Not that Rick was criticizing Richie. He already loved the boy. He intended to be his daddy.

Caleb brought the bassinet down from his room and

placed it in the den. Rick put the baby inside and returned to the kitchen, knowing he would easily hear the baby if he woke. "Thanks, Dad. Breakfast looks good."

"I remember when you kids were babies. Some nights I'd fix breakfast at four. Then we'd go back to sleep and have another one at seven. Takes lots of energy to manage everything."

"You and Mom are a great team."

"Yeah. Thank goodness we are again. I almost lost her because of my stupidity. I'm grateful she forgave me."

"We all are."

"Make sure you stay smart with Georgie."

"It's still hard to believe you're in favor of me and Georgie getting together. For so long you were—"

"Stupid. I'm not going to be that way anymore," Caleb assured him with a grin.

Georgie woke slowly, memories of the day before, replaying in her mind. She sat up just as slowly, feeling aches and pain all over her body.

She moaned and almost immediately heard a knock on her door. "Yes?"

"May I come in, Georgie?" Rick asked.

"Yes," she said, pulling the cover a little higher.

"I thought I heard you," he said as he approached the bed. "How are you this morning?"

"Fine," she said with determination. "Where's Richie?"

"Sleeping. Mom got up with him during the night. I've taken over now and she's gone back to bed. He's doing fine."

"Thank you. I'll take care of him from now on."

"You promised to stay in bed for four days," Rick hurriedly said.

"That doesn't mean I can't feed Richie."

"Patrick sent some pain pills home with you. He said if you'll take a couple in the beginning, you probably won't need the rest of them. But they'll help your muscles relax and heal faster."

She hesitated at his explanation. She wanted to heal faster, definitely.

"I'll bring you some breakfast. After that, you can take a pain pill and sleep a little more." He hurried out before she could argue with him.

Georgie closed her eyes, lying very still so her body wouldn't ache, and the next thing she knew, Rick was back with a full tray. He helped her sit up, putting pillows behind her.

She looked at the food, and was suddenly ravenous.

She'd eaten most of the meal when they heard Richie start crying.

"He's just like an alarm clock," Rick said, checking his watch.

"Please, can I see him?" Georgie longed to hold her baby.

"Yeah, I'll bring him in here and you can hold him while I'm making the bottle."

Rick soon appeared at the door, assuring the baby that noise wasn't necessary. Richie only screamed louder.

Georgie reached for her son and Rick put the baby in her arms.

"Dad is making the bottle," he told her.

She talked quietly to her son and gave Rick a bright smile.

"Here's the bottle," Caleb said from the door.

Rick reached for it and plopped the nipple into Richie's mouth. The sudden silence was a relief. "Thanks, Dad. That's a real help."

"I'm going to see if he woke your mom."

"I'm so sorry to cause so much trouble. I'll take care of him from now on," Georgie told Rick again.

"No, you won't. You promised Patrick four days in bed. It'll be okay. We're here for you. You and Richie are family, remember?" He waited, but she said nothing. So he added, "Besides, I love you."

Chapter 23

Caleb came into the kitchen for his midmorning cup of coffee, a habit he'd returned to once he and Carol became friends as well as lovers again.

"Looks like we might have a white Christmas," he announced as he sat down at the table.

"It's still a week until Christmas, Caleb," Carol said. "If it snows now, it will probably melt before Christmas Day."

"Probably so. How's Richie?" He'd taken a lot of interest in his newest grandson.

"He's doing well. Patrick increased the amount of formula he's getting and thinks he'll sleep six hours at a time." She beamed at her husband. "It's amazing that he's only three weeks old."

"Yes, it is. And I'm glad you'll get more sleep."

"It hasn't been too bad. With Rick taking the midnight feeding, Georgie is getting plenty of sleep in spite of getting up at 4:00 a.m. because I'm taking the eight o'clock feeding.''

"You've all worked together real well. I'm amazed at how well Rick has stuck with it.''

"He loves her.''

Her simple words brought a frown to Caleb's brow. "Yeah, but how does she feel about him? She seems kind of cold to him in my opinion.''

"Yes, she is. And he's getting frustrated. Yet I'd swear she cares about him. I'm not sure what the problem is.''

"So how long do we keep this up?''

"What do you mean? Are you going to throw Georgie and Richie out on their ears if she doesn't love Rick?''

Caleb knew he was in trouble. "Why wouldn't she love him?'' he asked, avoiding Carol's question. He didn't want to be back in the doghouse.

Carol sighed. "I don't know. But something is wrong.''

"Has he asked her?''

"No. He promised me he'd wait until she has her six-weeks examination. Then he'll talk to her again.''

"You talked him into waiting, I suppose.''

Carol slapped his mug of coffee on the table and put her hands on her hips. "Caleb Crawford! Three weeks ago you were saying I was always right. Have you changed your mind?''

He was not a slow-witted man. Immediately, he said, "No, of course not, honey. It's just that women are more patient. If it were me, I'd demand an answer now.''

"I think if Georgie's pushed in a corner now, when she's still recovering, her answer won't be what Rick wants. And whether she marries him or not, she's part of our family. We've told her that over and over again. Were we lying?''

"No, of course not. And whatever she does, Richie stays here. He's a Crawford!''

Carol sighed again. "He's Georgie's son, Caleb. She will decide where her son is raised. I swear, you're not thinking straight.''

"Aw, Carol, Rick is miserable. He's working long hours. Then he stays up until midnight to take care of Richie.''

"I know, Caleb. I'm worried about him. And I'm doing the best I can to help him. But in the end, it's Georgie's decision. She's become like one of my own daughters. I want her to be happy, as well.''

"Are you saying Rick can't make her happy?'' Caleb asked, his voice rising in agitation.

Carol stalked across the room and reached the cabinet where a cake waited. She cut a large piece and carried it over to Caleb. "Eat some cake. I'm going to see about Richie.'' She left the room, leaving a silent Caleb behind.

Georgie turned over and stared at the ceiling. She should get up and start doing the endless laundry. Her little boy created a pile of dirty clothes every day. It wasn't such a problem with Carol's washer and dryer. But Georgie wouldn't have those when she left here.

Thanks to Carol, she had three more weeks to regain her strength and get used to the constant demands a new baby made. Then she'd have to tell Rick she couldn't marry him, and find her own way in life.

She couldn't love him—no, that was wrong. She did love him. She'd love to marry him and live here, raising his children. But she couldn't do that. Not unless she was honest with him. And if she was, then he wouldn't be interested in her.

With a sigh, she shoved back the covers and pulled on the pair of jeans that Carol had bought for her. She'd also bought her several knit shirts and two dresses. Georgie couldn't run away this time. She'd have to pack and say her thank-yous. And leave the perfect family. But she'd known that all along.

None of them would have made the choices she'd made. And now she had to pay for them.

She went through the kitchen, saying hi to Calcb, on her way to the dining room, where Richie's bassinet stayed during the day. Carol was there changing his diaper while he complained that the bottle hadn't magically appeared to soothe his hunger.

"Is he learning patience?" Georgie asked with a smile.

"I don't think so, but he's suddenly interested in hearing our voices. Sometimes I've heard Rick whistle for him. That really grabs his attention."

"Rick is good with him."

"He surely is. But all my boys are good daddies. Except for Michael," Carol said, frowning. "I'm not sure he'll ever stop working long enough to find out."

"He's still young, Carol. I'm sure he'll get caught by some lady. After all, he's as handsome as his brothers."

"He is handsome. We'll see, I guess."

Georgie started to take the baby after Carol changed his diaper, but a look at Carol's expression had her saying, "If you don't mind feeding him, I'll start a load of laundry."

With a sigh of relief, Carol nodded in agreement. "It will be a pleasure."

"If he minds his manners," Georgie teased.

"Oh, he will."

Georgie headed for the laundry room, wondering if she could remain until her six weeks had passed. It wasn't a question of not being able to take care of her baby. The money in the trust fund was very generous. If she was careful, she could stay at home with her baby until he began school.

It would be lonely for both of them when they left the Crawfords. Having money wasn't nearly as important as having family.

Joe stopped by the Crawford ranch, parking his truck by the barn. He could see Rick out in the corral and wondered what was wrong with his brother that he was out like that on such a bitterly cold day? He was going to be frostbitten if he didn't get inside.

"Hey, Rick, come into the barn, out of the wind."

It seemed to Joe that Rick hesitated before he led the horse he was training into the barn. He put him in a stall and took a brush and began cleaning him, patting him and speaking to him in a calm, soothing voice.

Joe said nothing, just watched his brother. Finally, Rick put some fresh hay in the stall for the horse and came out, closing the door behind him.

"What are you doing here, Joe?"

"Came to see you about a pony."

"I don't have any ponies. You looking for one for Johnny?"

Joe laughed. "I think six weeks is a little young to be putting him in the saddle. This is for Julie. I wanted to ask you about Tex Drayton's ponies. Does he do a good job of training? And can I trust him?''

Rick stared outside for a moment before he answered. "Yeah. He's a good man. Isn't that where Pete got the pony for Drew?''

"Yeah, but I want something gentle for Julie. She's smaller than Drew. Delicate, you know?''

Rick gave a reluctant grin. "Yeah, I know. Tex will get her a gentle pony.''

"Okay, then. You doing all right? I haven't seen much of you in a while. You staying busy with the baby?''

"Some.''

"Pete was asking me if you and Georgie were getting married before Christmas,'' Joe said, watching his brother closely.

Rick turned his back to Joe. "Nope.''

Joe stepped forward and put a hand on his shoulder. "Anything I can do?''

"Nope. The lady doesn't appear to be interested. Besides, I promised Mom I'd wait to talk to her until after her six-week checkup.''

"When will that be?''

"The first week into the New Year.''

"Why did Mom want you to wait?''

"She says I should wait until Georgie is fully recovered from Richie's birth.''

"What if she's waiting for you to speak up?'' Joe cleared his throat. "You know, Anna and I didn't…well, we didn't tell each other the truth in the beginning and we had a few problems because of that.''

"I remember. But that's not the case here. I've told Georgie I love her. She never says anything. And she avoids my eyes. I've stopped telling her because it seems to embarrass her. I don't want her to feel uncomfortable here. Or to make her think she has to marry me to stay on. It's time for me to get my own place, anyway. I've been saving my money for a while now.''

"Whoa! Don't tell Mom I talked you into moving out. She'd never forgive me, or you, either. You're her last chick at home.''

"There's Michael.''

"No. Michael's been gone since he went off to college. He comes for short visits, but you know he never comes home to stay.''

"Yeah. He hasn't married, either.''

The two brothers stood there in silence, staring out at the blowing wind. "Life is funny, isn't it?'' Rick finally said. "Three months ago, I was satisfied to live at home. Life was easy. But ever since Georgie ended up here, life has gotten harder.''

"But more interesting?'' Joe asked.

Rick grinned. "Yeah, more interesting. But I'm not sure how long it will last. How did you know for sure Anna was the one?''

"Because she was the only one who'd put up with me?'' Joe grinned.

"Don't give me that. I've seen her look at you like you're the only man in the world.''

Joe's smile grew even larger. "Yeah. I'm a lucky man. Not handsome like you, but damned lucky.'' He shook Rick's shoulder. "Hey, man, don't give up on Georgie. Maybe something's bothering her that you can make go away. Send her flowers. Bring her little gifts. Court her.''

"Yeah, you're right. I haven't put a lot of effort into

it. I know! I'll offer to take her Christmas shopping. If I can get Mom to keep the baby.''

''Bring him over to Anna. Then you and Georgie can keep Johnny while Anna and I go shopping. Anna will be surprised.''

''Yeah, I just hope your wife still talks to you!'' Rick said with a laugh.

Joe was pleased to see his brother looking more like himself. And he vowed to pass the word on to the other family members who thought a wedding was imminent. Rick needed some family support.

Anna called Georgie the next day. ''I understand my husband made arrangements to exchange baby-sitting chores with you and Rick so we could all do our Christmas shopping. You did remember I have three children, didn't you, Georgie? If you want to back out, you'd better say so right now.''

''What? I don't know what you're talking about, Anna, but baby-sitting your three would be fine. They're very well behaved.''

''Bless you for saying that. Especially since you knew nothing about it. But if you don't mind, we'll go ahead with it.''

''I don't need to go shopping.''

''Didn't Carol tell you about drawing names? With so many of us, that makes shopping easier.''

''No. I ordered a gift for Carol and Caleb from a catalog, but I didn't know about drawing names.''

''You got Rick and Johnny,'' Anna said. ''We all agreed it sounded fixed, but it wasn't, I promise.''

''Then I guess I do need to shop. Thank you for telling me. I wonder why Carol didn't?''

''She said she might purchase gifts for you if you

didn't recover quickly. I'm sure she only wanted to make things easy for you.''

"I know," Georgie agreed. "Well, do you know when you want to go shopping? My schedule is open."

"Are you sure?" Anna asked. "It's just that I have some more Santa shopping to do. Julie's getting old enough that she doubts Santa is real. I'd like to keep her believing in him one more year."

"Of course. How about tomorrow? You can leave as soon as you get the kids off to school. We'll pick them up and feed them dinner. That will give you a full day."

"Oh, that would be wonderful."

After hanging up the phone, Georgie found Carol folding a load of laundry. "I hear we drew names for Christmas."

Carol gave her a sharp glance before looking away. "We started drawing names two years ago because there are so many of us. We didn't want anyone going crazy buying us all gifts."

"That's good thinking," Georgie said with a grin. "When were you going to tell me?"

"I was waiting to see if you would be able to shop."

"I'm able. And someone volunteered a baby-sitting exchange with Anna. So we're keeping her three tomorrow. I'll talk to Rick about picking up Julie and Hank from school. I told her we'd feed them supper."

"That's a great idea. I know how hard it is to do shopping when you have a lot of little kids with you."

Georgie smiled and excused herself. She'd been avoiding Rick since she and Richie had gotten home from the hospital. But now she put on her coat and headed for the barn.

"Rick?" she called as she shoved the door open.

The wind was sharp and she was glad to reach the protection of the barn.

Rick's head appeared above a stable wall. "Georgie? What's wrong?"

"Nothing major. I just had a question for you."

He slowly walked toward her. "What question?"

"Is it possible you volunteered me as a baby-sitter and forgot to tell me?"

Rick's guilt was obvious by the red color that flooded his cheeks. "I forgot to tell you, yes. I'm sorry."

Georgie couldn't hold back a laugh. That was why she tried to avoid him: she couldn't hide the pleasure she felt in his company. "Well, you get to pick up Julie and Hank tomorrow. That's the day Anna has chosen to shop."

"No problem. And what day did you decide to go shopping?"

"Well, I told Anna I didn't need to. I bought your parents a gift from a catalog, so it'll be delivered. But Anna told me about drawing names for Christmas. So I guess I do need to shop."

"Good. So do I. When shall we go?"

"I can't go with you, Rick. One of the names Richie and I drew is yours." Georgie looked away. "So I'll have to go by myself."

"Can't I just close my eyes when you tell me to?"

Georgie chuckled again. "I bet you always get your way, don't you?"

"You know better than that," he said, suddenly turning serious.

"Rick—" she protested. Then she gave up. "We can go together as long as you...as long as we stick to shopping," she finally finished.

"Well, of course. That's all I had in mind. I'll need some help. I drew Kelly's name."

"Oh. Maybe I'll call Lindsay and see if she has any ideas."

"Great plan. I knew you'd be a good co-conspirator. Do you need me to loan you some money?"

"No. Your father got his lawyer to provide me an allowance."

"All right. Shall we go day after tomorrow?"

Georgie drew a deep breath, trying to quell her excitement. "I suppose so. But we won't need to be gone all day, like Anna. We don't have as many to buy for."

"Speak for yourself, young lady. I haven't bought my parents anything, either, and I want to buy Richie something."

"Rick, you don't have to do that. After all, he won't know."

"One day he'll ask me what I gave him for his first Christmas. How will I be able to face him and say 'nothing'? Nope, I'm buying him a present."

"All right, something small."

Rick laughed and pulled her against him. "You don't get to tell me how much to spend or what to buy...yet."

And he kissed her.

Chapter 24

Georgie woke up early on their shopping day. She and Carol had baby-sat Anna's children yesterday, but the kids weren't much trouble. Hank had been tired from day care and even Julie took a rest after kindergarten. Little Johnny was an angel. In the afternoon, Georgie and Julie had played paper dolls and Hank had tried to play, too. Until Julie caught him trying to eat one of her paper dolls.

Anna had called several times to see if they were having any problems, and Carol or Georgie—whoever answered the phone—had assured her they were fine.

Today was Georgie's day. She'd put all her money in her purse. The allowance was generous, but she didn't mind if she spent it all. She'd get more the first of the year, and she owed the Crawfords so much.

And she had selfish reasons, too. She wanted to feel part of the family, to give gifts people would like. She'd discovered it was more fun to give than to receive. And she was celebrating her very first family Christmas.

But she also had to be on her guard. Rick could be so charming. He made everything so much fun. But she had to guard against any touching. The kiss he'd given her two days ago had been very persuasive. She shook her head. Okay, so she was easy to persuade.

So no touching today.

She began dressing. One of the dresses Carol had bought her was a denim jumper Georgie teamed with a blue plaid shirt. Her hair had grown longer than ever, so she pulled it back and braided it. As she finished, there was a knock on her door.

"Who is it?"

Rick swung open the door. "It's me. Are you ready?"

She looked at her watch. "But it's only eight o'clock. The stores don't open until ten."

"Wrong. Before Christmas they open at nine. Besides, we're going to Oklahoma City. It will take longer to get there."

"Well, you should've told me. I have to eat breakfast first."

"We're going out for breakfast. Five minutes."

She stared at the door for several of those minutes. Oh, boy, she was in trouble. He was in his command mode. But breakfast out? That might be fun.

She powdered her face and put on some lipstick. Then, after a look in the mirror, she hurried to Richie's bassinet.

Carol had already changed the baby and was feeding him his bottle. "Good morning, Georgie. I'll fix you breakfast as soon as I'm finished here."

"Rick promised to buy me breakfast. I just wanted to see Richie for a minute."

Carol took the bottle out of the baby's mouth and handed him to Georgie. She smiled down at her baby. He was such a handsome boy. Like his daddy and his cousins. "He looks like a Crawford, doesn't he?"

"Absolutely. Irresistible," Carol said with a smile.

"Don't forget Anna is coming to get him when she picks up her two after lunch."

"We've already talked. Just have fun shopping."

"Georgie?" Rick called from the kitchen.

"I think that means he's ready to go," Georgie said with a rueful smile. She handed her baby back to Carol. "We'll try not to be late."

"I won't worry. After all, you'll be with Rick."

After stopping at a diner for a breakfast of hot cakes, Rick drove on to an Oklahoma City mall. "Okay, Georgie, who do we shop for first?"

"I need to go to one of the big stores, to the cosmetics department and then the men's department."

"Who are you buying for in the men's department?" he growled, as if she were cheating on him.

"Your father," she said calmly. And you, she silently added. But she intended to keep her purchases a secret.

In the cosmetics department, she discovered a gift box in the perfume that Carol loved. It smelled like gardenias, and the box had powder, body lotion, soap and toilet water.

"Is that your favorite?" Rick asked.

"No, it's your mother's favorite, silly. I'm not shopping for me."

"Oh, yeah. Well, what kind of perfume do you wear?"

"I don't know. I haven't been able to afford much."

"Well, I think we should sample a few scents. You might find one for Santa to bring you." Rick winked at her, inviting her to pretend.

The saleslady willingly joined in their search, recommending certain scents that she said would suit Georgie. Georgie tried to hide her reaction, but she did find several she liked.

When she suggested they move on to the men's department, Rick said he wasn't sure they'd let him in with perfume sprayed all over him.

"I haven't seen any women running away when you pass by. Quite the opposite, in fact," Georgie pointed out.

Rick gave her a rakish grin. "I hadn't noticed. I'd better start looking."

She frowned and walked ahead of him, trying hard not to show her jealousy.

In the men's department, she found exactly what she wanted to get Caleb—a pocket knife with a bone handle. She knew he had a knife already, but it was old and missing a few blades. When Rick saw the knives, he took great interest in them, especially one with a black handle and extra blades. When she'd distracted him with some ties, Georgie asked the salesman to include the black knife for Rick. That would be Richie's gift to him.

"I asked Lindsay what Kelly would like, and she suggested a reading light, one of those that you can clip to the bed. She likes to read late at night," Georgie told Rick.

"Good idea. And I can buy her some books to read. I think they sell those lights in the bookstore."

They found the light, then they wandered the store, looking at books and calendars. Rick chose several books for Kelly. Georgie found a cowboy calendar and asked if Kelly would like that.

"Naw, honey, her first husband was a no-good rodeo bum. Kelly wouldn't like that at all."

"Oh, I'm glad you told me that. Poor Kelly."

"Yeah, but she's doing okay now. She's got Pete."

Georgie grinned. "And you're not prejudiced at all."

"Nope. Why don't we take all these packages to the truck before we find a place for lunch?"

"Already? But we just ate breakfast."

"Mercy, Georgie, it's almost noon. You sure like shopping, don't you?"

"I guess I do. I haven't done much of it. Sorry, we'll do as you suggested."

After a casual and enjoyable lunch, Georgie led Rick to the infants' department. She picked out an outfit for Johnny, then several things for Richie.

When she looked around for Rick, she found him studying a white teddy bear about Richie's size. "Isn't that bear bigger than my baby?" she asked.

"Richie will grow bigger in no time. And look, it's washable!"

"Carol has trained you well, Rick. It would be a lovely gift, but it's too expensive for a baby."

"Let me worry about that. What else do you want to look at?"

She hesitated, but when he gazed at her expectantly, she admitted, "I thought I might find something to wear for Christmas. Something that's mine."

"Good idea. Why don't you try that store?" He pointed to a boutique across the hall. "Lindsay used to shop there before she got into the business. I'll catch up with you in a few minutes."

To Georgie's surprise, she'd been shopping an hour before he returned. Time had flown by. Instead of acting impatient, he wanted to know what she'd found, and approved all her choices.

"I haven't tried them on. I'm trying to eliminate some before I do. I have way too many choices here."

"No you don't. I'm in the mood for a good fashion show. There's a chair here. Come out and show me all of them."

The saleslady nodded her approval. And with a sigh, Georgie went into the dressing room.

When all was said and done, she bought two outfits—one festive yet casual, the other was a navy-blue suit to wear to church.

While Georgie dressed again, Rick added another outfit that he particularly loved on her. He had it boxed up and hidden in another bag so she wouldn't see it.

"Now, what else do we need to shop for?"

"I can't think of anything except wrapping paper."

"Mom has plenty of that stuff."

"But I should buy—"

"You provided her with a new grandbaby. She won't mind sharing."

When they got in his truck, Georgie leaned back against the seat. "You know, Rick, that's the most fun I've ever had shopping. Do you think I'm addicted?"

Rick laughed. "No, honey. It's just a new experience for you."

"Well, I certainly enjoyed it. Thank you for making it so much fun."

"It was fun for me, too."

When he pulled off the road a few minutes later, she asked, "Why are we stopping here?"

"This restaurant serves really good steaks. I need some nourishment after all that hard work." He got out of the truck and came around to open her door.

"But Anna might be tired of taking care of Richie."

"Naw, I called. She said he's doing fine. Besides, she's got Joe to help her now that it's suppertime."

"But I feel guilty staying away so long."

"Georgie, she owes you. You kept all three of hers until after supper."

"I know, but I had your mother to help me."

"And Anna's got Joe. Besides, it was his idea."

Inside the restaurant, Georgie was surprised to find the lighting low and romantic. They were given an intimate corner table for two.

"Um, it's kind of dark in here," she told Rick.

"Yeah, like in a bedroom," he said with a grin. "Don't worry, Georgie. I promise I'll eat my steak and not you. And if you're good, I'll buy you dessert. They've got some cheesecake that'll melt in your mouth."

"I think I should pay for dinner. You bought lunch."

"And I'll be buying you dinner, too. No argument."

Georgie didn't know what to say. This was most definitely a date and she was worried where it might lead. The only man she'd slept with was Cal. She hadn't understood what was so exciting about sex. It was pleasant, but nothing earth-shattering. But she'd willingly make love with Rick. She wanted to make love with him. But she didn't want Carol and Caleb to think poorly of her after she'd gone.

Dinner was more fun than she expected. Rick kept

the conversation light, telling her about his childhood. She envied him the memories he had.

He told her about Joe picking out a pony for Julie, so she'd have one like Drew.

"But she's a little girl. And surely five is too young," Georgie said.

"To have a pony? Nope. Richie will need one by the time he's five, too. You've got to start early."

"We may not be living in the country. Horses and cities don't do well together." It was a subtle reminder that her life was not always going to be with the Crawfords.

"Richie is a Crawford. He belongs in the country."

"What about Michael? He's a Crawford and he lives in the city."

"He does at the moment, but he'll come back to the land someday. He's too involved in his career right now. And he hasn't found someone to share his life." Rick looked at Georgie, his gaze steady. "That makes a difference."

"I suppose it does."

"You know it does. You and Cal were planning on settling down, what with the baby on his way. If Cal hadn't been killed, he'd be taking care of both of you."

She stiffened. "I can take care of my baby without him. Though, of course, I wish he were here," she added, hoping she sounded sincere.

"Do you miss him?" Rick asked.

She didn't want to answer that question. "I'd rather not talk about Cal."

Rick studied his steak, saying nothing. Then he looked up and smiled. "Right. What do you think Mom and Dad are getting you for Christmas?"

"Getting me? I don't know what you're talking

about!'' she exclaimed. ''I'm buying them something to thank them for all the help they've given me. They're not getting me a gift.''

''They always buy something for all of us. We call them our Santa gifts, but we're too old to believe in Santa, you know.''

''I don't—they shouldn't buy me anything! Tell them, Rick, please?'' She fought to keep tears from her eyes.

''Honey, I can't do that. Dad would tan my backside if I tried to tell him what to do. If they buy you something, it will be because they love you. That's the best gift of all.''

She felt her tears begin to fall. She didn't need Rick to tell her that. Love was a gift she'd never received until she met Helen and Cal. And until she met the Crawfords.

Rick moved his chair so that it was right beside her, and put his arm around her shoulders. ''Don't cry, sugar. You're the most lovable person I know. It's all your fault. I've tried to resist you, but I can't.'' He kissed her gently on the lips. Before she could protest, he moved back to his side of the table. ''Eat up. They're bringing the cheesecake.''

When the two of them reached home later that night, after picking up Richie, Rick caught her arm as she started to get out of the truck. ''Georgie, I had a great time today. We make a good team.''

''I had fun, too. Thank you.''

He pulled her toward him and kissed her again, as he had two nights ago.

''Rick, you've got to stop that. We're not...I have to leave in January.''

''Have you told Mom and Dad that?'' Rick asked

"No, but I'm sure they expect me to leave. I—I have the trust fund and, thanks to you, my baby is here safely. It's time for me to take charge of my life."

"The house will seem empty if you and Richie leave."

"I have to go!" She pulled free and got out of the truck, almost running for the back door, afraid he might catch her again. It would take forever to get to sleep as it was. She'd be longing for more of his kisses.

Chapter 25

On Friday, Georgie got a call from Kelly telling her the entire family was going to see a movie. "You know all the good movies come out right before Christmas."

"Really?" Georgie knew no such thing. She'd seldom gone to the movies. It wasn't in her budget. "Maybe I should baby-sit for you."

"Nope. Even Carol and Caleb are coming with us. I've hired two ladies who run the nursery at church to come to Carol's and take care of all the kids."

Georgie couldn't think of anything to say except thank you. She went into her room and took down the casual outfit she'd bought. It would be perfect for an evening at the movies. She was excited about having something new to wear.

The outing was enjoyable. But when they all came back to Carol and Caleb's, everyone dispersed quickly, anxious to get their children home to bed. Rick walked Georgie to her bedroom door and wrapped his arms around her, kissing her good-night. After three kisses, she broke away.

"I think you'd better go," she whispered, not looking at his handsome face.

"Why?" Rick asked, still holding her in his arms.

"It's too...too tempting."

"Good."

"Rick..."

"Yes, honey?"

"Never mind. Just go to bed."

He kissed her one more time. Then, with his chest heaving, he hurried away.

Stepping into her room, Georgie closed the door and leaned against it. She wanted so much to invite Rick to her bed. To share the greatest intimacy with him.

It had been different with Cal. She'd accepted intimacy with him because she thought it was the price to pay for his and Helen's care and friendship.

But with Rick, she wanted the intimacy herself— even if she had to go away and leave him afterward. At least she would have her memories.

The tree was up, the decorations shining in the soft light of the twinkling bulbs. Packages were piling up under the tree. Carol was baking, filling the house with delicious aromas. Cards arrived daily in the mail and then hung on the wall for everyone to see.

Georgie thought of the many Christmases she'd had alone, with no presents, no tree, no cards.

"Carol, Christmas is so wonderful here. Do you ever get tired of all the work?" she asked one afternoon.

"No, Georgie. I love to bake, and the tree is my favorite part. The cards we send out are a way to contact our friends, and the cards we receive are always wonderful.''

''I think so, too. Is there anything more I can do to help?''

''You're already doing all my wrapping, hanging the cards and helping me in the kitchen. And you're now doing all the feedings with Richie, too, except for Rick's.''

''That's because he won't let me do it. I'm afraid he's not getting enough sleep, but he won't let me relieve him.''

''He loves little Richie. I do, too. After Christmas, I think I should get to feed him every once in a while,'' Carol said with a smile.

''Well, of course…until we leave.''

Carol gave her a quick look and turned her attention to the cookie dough she was rolling out. ''Want to help me cut out these cookies? It'll go so much faster. Then I'll mix icing in various colors and you can help decorate.''

''Of course,'' Georgie agreed.

An hour before dinnertime, Carol called Rick to come help Georgie with the cooking, so she could prepare the meal. ''You don't mind, Georgie, do you?''

''Of course not, Carol. Rick makes everything fun,'' she assured her with a smile. And it was the truth. It just made the thought of leaving that much harder.

As predicted, Rick brought his teasing laugh and willing hands to the task. Georgie couldn't hold back her smiles and laughter.

''This will be even more fun when Richie is old enough to help us. Imagine Christmas morning when he can tear into the packages under the tree,'' Rick said.

"I think he might get spoiled quickly," Georgie said, not bothering to remind him she was leaving. He knew her plans. He was just ignoring them.

"We have a lot to be thankful for. But I don't think we should feel guilty. Mom fixes food for people who don't have a lot. We make sure families with no gifts for their children receive some. And we teach our children to share, too. And you know giving can be as much fun—or more so—than receiving."

Georgie didn't argue about his defense of their Christmas celebrations. She'd discovered what he said was true. She intended to raise her son the same way. But there would only be the two of them. Or maybe they could come back every once in a while for a Crawford Christmas.

But that thought disappeared as she imagined coming to visit and meeting Rick's wife and their children. How painful that would be!

When the cookies were iced and ready for eating, Rick picked one of his favorites that Georgie had made. "I'm the quality control man doing an inspection." He took a big bite of the cookie. "Mmm, perfect, Georgie. And it looks good, too."

He reached for another and Georgie slapped his hand. "No more. You've made your evaluation and I don't want you to ruin your appetite for dinner."

"Oh, Georgie, come on. Only one cookie?"

"If you expect to raise well-behaved children, you have to set a good example," she said, looking down her nose at him.

"My children will be the best, because their mama is one tough cookie!" he exclaimed, a big grin on his face. He put his arms around Georgie and danced her around the kitchen, while Carol clapped.

Georgie laughed, unable to resist the sheer joy. Another memory to tuck away for rainy days.

Christmas morning finally arrived. Each of the Crawford families had their own private Christmas celebration early that morning. Then they all came over to Carol and Caleb's house. Georgie quietly observed every moment, wanting to make memories to share with her son when he was older.

Carol received many kisses, as did Georgie, to her surprise, and the men all shook Caleb's hand. He handled the eggnog, one with a little alcohol, and one without for the children and anyone else who preferred it. Carol had made sticky buns, in case someone had missed breakfast because of the excitement. Michael attacked them at once, saying he purposely hadn't eaten breakfast so he'd have a lot of room for his mother's cooking.

"Wait until you try one of Georgie's Christmas cookies," Rick bragged.

"Your mother made the dough. I just decorated them," she reminded him.

Before he could answer, Michael said, "I don't mind testing them right now. Where are they?" He looked around. "Hey, Mom, where are the Christmas cookies?"

"Right here, dear. I just put out a plate."

Georgie stood back as several children and grownups hurried to snatch a cookie. There was so much going on, she couldn't keep up with everything.

Then Carol ordered everyone to sit down around the tree. She had Drew and Julie deliver the presents as Caleb read the names on the tags. Since everyone waited for each gift to be opened in turn, the process took a while.

Georgie enjoyed every moment. She'd ordered Carol and Caleb a door mat that said Welcome to the Crawfords, in addition to the presents she'd bought on her shopping trip with Rick. And there were a lot of gifts for Richie, giving him a full wardrobe.

"You've all been so generous," she said, tears in her eyes. When she heard her son cry out for his bottle, she fed him in front of the tree. His eyes widened at all the excited cries of delight and squeals of laughter, sounds he wasn't used to. A couple of times he was startled, but Rick, sitting next to Georgie, would take him and talk to him until he relaxed.

After Richie finished his bottle, Rick held up the white teddy bear. Again the baby's eyes widened. Rick moved it closer so he could feel it. Richie immediately opened his mouth to taste it.

"Hey, little guy, try the cookies, not the bear," Rick protested. His brothers laughed, telling tales about strange things Rick had tried to eat as a baby.

"He's definitely like you, Rick," Michael said.

The silence that suddenly fell was awkward, but Carol thought of another story that made everyone laugh again.

The rest of the day passed in a haze. There was the big meal at noon, even more impressive than Thanksgiving. But no one left after it was over. Kelly's mother and her husband, Rafe, came over to visit. Neighbors dropped by, bringing food as well. During the afternoon, Caleb and Carol made a few neighborly calls, but their children stayed home, visiting with each other.

Pete had brought Drew's pony and Joe had brought Julie's. They took both children out for a riding lesson. Georgie joined the others to watch the event, worried about safety. But she discovered Joe and Pete were thorough in their instruction and the children were very safe.

That evening, everyone dined on leftovers. After that, as the children grew sleepy, the various families said their goodbyes. Georgie hated for everyone to leave and the day to end. It had been so magical.

Rick came up behind her and put his arms around her. "I suggest we use your gift from Mom and Dad to end the day. A good whipping in chess will keep you humble."

Carol and Caleb had bought her a beautiful chess set that she would treasure all her life. Rick was right. It was the perfect way to end the evening. "And if I win?"

"We'll have to keep playing until I win," he assured her, that teasing grin in place.

Two hours later, when Carol poked her head in the room, they were still playing. "Are you two going to stay up all night?"

"We may. We've played three games and she's won two. I've got to at least beat her again," Rick pointed out, his gaze remaining on the chessboard.

"Carol, today was wonderful, and thank you so much for the chess set. It's beautiful," Georgie said.

"That was Caleb's idea. He said you were so good at the game, you needed your own set."

Georgie was so touched by Caleb's about-face in how he treated her. "That's so kind of him."

"Yes. He has his good points," Carol agreed with a smile. "We're going to bed, and everything is locked up. Rick, turn off the lights when you go to bed."

"Yes, Mom."

About half an hour later, Rick won for the second time. He did a dance around Georgie's room, celebrating his win. "I'm going to have to practice before I take you on again," he said after he stopped dancing. "You're tough."

Georgie smiled. "I had a good teacher."

He pulled her up into his arms. "You must mean that damn book instead of me!"

"No, I meant you, silly. You taught me the basics."

He gave her a quick kiss. "Well, hell, anyone could've done that."

"You're going to have to watch your language around Richie. I don't want him saying bad words all the time."

"Right. But if you leave, like you've been threatening to do, I won't be around him that much." Rick's voice was hard, as if he were angry.

"I don't want to leave, Rick. But I can't live off Carol and Caleb forever. They've given me so much."

"How about I build us a house nearby? Then you could stay and not live with Mom and Dad."

She didn't answer, but pushed away from him. She sank back down on the bed.

He stared at her. Then he moved the chessboard and pieces to her bedside table. Sinking down beside her, he pulled her against him and kissed her. Then, lifting his head, he said, "I wonder what you're thinking when I kiss you. I'm not wrong, am I? You want me as much as I want you."

Georgie lowered her gaze. She knew if he saw her eyes, he'd know he was right. "What would Carol think? I don't want to disappoint her."

"That's your only reason?" He kissed her again... and again.

In no time, they were stretched out on the bed, in each other's arms, their bodies pressed together from their chest to their toes. Georgie felt sure steam was rising from their bodies, but she couldn't pull back. His kisses were so sweet. And his hands roaming her body felt so wonderful.

When he began undressing her, she willingly helped him, then started working on his clothing, too. With their skin bare to each other's touch, the heat soared.

When Rick pulled back to grab his jeans, she thought he was leaving. "No, Rick, don't go!"

"I'm not leaving, baby. I'm getting a condom to protect you."

Relief filled her and she reached for him again, loving the feel of his skin. When Rick again began kissing her, loving her breasts, she quickly moved beyond thought to pure feeling. She was exactly where she wanted to be.

"Georgie," Rick whispered, his voice hoarse, "it's not too soon, is it? Did the doctor say?"

Dr. Wilson hadn't specifically mentioned the topic, but he'd been impressed with Georgie's fast healing. "I'm fine," she assured Rick, eager for him to take possession of her. At her words, he lifted himself over her and entered her. She was tight, but he eased his way in, holding her against him.

The heat built even more, and after a moment he began to move. Georgie was astounded by the sense of belonging, of the rightness she felt. She also began to understand the hunger some women talked about.

When their bodies reached a fever pitch, she began to tremble, then gave a cry of completion and sank back. "Rick," she said, breathlessly. "I never...it wasn't like t-this with...I love you."

He lay on top of her, heavy in his completion. When

he started to move, she held him in place. "I'm too heavy for you, honey."

"I'm okay. Don't leave yet."

"You think I'm going to leave?" He gave a lazy chuckle. "Never in a million years."

And that's when Georgie knew she'd made a big mistake.

Rick supposed he should be glad Richie was as timely as an alarm clock. He and Georgie had fallen asleep in each other's arms. He crawled out of bed, donned his clothes and hurried to the bassinet in the dining room.

After changing the baby's diaper, Rick hurried to the kitchen and prepared a bottle. In no time, he had the baby quietly feeding in his arms.

"Hey, little guy, I think I persuaded your mom not to leave. She wanted me as much as I wanted her, which was a powerful amount. We're going to be a family, the three of us. I'm going to be your daddy, which is only right, since I brought you into this world." He leaned down and kissed Richie's soft baby cheek.

"Life is going to be so good, Richie. I never thought I'd fall in love, but your mom won my heart right away." He began to sing a lullaby as Richie's eyes began to drop. "Hush little baby, don't you cry." Between him and Georgie, Richie would be well cared for. And maybe he'd have brothers and sisters, too.

Rick was willing. Of course, they'd need to wait awhile to make more kids, but they could practice until then. He grinned at the thought. Oh, yeah. Practicing would be great.

Once he tucked Richie back in his bassinet, he returned to Georgie's room, stripping again and sliding under the covers. When he reached for her, she didn't protest. Of course, she was still asleep, but she seemed to recognize his touch. At least he liked to think so.

He couldn't resist touching her again. Holding her against him, he soon fell into a contented sleep.

Carol sat at the kitchen table, enjoying a second cup of coffee, thinking about Christmas. It had been a good one and she hoped Georgie had enjoyed it.

The sound of Caleb coming back in got her moving. He'd gone out to be sure the skeleton staff was taking care of the animals. It was colder than ever out there. They hadn't had a white Christmas, but they might have a white day after Christmas.

She poured him a cup of hot coffee and put it down at his place before she sat again.

"Thanks, hon," he said, spotting his cup at once. He touched his cold hand to her cheek and she yelped in surprise.

"What are you trying to do? Freeze me to death?" she protested.

"I could make it up to you if you want to go upstairs," he suggested, a big grin on his face.

He'd made love to her last night. It seemed he was trying to make up for the time they'd spent apart. And she wasn't complaining. "Want a leftover sticky bun or Christmas cookies with your coffee?"

"I'd rather have some of your coconut pie. It's my favorite."

Carol had already cut him a piece, knowing what he would say. She took it out of the fridge and put it in front of him.

"You think you're pretty smart, don't you?" Caleb teased, smiling at her.

"You've been asking for the same thing for the past twenty years. I thought I'd just be prepared."

He reached out a hand. "I can't believe I wasted all that time apart from you, honey. You make my life worthwhile." He leaned over and kissed her. "Sure you don't want to go upstairs?"

"Tonight, sweetheart. I have to fix breakfast for Georgie. Did you find Rick in the barn? He should come in for coffee at least. He hasn't been in the kitchen yet this morning."

"Maybe something came up. He didn't leave a message, did he?"

"No. I—"

Richie's voice alarm interrupted her. Carol jumped up. "I guess Georgie is sleeping in. I'll go get the baby."

"I'll get the bottle ready," Caleb agreed, leaving his hot coffee to help his wife.

As usual, Richie continued to scream while his diaper was changed, in spite of Carol's efforts to soothe him. As she brought him to the kitchen, the door to Georgie's bedroom opened. Both Carol and Caleb turned in that direction, expecting Georgie to appear.

Instead, Rick emerged at a run, trying to button up his jeans. He was shirtless and barefoot.

He came to an abrupt halt when he realized his parents were staring at him. He took the bottle from his father and slid it into Richie's mouth, cutting off the siren. With a big sigh, he looked from Caleb to Carol.

"Um, Mom, if you'll keep holding him for a minute, I'll find my shirt and some socks. The floor is cold."

Without a word, Carol grasped the bottle. Rick

kissed the baby's forehead before he returned to Georgie's room. When he emerged a couple of minutes later, he was clothed in what he'd worn yesterday. He took the baby from his mother and settled at the table.

"I'll get you some coffee," Carol said.

Caleb wasn't as polite. "I assume what went on in there means there's gonna be a wedding?"

"Of course it does!" Rick was upset that his father would think anything else. "Georgie and I are going to marry. And I'm going to be this little guy's father."

Carol and Caleb gave him their heartfelt congratulations.

Rick received their warm words in a haze of happiness. Last night had been wonderful, and he could look forward to sharing a bed with Georgie for the rest of his life.

When he heard sounds in the bedroom behind the kitchen, he was eager to return to Georgie's side. Maybe collect a few more kisses.

"I'll finish Richie's feeding if you want to go talk to Georgie," Carol offered.

Rick didn't hesitate. "I'll be back in a minute."

He hurried in, finding Georgie dressed. He pulled her into his arms and kissed her as he had last night. She didn't protest, which pleased him. But when his lips began kissing her neck, then descending to the opening in her blouse, she pushed him away.

"Georgie, let's go back to bed. Mom's feeding Richie."

She had been moving around the room. She stopped and looked at him. "No, I can't."

"Why—?" he began, but stopped when he realized she was packing. "What are you doing?"

"I'm packing."

"I can see that. Why?"

"Because I have to leave. I can't face your parents."

Rick believed the love she'd shown him last night was real. But if it was, why was she leaving?

"Georgie, last night you said you loved me. Why would you want to leave? We can have it all. You, me and Richie are a family. Isn't that what you wanted?"

"Yes. But I can't take what I want and continue to lie to you."

"To me? You're lying to me? You don't love me?" He took a step toward her and she backed away.

"I love you, Rick, but I've lied to you and your parents. Surely, if nothing else, we've all learned what lies can do."

Rick stared at her in dismay. "If you love me, tell me the truth."

"I can't," she protested, turning away from him once more.

"Georgie, I love you. And I'm not letting you run away. You can't be that much of a coward!"

His harsh words hurt her, he could tell. But he'd do whatever was necessary to get to the core of the problem.

Their voices had gotten louder, and a moment later Caleb appeared in the doorway. "Maybe you two would like to join us in the kitchen. I wouldn't enter into your argument, but we heard our names mentioned and your mom wants everyone to sit down at the table and talk."

"No, please, I can't," Georgie whispered.

Rick's voice was stern. "You have no choice. I want to know what's going on in your head that you could say you love me like you did last night and then walk away from me this morning."

Chapter 26

Georgie sat at the kitchen table as Rick insisted, but said nothing.

"Georgie, you've got to explain what's going on," he stated, almost pleading. "We made love last night. You told me you loved me. This morning you start packing? That doesn't make sense."

"I have to go," she whispered.

"But why, dear?" Carol asked. "I know Caleb was against you marrying Rick at first, but he truly has changed."

"I know. He's been wonderful these last few weeks. But I can't stay."

Rick sat still, trying to contain his anger. But he finally jumped up and began pacing the kitchen. "Did I do something that made you want to punish me?"

She shook her head.

"It's not Mom and Dad. It's not me. So why do you have to go?"

"I...I lied. I misled you. And that's the one thing I can't— I already caused a lot of trouble. I can't stay. I don't deserve to stay."

"What did you lie about?" Rick demanded.

Georgie shook her head.

"Do you want to punish Richie?"

She looked shocked. "No! Never!"

"Don't you think Richie would be happy here, with me as his daddy?"

"Of course he would, but—but I can't stay."

"But you still haven't explained why," Rick pointed out. "Georgie, you've got to tell me why or I'll follow you wherever you go."

"I lied about Cal." Her voice was very quiet, and she said those words as if facing execution, determined to take her punishment with courage.

"What do you mean?" Caleb demanded. "Isn't Richie Cal's son?"

She nodded her head.

"Then what in hell are you talking about?" Caleb said.

Georgie covered her face with her hands.

Carol patted Caleb's arm. "Calm down, dear. This is hard for Georgie."

"But she's not making sense. We know Richie is Cal's baby. We have the DNA test. What aren't you telling us?"

"Damn it, Georgie, what is it? Tell us so we won't make any wild guesses anymore!" Rick pleaded.

"I—I didn't love Cal." She covered her face again, sure they would condemn her.

Instead, all she heard was silence.

"I know I've shocked you. I didn't realize...Helen

and Cal were so kind to me. I didn't really know...I wanted to be a part of their family.''

Rick pulled her hands down again. ''That's your horrible lie?''

Tears flooded her cheeks as she nodded again, her gaze on her hands, held in Rick's grasp.

''Is that why you won't marry Rick? Because you don't love him?'' Caleb asked.

''Dad!'' Rick protested.

''No,'' Georgie said. ''I love Rick. But I don't deserve to be happy. I lied. I should've told you, but I was afraid I'd have to leave.''

She was crying by now, her words interspersed with her sobs.

Carol leaned forward. ''Georgie, how do you know you love Rick?''

''Because I feel differently about him. I love being with him. I want him to hold me, touch me. I want to always be near him.''

''But you think you should leave because you didn't love Cal?'' Rick asked. ''Don't you think you're being a little hard on yourself?''

''Look at the problems I caused your parents because of my lie. How could I even think of marrying you when I haven't been honest!''

Rick pulled her up from her chair and cradled her against him. ''Do you know how happy I am that you lied? I want you to love only me. I'm selfish, I know, but you and Richie belong to me.''

''You're glad I lied?'' Georgie sounded puzzled.

''Yeah. I wanted your love all to myself.''

''But aren't you worried that I might be loving you for your family?''

He grinned. ''I might be, if we hadn't spent last

night together. I don't think you're that good a liar, honey.''

''Is that why you had Cal's baby? To be a part of their family?'' Carol asked.

''Yes. I was so thrilled to feel that way, I—I thought if I gave Cal what he wanted, he'd let me be a part of them forever. It was wrong, I know, but—''

''What was wrong, Georgie,'' Rick said, holding her against him, ''is that you weren't loved by your mother. Our children will all know they're loved. They won't ever have to lie because they want to belong. Agreed?''

''Yes, but I don't deserve to have everything so wonderful.''

''But I don't deserve to be miserable, do I?''

''Oh, no, Rick,'' she assured him her arms going around his neck. ''You should be loved. But Cal should have been, too. He was a good man.''

''I'm sure he was. But he loved you, and you were faithful to him. I think he died happy. He wouldn't be if he knew about Leon's bad treatment of you, but I'm sure he'd want you to be happy. You owe it to Cal.''

''That's true,'' Carol affirmed, watching Georgie carefully.

Georgie hid her face against Rick's chest, saying nothing.

Caleb spoke up. ''If Cal was as good a man as you've said, Georgie, he'd want you and his baby to be happy. The most important thing you can do for Cal is make sure Richie gets the love and care he deserves.'' Caleb reached out and caught Carol's hand. ''And that's being raised with Cal's family here in Oklahoma.''

Tears were still streaming from Georgie's eyes. Rick

scooped her up into his arms. "I'm taking her to lie down. I think she's worn-out."

His mother nodded, holding Richie in one arm. "I'll take care of the baby."

"We will," Caleb added.

Rick carried Georgie into her bedroom. After he laid her down on the bed, he joined her, holding her against him. "Do you remember that lullaby, 'Hush, little baby, don't you cry'? I sang what I could remember to Richie the other night. We're going to raise him to be happy, not to cry. And I want you to be happy. I need you to be. You have to be a part of my family for *me* to be happy."

"But it's not fair. Cal didn't…"

"I know. But that's not my fault. And it's not your fault. I think he was happy when he died, and that's all we can ask for. So hush, Georgie. Don't cry."

"Do you think Cal would want me and Richie to be a part of his family?"

"I'm sure he would. We're going to provide for Richie and raise him well. And I'm going to keep you happy. And we'll try to help everyone we come in contact with to be happy. That's what we're supposed to do."

"I think so, too. But I still don't quite feel I deserve you—all this happiness and love…Oh, Rick, I love you so much," she whispered.

"That's what I want to hear."

She put her arms around his neck. "I'll say it every day of our lives."

"Me, too," he agreed. Then he kissed her.

Epilogue

Two Years Later

On Christmas Eve Georgie was placing presents under the tree, their first tree in their new house, when she felt a twinge in her back.

"Uh-oh," she said, then slowly and carefully straightened.

Rick, carrying more presents in from a closet, raised one eyebrow. "What's wrong, sweetheart? Did you lift something too heavy for you?"

"No. I don't think so. But I don't think I'll be here in the morning."

"What are you talking about?" Rick asked, concern in his voice.

"I think I just started labor."

Rick rapidly set down the gifts and reached for Georgie. "But Patrick said you had another two weeks."

"You remember Richie arriving early, don't you?" she asked, smiling until another pain came. "Oh, my. Those are close together. I hope Patrick won't mind us calling on Christmas Eve."

Rick led her to the sofa. "Sit down. I'll call Mom. She'll come take care of Richie."

"I'll get Richie's clothes together."

Rick turned around and kissed her. "You stay put. I'll take care of that. Any more pains?" he asked.

She started to say no, but a contraction struck at just that moment. She tried to breathe through it, but it was harder than with the previous one.

Rick dialed his mother and asked her to come over. Then he called Patrick. "Sorry, pal, but it looks like you're going to be delivering our baby tonight instead of celebrating Christmas Eve."

"How are her pains?" Patrick asked. "Are they closer than five minutes apart?"

"Oh, yeah. About two minutes?" Since his last words were a question, Georgie nodded.

"Well, get her here fast. I'd like the chance to deliver one of your children. I suspect she'll be a very early Christmas present."

"Right. Five minutes."

"It will take longer than that, Rick," Georgie said, then gasped. Another pain, and it hadn't been two minutes. "We have to hurry."

She heard a car outside. "Rick? I think your parents are here already."

"Don't worry, hon. I guess Mom and Dad drove faster than I thought." He swung open the door. Carol rushed in.

"Haven't you left yet?"

"Yeah, Mom. We got there an hour ago," Rick said with a laugh.

"Don't be rude to your mother!" Caleb said. "She's worried."

"Right, Dad. We're leaving. The pains are coming quick. I'll call after we get to the hospital."

Georgie gasped again. "Rick!"

"We're going, honey. Dad, can you carry her suitcase? I'll get Georgie." Rick helped her up and started to the door.

Carol came in carrying Richie.

"Daddy? Did Santa come?" the boy asked drowsily.

"Soon, Son, soon. He's bringing you a little sister. You go with Grandma, and I'll see you in a little while." He leaned over and kissed Richie goodbye. Then he helped Georgie kiss the boy.

"Be good for Grandma," Georgie whispered.

"He will," Caleb said. "Get her to the hospital before you have to deliver another child."

"You're right, Dad, as always."

With a grin, Rick helped Georgie to the car. And this time, they actually made it to the hospital.

*   *   *   *   *

Look for Judy's next return,
RANDALL RENEGADE,
available in October from Harlequin Intrigue.

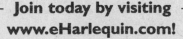